MEANWHILE...

MURDER!

BUMPER
COLLECTION OF
29 DETECTIVE
STORIES

FOREWORD BY JACK HEATH

I0593159

Copyright ©2022 Meanwhile Murder

FIRST EDITION: 2022

978-0-6481472-9-9 (pbk)
978-0-9872863-0-7 (ebk)

The moral right of the author has been asserted.
Foreword © Jack Heath
Physics Police © Jack Heath
It could be Friday © Charmaine Clancy
How to Solve Mysteries © Roger Bray
Rounder © Chris Radge
Crossings © Gina Pinto
The Juggle © Emma Rennison
Unsolved © Megan Steele
The Clone Syndicate © Holly Sydelle
Ice Queen © JC Lesley
It's all Chekhov's fault © Alexia Leigh
The Watery Grave © ZZ Anders
Paddy O'Malley's Wake © Robin Martin Thomas
Undetected © Christine Betts and Kate Kelsen
Ida and Squizzy © Frank Prem
Death List © Victoria Vanstone
Who stole the Choos © Debbie Kahl
Spice © Georgina Ballantine
Calamity in the Community © Lea Scott
Hide and Seek © Danielle Hughes
Tomatso and Monty © Paul Smith
The Motive © Maria Parenti
The Next Wave © Raelene Purtill
Honey © Michaela Sanderson
Nothing ever happens in Anafi © Elizabeth Spratt
The Eye of Picasso © Jenny Woolsey
Last Kill and Testament © Gary David
A Case of Honour © Sharon Thrupp
Liberum Mortis © LR Johnson
Twice a Killer © Diane Edwards

For information contact Info@RainforestWritingRetreat.com
Rainforest Writing Retreat is not responsible for websites (or their content) that are not owned by Rainforest Writing Retreat.
Cover layout by Self-Publishing Lab and Charmaine Clancy.
Interior layout by Self-Publishing Lab and Christine Titheradge.

OTHER BOOKS IN THIS SERIES

CONTENTS

FOREWORD

Writers are odd creatures. If you're lucky enough to spot one in the wild, you'll see that it is quiet, cautious, and averse to sunlight. There is ongoing debate about whether they are rare or merely shy. Several times they've been added to and subsequently removed from the endangered species list.

Typically, a person who talks so much about writing is not a writer. But the denizens of this retreat—sanctuary? Zoo?—were the real deal. Many were already published. Some were even award-winning. When it came time to put pen to paper, silence fell, as though they had spotted their prey, and didn't want to spook it. Then they scribbled like their lives depended on it.

How fortunate you are, dear reader, that these extraordinary animals chose crime—the best genre!—with which to entertain you. In this anthology you'll find devious detectives, creepy criminals and preposterous plots aplenty*. Enjoy. By the time you're finished, you may despair of ever having the skills to join them on a future retreat. I'd nevertheless encourage you to try! You'll find them a wonderfully welcoming bunch.

—Jack Heath, bestselling author of *Kill Your Brother*

POLICE PHYSICS

JACK HEATH

Beep. Constable Audrey Fennell checked the radar gun, and nearly swallowed her spearmint gum. 1.41 times the speed of light. She'd never seen a reading that high.

She punched the siren, hit the accelerator and swerved onto the road. Coffee sloshed around inside the takeaway cup as gravel gave way to blacktop under her tyres. Soon she was amongst the traffic. Her vehicle was unmarked, but the early morning commuters got out of her way pronto, bumping up onto the shoulder of the road.

Fennell hadn't seen the speeding car. It was against the law to observe a vehicle's position and its velocity at the same time. But the onboard computer speculated, with 84% certainty, that it was a white sedan.

That wasn't very useful. Half the cars out here were white sedans, including hers. Still, Fennell found herself grinning with anticipation. Sergeant McDonagh was running a contest to see who could issue the biggest fine. Fennell's name had been pinned to the very bottom of the board. She had busted a couple of men not conserving mass, and one lady not reacting to an action in an equal and opposite way, but that was it. A traffic violation for travelling at 1.41 times light speed? Unheard of.

Or was it? A memory tickled the back of Fennell's brain, but it was gone too fast to catch, like even her thoughts couldn't keep up with her at this speed.

Anyway, the fine would be huge. The prize was hers—if she could catch up. She floored it, screaming through the city. There was a sonic boom as she broke the sound barrier. Soon she was approaching the light barrier, too. The world fractured at the edges, kaleidoscoping. The reinforced windscreen vibrated under the strain as the air pushed back against it.

Fennell pressed the transmitter. 'Pull over! You are breaking the laws of physics!'

It was illegal for information to travel faster than light, so the other driver wouldn't receive the message until he slowed down. But it was protocol to say it anyway, and this time, Fennell was determined to do things by the book.

She had once been a detective, and a damn good one, no matter what anybody said. She would be deputy chief by now, if she hadn't arrested Damian Reynor. The kid had been organising his apartment with the doors and windows shut—or, as it had been written up in the police report, 'decreasing entropy in a closed system'. It would have been a nice bust, if Raynor hadn't been the son of a cabinet minister. Strings were pulled, Reynor walked, and Fennell found herself demoted.

2

Officially, she'd been disciplined for writing the wrong time on the arrest report. But actually, she'd left it blank. Most detectives did that, since the bodycam clock was more reliable. The wrong time had been filled in for her, probably by McDonagh. Scratching the minister's back, hoping someday the politician would return the favour.

So Fennell was a constable again, like the last four years had never happened. She needed to work her way back up to the top.

Her colleagues in uniform acted like she thought she was better than them, because she used to be a hotshot detective. They were right. The sooner she got herself promoted out of here, the better. But it was hard, when McDonagh kept giving her stupid tasks. He liked to watch her chase her own tail.

Fennell zoomed up the ramp and onto the R7 parkway, jaw clenched, gloved hands strangling the steering wheel. She kept the pedal to the metal, and soon felt the familiar creak of bone and clench of heart. There was a blinding flash, the visual equivalent of a sonic boom, as she broke the lightspeed barrier. It was legal to do that, in a pursuit situation.

She shot across a bridge, the river below glittering in the dawn light, and hurtled along the parkway. She still couldn't see the other vehicle.

Fennell pushed past 1.1 times lightspeed, then 1.2. Her vision swam for a second, but stabilised as she hit 1.3. Even the nausea couldn't keep up with her at this speed.

The other car still wasn't visible. Something flashed through her mind: ghost car.

She remembered now—the stories in the bullpen. Rumours of a driver hurtling through the metro area at crazy illegal speeds, in

3

a different car every time. Sometimes cops gave chase but couldn't keep up, and the vehicle vanished ahead of them. Other times the patrol car vanished too, the officer inside never to be seen again.

If Fennell really was pursuing the legendary ghost car, then this wasn't just about a traffic ticket anymore. Four cops were missing. This was a homicide investigation.

It was like she was a detective again.

A warning light flashed. Fennell had been told to never go past 1.414 times light speed. McDonagh bellowed it to the bullpen every other day, his rough voice like the gargling of crushed peanuts. But Fennell couldn't remember the reason. The car's battery might explode, maybe?

She'd have to risk it. The ghost car was still too far ahead to see. She didn't want to lose it.

At 1.4, the whining of the motor became a scream. Her car shook like an old washing machine.

When she hit 1.414, a loud thud came from the boot. Like the sonic boom from before—the breaking of another barrier, this time, a mathematical one. But she'd done it. The ghost car appeared in front of her, the tyres flinging tiny rocks at her windscreen. It was indeed a white sedan. Touché, computer, Fennell thought. She eased back to 1.4 flat...

Then saw that a second car had appeared behind her. She was sandwiched between the two vehicles. This was some kind of trap! Possibly a hit—physics cops weren't popular, especially among scientists.

Was that what had happened to the other cops, who had pursued the ghost car and vanished? Had they been sandwiched and assassinated by rogue physicists?

But Fennell was better than them. She had to be.

Fennell rocketed over a second bridge, the ground shrouded in fog far below. She didn't remember this road having two bridges. She didn't know the area well enough to escape.

She needed to run the plates of the car in front. See which science gang she was dealing with. The Curies? The Lavoisers? Fennell punched the license number into the onboard computer.

Error. Maybe it couldn't communicate with the station while she was on this side of the lightspeed barrier. As she went to punch in the plate number a second time, she realised it was her own.

She looked up, astonished. Yes—the car in front was hers.

She checked the mirror. The car behind was hers, too. She could even make out her own face behind the wheel. She could see the horror in her own eyes, as she realised what was happening, and what had happened to those other missing cops, the ones who had suddenly ceased to exist.

Fennell hurtled over the same bridge for the third, hundredth, millionth time. The rest of the universe had already moved on without her. She was pursuing herself. She had been since time began, and she was doomed to continue forever.

IT COULD BE FRIDAY

CHARMAINE CLANCY

You remember your name. That's the last thing you cling to in the darkness, in the void as you fall. You scratch at it, claw and clutch it tight in your bony fingers. Once you lose the name, it will all be gone. The name proves you are here. You're alive. You are a real person. You're Terry.

Lose one, win the other.

There is so much already fading.... you forget the name of your neighbour, the cup of tea you poured turned tepid, how old you are this birthday, or even to go to the bathroom before you need to urinate. But you remember your name.

Terry can accept the loss of dignity and independence, the stream of strangers claiming to be family, even the hours that slip away in a blink. He is good at loss. Not his name though. He isn't losing that. No sir.

'Terry. Terry. I'm Terry.' Right now, Terry can't remember much else.

The scent of night hangs heavy in the air, it smells of dirt and heat and emptiness. He sways, unsteady in the darkness and stares through shadows for some spark of recall. A dim, flickering streetlight nearby barely illuminates a tree, its branches spreading toward him, reaching.

Without any idea of what else to do, Terry waits. If you wait, someone comes to get you. He's been here before. Maybe not here, but somewhere. They always find you... but does he want to be found?

The sky bursts orange and soft streaks of light. There is a street, sometimes a car drives by. This is a park. Terry's standing in a park. Behind him is a red and blue slide, a BBQ, and sheltered benches. A woman jogs past, her hair flapping behind her like a defiant flag. Her shampoo is mint.

'Hello?' Terry asks, but the girl jogs on, to the corner past the fig tree, turns right and never looks his way. Maybe there will be another girl. Penny? She never came. Or did she? Penny wore the yellow dress. That was in a park. Or maybe a church. No. She didn't come because she saw, something, someone. Valerie came, so he married her.

Lose one, win the other.

A man with a dog. Terry doesn't speak this time. The dog puts him off. It is fat and black and its tongue flaps about its gums. He stays very still so the dog does not see him. Someone will come.

They always come and take him back. He remembers that. Sometimes they are cross. He looks down. Good, he's not naked this time. Shirt, tie, pants, and shoes, all accounted for. There's no coat, perhaps he left it somewhere. He turns left and right.

He does not see his coat. Terry twists his wrist and is surprised he is in fact wearing a watch. It has a big round black face and the numbers blink large and green. Nice, but it's not his watch. Not his father's watch that hung loose on his wrist as a boy. The wrong watch says 5:45am. Is that important?

Yes.

You only check the time if you are waiting for someone, expecting someone. Everyone knows that. Yes sir. Terry is *supposed* to be here, someone is coming for him. Not Penny, that was a different day. It'll be Tony. It's always Tony. He will come, and you better believe when Tony comes for you, you best be waiting.

Terry shudders. No matter how many times he tries to get away, it turns out the same. Tony will find him. He'll have to stay right here.

More people stride past, most speak into phones while juggling bags and steaming paper and plastic cups. Coffee. Its smell, a gravelly, warm welcome. They're in suits, even the women. None of them wear a yellow dress and they ignore Terry, even though he waves. Terry wants coffee. Did he already have coffee? He decides to use the toilet in the block by the slide. If he had coffee, he should pee.

Did he go? He raises a palm above his brow and squints into the surfacing sun. He looks away again. Cataracts. You have to watch out for cataracts. A shiny white beast pulls into the kerb.

'Valiant Charger,' he mumbles, '1971.' He adds a whistle, but it's mostly just spittle.

Two young men clamber out, both sporting baggy jeans sitting ridiculously low on their hips. One hunches the way only tall people do, a hood pulled so far over it almost covers his eyes, the other is a dumpy man with red blotchy cheeks and a sweaty forehead. They give no more than a sneering glance Terry's way, then lean on the bonnet of the beauty and fold their arms in unison.

'Where is he then? Gordo said the guy'd be here at nine-thirty.' The lanky one has an angry cigarette-smoke voice.

You can always sense when evil approaches, it breathes onto the tiny hairs on your skin, seeps under and chills you through your shivering bones. In the rising sun he forms a long lean shadow. Terry glances to his right and there, stands a man looking for all the world relaxed and at home in this absurd little park, like he comes here every day to smoke his Camels and lean against the swing frame. Even in his sharply cut pinstripe suit, he doesn't look out of place. This could be *his* park, his own private land, and everyone else is merely a visitor. Every place he occupies is his, and as he casually steps forward, his air suggests you'd better have a good excuse for interrupting him.

Terry gawks. Not because the man tosses his cigarette butt right into the sandpit, but because he looks like...

No matter how much your head knows a thing, you can still be deceived. This man could be Tony, the same sneering grin contrasting with the laughter reflected in his eyes. He is Tony, the last time Terry saw him. Except he can't be. That was, what? Forty? Fifty years ago? Tony would be an old man now.

The man who could be Tony addressed the two goons, 'You morons were supposed to be here half an hour ago.'

They stop, look at each other and then back to him. The lanky one starts, 'Who the Fu—'

'You want to be a wise guy, or we going to do this?' Tony clearly has no patience for these kids today. All smart mouths, but no backbone to stand.

'This has to be the guy.' Pudgy wipes sweat from his brow and shrugs. They introduce themselves, Jarod, and Jayden. Tony assures them he doesn't care; he yanks open the heavy metal door and slides into the backseat. And because nobody tells him not to, Terry gets in too.

When they pull up outside the house, Terry isn't sure if it was a long drive or a short one. Car trips are often like that. He doesn't even know how long they've sat parked here while... what are their names? Jarod and Jayden. He smiles, names don't usually come that easily. He wants to announce this accomplishment, but Tony's impatient expression keeps him silent. Besides, he can't recall which name belongs to the red-cheeked fat kid and which one is for lanky. Still. He remembered *both* names. Maybe Terry practiced saying their names over and over the way he was shown by... nurse... doctor... anyway, he's uncertain how much time passes while Jarod and Jayden argue about how this should 'go down'.

'Got a piece?' Tony's voice is smooth.

'Yeah, course,' Lanky scowls into the rear-vision mirror.

'Hand it over.'

'But...' He doesn't finish. One cold glance from Tony is enough. Instead, he thumps his fat friend on the arm and Pudgy reaches under his seat and pulls out a handgun. Tony takes it and turns it over in his hands, running his fingers over the smooth metal. He holds it up and stares straight down the barrel at an imaginary target. He mouths the word 'bang' and flicks the gun slightly up, apparently pleased with his hit.

Terry flinches. The last time he'd seen a gun, was... the girl? No, there must have been others. Maybe. You can convince yourself a memory is the most recent because it's the most painful. You treasure your earliest pains; the first time you truly disappointed your mother, your first fall from a bike, your first heartbreak. You place them like trophies on the shelf in your mind. Terry is no different, it's just he misplaces the shelf.

Next, the fatter of the two screams, 'Oh Jesus!'

No, not next. There are other things. A man and a woman hogtied on the floor, their wrists and ankles bound with cable ties. The sobbing and whimpering, and her cussing such terrible words, spitting each syllable.

The lanky man kicks her in the stomach.

Terry crouches downs, it takes two goes, your knees don't hinge easily after a certain age. 'Don't swear dear, I think it's making them angrier.'

'Fuck off... you... fucking... old prick,' is her reply.

Terry glances from one face to the other. The guards get upset when one of the inmates swears. Any minute now someone will come to make her take the pills. You don't want the pills, they cloud your mind so you can't even tell when you poo. All you can do is sit and rock and wait for the smell of death to cease. The pills take your name. You *need* your name. It's all there is between you and the emptiness. And if you're caught too close to someone having a 'turn', chances are you'll get the pills too. Best to move away. Yes sir.

'Move.' Tony's voice is smooth and cold, like an unforgiving parent.

Terry stands, and yelps when his left knee explodes. He reaches out and grabs at Jarod, or maybe this one was Jayden.

'Hey, you gonna be okay?' Sweat trickles down the rounded temples of Pudgy.

Gritting his teeth, Terry nods, ignoring the deep purply-red that shrieks into his vision.

Tony snaps, 'If you two are done making out, let's get on with this.' He pulls the gun from his belt and points it at the temple of the cussing girl.

'I'm not telling you fucking bastards anything!'

'I don't expect you to. But he will.' Tony nods his head to the man on the floor, now groaning the words 'oh god, oh god' over and over. Grinning, Tony parts his lips and whistles the first bars to 'Stairway to Heaven'.

Lose one, win the other.

His finger squeezes and the hammer clicks.

There is no bang. Just the smell of blackness. It hits strong and thick, a stench that forces your eyes shut. It doesn't stop there, blackness eats down your windpipe and burns your lungs, it fills your gut with bile and squeezes your testicles.

Kids squeal down the slide and a group of people laugh and talk by the BBQ. They huddle and merge like they belong. There might be sausages, it smells like sausages. Is he hungry?

Perhaps Terry is with the people with the sausages and clinking glasses. Maybe he knows these kids. His grandchildren?

Does he have grandchildren? They seem like something you should have. Right now, he's not sure if he has a wife...or ever had one.

He has just made up his mind to speak with the older woman in the group, she is rounder and not laughing as loud as the others, when he spots the green metal sign, poxed with dints from years of cricket games and aggressive batsmen, but still legible. *Morton Park.*

You don't always know why you remember something, first there is a flash of familiarity, almost like ownership. You know this, this is your memory, it belongs to you. You're Terry.

'I'm Terry.' He is pleased that it sounds right.

Encouraged, Terry continues, 'Morton Park.' He rolls the name over in his mouth, like a hard-boiled sweet, releasing little flavour at first, but promising more as you work it around and over your tongue. And here it comes. He is *meant* to be here.

'You're meeting someone,' a soft voice reminds him. His voice. Although it sounds much raspier than he expected. Not a young man's voice.

'Morton Park,' he tries again and this time there is more. A girl. She's pretty. A pretty girl called...Valerie...no. That's not a real name. Something else. There are so many girl's names these days. You can't possibly distinguish between them. Maria. That's a girl's name, just not this girl.

Lose one, win the other.

His mother was Maria. She took him to church every Sunday morning, she'd make him wear his father's white shirt and coat and tie. Even in summer. They smelled of camphor. On the way out of the house she'd stop by the hall table, pour water from the ceramic jug, adorned with tiny blue and white painted flowers, splash her hands in and then smooth down his stubborn cowlick. Father Dominic once joked that a cowlick was the sign of possession in a child. This terrified his mother, so she'd plaster his black wave down tight against his forehead. Then they'd trudge through the dusty streets with his younger brothers.

'Giorgio will be a doctor, he will make us all rich. Paul is lazy. But Tony, he will be a priest and he will make his mamma so proud. Don't you think?'

He'd nod to make Mamma happy. She only had happy or angry, and you didn't want the angry.

Mamma was gone and Tony did not become a priest. Paul did though.

Lose one, win the other.

Paul will not come for Terry. He is done with all of them. He'd said so at church. A funeral? He could always see the black in Tony's soul. There's no hiding that sort of thing from a man who knows God personally. No sir.

Tony will come.

Penny! That was her name. She almost always wore sunshine and lemons and smelled like yellow. Not anymore. She's gone.

She'd liked Tony first. Terry knew, he understood. Tony's quick succession in growing his regions and building his 'family' came down to his lack of fear. As a kid, he'd meet any dare. When they sat on the train lines, Tony would be the last to leap off as the train pounded past, clanging its bell. Sometimes the driver would lean out and mouth obscenities. The boys would pat Tony on the back. At every school they attended, he'd go up on the first day and punch the biggest kid in the face, without warning.

Sometimes he'd go down, having the weakness of never protecting his face. It wouldn't matter. Either way he'd win.

No one could say the boys went without. Mamma worked days cleaning houses and nights cleaning factories, just so they'd always have good fresh food, which, to the amusement of their neighbours, they grew in their back yard. Mamma didn't like supermarkets, she only went for milk whenever Elsie, their grey and white woolly goat, couldn't produce. Still, Tony saw every other boy at their catholic school as having more. He wanted it. The nice suits, the connections, the girls. All of it. When you want something bad enough, you don't stop to think about the cost. It cost Tony, but he got there.

Tony built his connections, ruled Melbourne. Grew his mob, his family. In the process, lost his real family. First Mamma, then Paul.

Lose one, win the other.

Terry is meeting Tony here. Isn't he?

It isn't Penny. He knows that. This is important. There is no Penny, only Valerie. His head throbs as he strains to remember if Valerie is still alive. He hopes she is. He sometimes gets things like that muddled. He'd lose her in his thoughts, like car keys misplaced. He'd search in his mind, through the bureau drawers, on the kitchen bench, the coffee table, but the memory wouldn't be found. Not until you gave up.

Valerie is good with names. She'd remember for him. Maybe she's coming for him now? He turns about, wondering if he'll recognise her. She doesn't wear yellow anymore.

A flash of the woman on the floor. Lying still. Her sunny dress splattered in red. The lanky one, Jared, pointing the gun at Tony.

No. He's not in that house. He's in a park. Parks are nice places. That other thing is just a nightmare of sorts. You have to remind yourself that nightmares aren't real.

Terry's hands form tight fists and bang on his chest as it tightens and a white burn runs all the way down his left arm and up his neck, right up to pulsate through his cheekbone, and up farther, behind his left eye. He gasps. Pictures scream into his mind, some still, some moving. The people. Dead. Tony. Jared. The girl. They mustn't know they're just nightmares.

'Oh god, oh god, oh god,' The man on the floor cries over and over.

Was that today? Has it happened yet? The sky is grey and the streetlights flicker on once again. Terry is woozy. He staggers toward the swing. Tipping left then right, finally finding his way in the dim light to a rubber seat suspended by two strong chains. He grips the chains and lowers himself down.

Still the images bellow, taunting, accusing.

He lowers his face between his knees. That's something you do when you've had a shock. Or is that for a fainting spell?

He can still smell the tangy Brylcreem glistening in Tony's hair, trying, and failing to hold down the devil's mark.

Tony laughing. A hearty laugh. *That was a good one.* He opens his palm and dribbles the bullets onto the floor, each one tapping as it bounces, little bronze promises, just inches from the girl's face. And her, in the yellow dress, tears streaking her pretty face.

'Shall we try that again?' Tony picks up one of the bullets, pulls down the magazine and slides it in before snapping the chamber back into place.

'Bastard. Fucking bastard,' she weeps, but the fight is out of her. Not yellow, she wears a large white t-shirt and faded blue jeans, now darkly stained. The stench of urine stings the air like the colour silver. She tells the boys where they can find the stash.

Lanky makes Pudgy pull the dead palm up out of the large pot. He reaches down and holds up a plastic wrapped package. 'It's here.'

The girl is alive. Tony is dead. Terry knows that. He just knows it.

Lose one, win the other.

If only you could choose which memories stay and which ones fade off forever. Terry would much prefer to recall a nostalgic moment from childhood, of flying high on a swing just like this one, the wind in your face. There must have been swings in his past...parks...BBQs. No such images arise. Only the other ones.

The roaring gunfire. Once, twice, three times. Tony's gun. No. Not his. Jared pointing and firing. The man hogtied. Twice into his back, then once more. The man's cries to God now silent.

Jared swinging his lanky frame to the girl. Terry reaching to Tony for help. Gone. Where did Tony go? Terry was *not* like Tony. He knew fear. Old age gifts terrors; dogs, loud people, angry people, the pills...and losing himself, his name. But not death. He's not afraid of that. No sir. Terry falls against Jared with all his feeble strength.

Explosion. Loud and bright, it smells red and orange, like fireworks.

Next, the fatter of the two screams, 'Oh Jesus!'

Jared regains his balance, this time pointing the weapon at his pudgy friend. Pudgy lifts a gun from the bottom of the empty pot and fires without aiming.

Terry sits up in the swing, rubbing his eyes, rubbing away the images. He sucks in his breath three times. A little better. Pushing with his heels he rocks back and forth. Shadows cross over and everything is getting dark. He is in a park. On the street out front, cars drive by, their headlights on. None of them stop. They might not see him here. Maybe he should walk over and wave to them?

Things happen very fast, and you find yourself places you shouldn't be. They would be cross with him. It's not like you mean to wander off. You start off looking for a bite to eat, a biscuit, maybe a slice of ginger cake, on Fridays there's ginger cake, and then everyone is mad at you because you're in the wrong place and you haven't taken your medication. Has he taken his medication? He remembers swallowing pills...although that might have been yesterday. Days get lost. At least he has today. It could be Friday. Or maybe Tuesday.

Lose one, win the other.

A car beeps its horn. Terry turns away. It's dark and he doesn't know this car. He shouldn't speak to the person in there. They might ask his name. It gets stuck in his throat sometimes. T. T. Terry. That's it. He is Terry.

You must never forget your name, no sir. It's all you've got to keep you safe. People will find you if you have the wrong name. He remembers the young detective telling him that.

'Don't forget, you are Terry now.' Is the detective old now?

This car is looking for someone else. They might think Terry is that person. He's not.

'I'm Terry. Terry. Terry. Terry,' he says defiantly to the car, but only in a soft voice. He doesn't really want the driver to hear him. Terry looks about. He's in a park. He should go and hide behind that big tree.

He leans around the trunk. 'Hello?'

'Tony?' The girl in the yellow dress quickens her pace until she is right before him. Her face is different.

'Oh my, we've been looking *everywhere* for you, you silly old thing.' She looks about, as though she's with a crowd of people. None of them appear.

He reaches out, his hands shaking, how long have they been shaking like this? 'Penny? Penny did we get married?'

A grin curves up her pretty pale lips and one eyebrow lifts higher than the other. 'I'm Chloe, remember? And no, we are not married, you cheeky bugger.' She clasps his arm. He wobbles the first few steps.

'Come on Tony, we have to go, even the police are out looking for you.'

The police? You don't want the police after you. They're worse than the connected guys. The police know how to put you in the Yarra River, so you never surface.

You know when you need to remember a thing, but you don't always know *what* it is you need to remember.

'I'm Terry. My name is Terry.'

Chloe blinks at him as if he'd just told her the sky is dirty brown and smells like rancid death... which it sometimes does. 'I know. I *said* Terry. Come on now, I've got a bottle of water for you in the van. We need to get some fluids into you, don't we?'

Terry nods. Yes. That's very important.

Chloe pauses. 'Terry? Is that blood on your shirt? Have you hurt yourself?' She shouts the last part, as if he might not understand.

He doesn't understand.

The girl in the yellow dress, no, it is a duck-egg blue uniform, tightens her grip on Terry's arm and leads him toward a parked van.

This isn't Penny.

She helps him up into his seat, it is high, so she gives him a push. 'Doctor Radcliffe is going to be so cross with you Terry.' Her face softens when she notices the fear in his eyes. She rubs his arm. 'Still, Val will be relieved to see you're okay.'

Terry smiles.

Lose one, win the other.

HOW TO SOLVE MYSTERIES

ROGER BRAY

In Ireland, they have the myth of the sin-eater. The idea being that when someone dies, their casket is open and plates of food are placed on the body. The sin-eater comes along and eats the food and it's believed they take on the sins of the deceased, so they can pass onto wherever they go next. I believe police are the sin-eaters of society. Police take on the roles that no one else wants.

So, the first thing a police officer does when they turn up is to work out if this is actually a crime scene or not. I've been to plenty of call-outs where it looks like a crime scene, but it's not, and vice-versa. One that I remember was when the neighbours rang up, in an absolute panic. They were convinced the woman two doors down was being attacked. There was shouting, breaking glass and all that. We arrived and found a woman cut to ribbons, she was actually bleeding out when we got there. Her house was trashed and the bathroom was smashed up. The woman was sent off to hospital and we had a crime scene on our hands. Who would do such a thing? There we are, a few hours later, making notes, checking for evidence and we get a call from the hospital. They said, don't worry about it, not a crime. Turns out, the woman had an epileptic fit and hurt herself. Looked like a crime scene, but not a crime scene.

Of course, not all call-outs are accidents.

Another example, was a call out we got for a couple who had recently moved into a new townhouse upon retirement. They'd apparently lived a happy life, but suddenly the woman had become despondent and threatened to kill herself. This was out of character, so her husband would occasionally call us when he was worried she might take action. We'd go out there and talk to her to see if further action needed to be taken, but she'd always assure us she would be okay.

One day, we get the inevitable phone call. She's dead. I wasn't on that day, but the police went out there, they checked it out and there she was, on the bed, dead. The uniform on thought, hmm, okay, I'm not happy about this. So they called up CID (Crime Investigation Unit). They send someone out and they say they think its suicide. She'd probably taken a handful of tablets. She was lying in bed and looked pretty peaceful. They figured the post-mortem will figure it out, they'll take some samples, do some tests and the answer will become evident.

So, they call up the doctor. The process is, you can't remove the body until it's dead and you need someone with a medical degree to say it's dead. Even if it is in pieces or been there for seven months. Anyway, he turns up, checks the eyes, and declares her dead. The next step is to have the body removed.

By this stage, all the police are out the front having a bit of a chat, when one of the undertakers comes out. He said, 'Hey, guys, did anyone mention the knife?'

Turns out, when they pulled the sheet down, there was a carving knife sticking out of her side, right into her heart.

Now, it was eventually established that it was actually a suicide and that's how she had done it, but you can see how this could have been a crime-scene that did not initially look like a crime-scene.

So, sometimes you go to a crime and you just don't know. There is nothing worse than treating a scene like it's not a crime and then finding out it is, because in the meantime, you may have destroyed important evidence. You just know there's a smart defence lawyer out there waiting for you to mess up. No uniform wants to stand in court and watch a guilty person walk free because of a mistake they made.

But police work is not just about the evidence and crime scene. There is also the need to use strategies when talking to suspects. A great interrogation technique is silence.

People like to fill in gaps. They do not like silence. If you put a question to someone, you then just sit there and look at them. Eventually, they'll crack and say something. You'll see them, they start getting nervous. Sometimes when you drop an allegation on someone, they'll just give you the bare minimum. But you say nothing. Then they'll add a bit more and a bit more. Eventually, they're telling you about when their mum first brought them home from hospital. You can't shut them up. One time, I caught a young man stealing a car. By keeping my mouth shut, he ended up telling me about around nineteen other cars he'd stolen.

Police officers are human and they want to fill in the gaps too, so we have to tell the young uniforms that are new on the job to shut up and let the suspect sweat it out.

One aspect of police work the public probably doesn't think too much about is the smell of death. One scent, never forgotten. It's almost impossible to describe what a dead body that's been left for a few days, where the temperature has risen, smells like.

It's not just the odour that haunts you. I remember going to this one job where a guy had gotten a letter from his bank telling him he'd received a cheque and the excitement must have been too much for him. He just died. Had a heart attack. His real estate agent found him. I enter his home and think, 'He looks like Santa.' But it wasn't a big white beard he was sporting, it was maggots. Thousands of maggots.

If the temperature is up, when you approach a house with a dead body in it, you know. There are blowflies at the window. They steam up the window, there's so many of them.

There are a lot of grotesque images I could tell you about finding a body. But it's the smell of death I could never find the words to describe. Only that it stays with you. We take it on and continue because it's our job.

We are the police, the detectives. We are the sin-eaters.

ROUNDER

CHRIS RADGE

*D*ew glistened on the antiquated rails of the local park's rounder. But the six teens dressed to impress were not crying with laughter. They were permanently silenced by death.

For almost sixteen years, Detective Jeffery Ryan had not stepped foot in Yorks Knob. But now he was back, and the memories of his brother's murder still haunted him.

Nothing had changed. It was the same muggy coastal town he'd grown up in. The same corner shop he'd stolen sweets from. Hell, it was the same park he'd seen her that night.

'Somebody, turn that friggen thing off.' Ryan – the name everybody called him by – stabbed a finger towards the newest party drug machine to hit the streets of the north Queensland town. It looked like a brass Turkish Hookah smoking device, except this one was glass with clear medical tubing snaking from the centre of its six separate compartments. As far as he could tell, it seemed to be designed to distribute an injectable, simultaneous roulette of drugs.

'We've tried sir, but we can't find the off switch'

Irritated, Ryan said 'Just leave it!' Making a mental note to turn it off himself.

'Geezuz.'

'Excuse me Sir?' one of the constables asked.

'That.' Ryan's pen shook slightly as he recognised the five-cent size insignia of a skull, crossed rifles, and a single marijuana leaf etched on the side of the glass. Leaning closer to the device, he noticed what looked like tiny black berries or beads floating in each section.

'Can you get a decent shot of both of these?' he asked the forensic photographer and sat back on his haunches to think as pain thumped through his knees.

Ryan, at the age of ten, had seen the same Mexican Drug Cartel symbol on an empty g-packet clenched in his older brother's hand on the day of the drive-by shooting. His young mind froze, as warm blood pumped from his brother's neck and puddled around his white converse sneakers. Sticky blood from a flesh wound at his temple, trickled into his eye blurring his vision. But his mind would not register the pain or what had happened, not until an officer guided him away from the Pinto Park rounder and his brother's lifeless body. He'd idolised his big brother. Wanted to be like him, wore his cap down low over his eyes like him, and had that same lazy hip strut just like him.

He knew now, his brother had been dealing, and had a *g* stolen. *Just vanished*, was the word on the streets and why the Cartel had blown his brother away. The take down had only lasted a moment, but it was etched into his memory, replaying over and over, and the reason he'd became a cop.

But now, he had a job to do, and focused in on the six adolescents that lay slumped and lifeless in front of him. He could see no indication why these teens would cut their lives short. But he understood the delicious nothingness the drugs represented.

Don't listen to the voices. He remembered the mantra from his stay in rehab years ago, a narcotic side effect from working undercover. He had to push it all aside, and his focus returned to the immediate crime scene.

All but one of the six teens sat with their backs against the rounder's cold metal rails.

Fibre optic flashes of multi-coloured light radiated from the Drip Tubing fountaining from centre of the glass automatic drug dispenser. He traced one to the tubes — strangely lit up like Christmas rope light— to a pulseless arm extended in early rigor mortis.

Was this the allure?

He tapped the clear tubing with his pen. *Blinking veins? I suspect this is a first outing for this device. But why test it on kids? And why these kids?* He squinted in thought. *Was this going to be the next big thing on the street?* His annoyance increased visualising future evening crime scenes lit up like discos. He looked down at the only teen — he guessed was a girl because of her eighties bedazzled jacket that seemed strangely familiar — sprawled face down across the legs of a dark-haired boy, her blood-matted hair staining the boy's mustard brown pants.

'Well, looky here.' His attention moved to the sitting teen. Flecked spittle dripped from the boy's mouth. It looked like... He moved closer. *Is that chocolate cake?* He scanned the area. *There.* He squatted, reached down towards the victim's hand and retrieved the empty plastic sandwich bag and snapped it open. Sniffing deeply, he breathed in the chocolaty sweet mustiness.

'I knew it, Shroomies.' Crunching pain surged through is knees as he stood up.

'Pardon?' the forensic photographer looked up from her camera.

'Truffle Trip, you know, Magic Mushrooms baked into Brownies.' he said breathing out the pain. 'That's what the street kids call 'em. And this...' He took another sniff. '... I would say is Mexican.'

He snapped the evidence bag closed, glad there were only crumbs left. Lifting the blue and white chequered crime scene tape high so he wouldn't have to crouch, he held out the bag.

'Log that, will ya,' he said to the nearest constable as he dry swallowed another pain pill.

A wailing woman in a tight snakeskin dress hobbled towards the crime scene.

'Jace.' Her pencil-thin heels pierced the damp morning ground while her matching handbag swung back and forth on her elbow like a church bell.

Ryan recognised the woman as Sonya Rodriguez, the wife of local Australian Cartel Lord Michael Rodriquez, from reports, and vaguely from his childhood.

Is this some kind of turf war between the Aussie and Mexican Cartels? From all reports they had been laying low since his brother's death, the case perpetually in appeal and in continuance.

Not low enough, he thought. *But why now? It makes no sense.* Chaos interrupted him before he could make any real connections.

The hobbling woman's head snapped back as her stiletto heel broke and her ankle twisted. She'd gone down hard, like she'd been tackled from behind by a pro football player. The comedic scene was forgotten as another woman in blue phlebotomist scrubs easily hurdled the fallen woman.

'Scar.' The loud piercing cry escaped her.

The name meant nothing to him, but that voice.

Debra?

His high school sweetheart, *could it be?* He'd not seen her for almost sixteen years. She came to a skidding halt on the dewy grass, his arms and the blue and white chequered crime scene tape stopping her from going any further.

'Oh no. Please God, no.' Debra's eyes scanned the scene.

'D!' Ryan's green eyes flashed a questioning look using the high school nickname he'd given her so many years ago.

'Jeff?' Her voice wobbled, as she crumpled into him like a rag doll.

'Do you know someone here?'

He felt her push herself away from him, and point towards the face down girl.

'I got a... a message from my daughter, Scarlet.' And held her phone up to him, the LED screen lighting up his face.

The words in the blue message bubble blurred. Taking the phone, he adjusted the distance and the words became clearer.

'Park rounder help'.

Placing the phone in another evidence bag, he Pocketed the phone.

31

'Hey.'

'It's evidence D. I will get it back to you as soon as I can.'

She seemed to accept the explanation easily, but tried to push past him.

'D, you don't want to go in there.' Salt laced wind whipped at her hair as she collapsed back into him.

'But, it's Scar...' Her voice wined. 'That's my favourite denim jacket. The one I bedazzled in Home Ec. She is always borrowing it.'

He watched as her eyes settled on the boy her daughter was slumped over.

'Oh, Scar.' She said, angry disappointment in her voice. Why, the hell are you with *that* cartel boy Jace.' She stabbed a finger towards the slumped boy.

Ryan zeroed in on the familiar jacket as his mind rewound to 2006 and the intimate night fifteen-year-old Debra and he had shared. They'd been in love. Well, that's what he'd thought. Debra had been an independent wilful girl and he loved that about her. He'd offered, but she insisted on walking herself home that night saying she had to be home before her mother's curfew. But she'd left her favourite jacket, so he'd gone after her.

Turning the corner to Pinto Park, he saw her at the rounder, with Michael, one of the Australian cartel boys. The boy's arm had been draped around her shoulder like he owned her. He stood, silent, and watched as she took a swig of his beer.

What the hell was she thinking! She didn't even try to leave.

Pain clenched at his heart, and he'd dropped her jacket at his feet, immediately about-faced and knew then he'd be getting out of Yorks Knob. His plan had come quickly. He'd join the police academy, when he was old enough, and become a homicide detective, bring his brother's killers to justice, and bury any thought of her.

Residual anger flared in his voice as he yelled to the officer on the core crime-scene perimeter.

'Get the rest of 'em outta here!' He indicated towards the early morning dog walkers and runners. 'And give that woman a hand.' He pointed at Sonya in her tight, snakeskin dress lying flat out like a lizard. *Serves her right,* he thought still harbouring angry thoughts against her family.

'Take 'em down the station and get their statements.' Ryan ran his fingers through his dark peppered hair and reluctantly peeled Debra from him. 'You have to go with them, D. I will let you know more about Scarlet,' he looked deep into her ocean-blue eyes. 'When I can?'

'Everything?' Her eyes pleaded with him, still not moving an inch.

'Yes, everything' He turned her towards a waiting squad car and watched her leave.

Pulling out his flip pocket notebook, he wrote.

- *Mexican insignia on device.*

- *Proto type?*

- *Australian Cartel somehow involved. Wife, Sonya Rodriguez's son Jace, victim on Rounder.*

- *Debra Turner's daughter Scarlet. Victim on Rounder. Possible friends with Cartel son.*

- *Other four victims' identities. TBC.*
- *Wait for coroner's decision on all victims.*

Snapping on a fresh pair of gloves, he noticed an open black doctor's bag just behind the boy he now knew as Jace. Closing the bag with his pen, he squinted at the gold initials embossed on the side.

'D.T.?'

Adding the evidence information to his notebook he glanced down to see the clear flashing tubbing of the IV travel under the face-down girl, and down the side of the rounder. He shuffled closer and lifted the arm of the girl he now knew as Scarlet Turner.

'She didn't get it in!' He reached across the body to turn her over.

'Stop!' Doc Carol, the Forensic Pathologist entered the crime scene. She'd worked with him on the crocodile-bikie case earlier that year, and pointed to the detective's black, patent-leather Oxfords his ex-wife had bought him. Jutting from the curved toe was the tip of a flashing needle slowly dripping its deadly contents.

Startled, Ryan dropped the girl's arm, and it slapped like a wet fish hard against the worn wooden rounder boards.

A groan.

The entire crime scene halted. Shallow nasally breaths pierced the silence. Snatching the arm back, he felt for a heartbeat.

'We've got a live one here! The pulse is... faint, but it's there. Call an ambulance. Let's get her to a hospital, pronto.'

Head down, Doc Carol took the other five teens' pulses and shook her head after each one.

'Are you right if I go to the hospital with this one?' he asked Doc Carol.

'Yes, do what you need. I will have a report to you as soon as I've processed the scene.'

'Can you also get an analysis on these black floating objects in the glass drug machine?' He pointed with his pen.

'Will do,' she nodded.

He followed the ambulance, knew, this was his best bet for answers. Picking up the two-way radio he said, 'Detective Jeffery Ryan from the rounder incident in Pinto Park, Yorks Knob. One of the kids are alive, but unconscious. Following for a possible interview. The squad car with Debra Turner, please proceed to the Cairn's District Hospital.'

Scarlet had been mega pissed at her mother. She'd had a secret crush on Jace, and she'd never given her a real reason to stay away. She'd just said, '*that* whole family is out of bounds, and we are not having this conversation, young lady.'

Scarlet seethed inside making her even more determined to meet Jace at the Rounder that night.

'Bring your mothers medical bag. It's Scarlet, right?' he'd said to her at school that day, and gave her a quick squeeze around the shoulders. 'I think we will be needing it.'

That was all the encouragement she needed. But she had a sneaky feeling this would have something to do with drugs. She really wasn't interested, but she didn't want to be the goody two shoes either, and on occasion had wondered what it would be like, even just once.

The other two girls and three boys were all part of the Cartel family, cousins, and these girls were real bitches. But now, they were pleased to see her, even sharing their special brownies. Her mouth closed over the sweet gooey chocolaty texture with a grassy mushroom undertone.

Disgusting, she thought and went to spit it out on the grass, but saw five sets of eyes watching her closely, and swallowed.

'Snatching this *gear filled* Hookah machine from our front gates before our parents saw was a stroke of luck.' Jace said, excited to test the unusual machine out. 'Let's get this party started,' and he flicked the switch to start the battery-operated drug machine flashing.

Scarlet took another small bite of her brownie, hoping it would give her the mettle she needed, and reached for her mother's black doctor's bag only just visible in the darkness.

Done, the other five were hooked up, including the now slurring Jace, and they were now waiting for her. How the medical tubing was flashing, she had no idea. Squinting closer, she could barely see the fibreoptic, hair size wire. But in the pre-dawn light, it looked pretty cool, and she hurried to hook herself up.

Scar tied the red cylindrical rubber tourniquet tightly just above her elbow just like she'd seen her mother do countless times before. She touched the little blue engorged vein, and the bulge bounced back.

'Perfect.' Using the torch app on her phone, she guided the beam of light to the crook of her elbow. The needle pierced her skin like a mosquito bite.

'Ouch'. Her heart banged hard against her chest, as she dug around for the vein she knew was just under the skin. The thought of the cloud-like feeling and the juice she was about to welcome into her body, made her hand shake ever so slightly. Bam, the needle pierced straight through the other side of the blood vessel.

'Frig', she mumbled and poked the needle tip around some more trying to locate the dark vein again. But the brutality of the act was nothing compared to the need to be part of this group.

The other five were already feeling the effects, eyes closed and heads resting against the rounders curved pipe bars staring mindlessly at the stars.

Scar fumbled, dropping the needle into the dirt.

'Damn it.' She started to doubt herself.

'Car'mon Scar.' Jace slurred.

She scrambled to get another needle set up. She knew she had to get this one in or be an outcast once again. And this time, for the rest of her senior year. She didn't think she could live through another six months of humiliation, and lose her one chance with Jace.

'C'mon Scar,' she babbled mimicking Jace, her mind fogging and starting to lose focus. She took a big breath and mentally prepared for the pinching she knew was coming, fumbled, and dropped the needle for a second time.

'For fuck's sake Scarlet, get yourself together.'

The rhythm of her heart slowed from the effects of the Shroomies. She glanced over to see Jace's head tilted at a weird angle and the pupils of his eyes dilated. Pink bloody foam, dotted with brownie crumbs, dribbled from his perfect kissable lips to his crisp white shirt and leather jacket.

'Oh shit, this is actually going down,' she slurred. On her feet now, she juggled the phone from her pocket and sent a text her mother's number.

Park rounder help

This was all she could type before she stumbled and fell forwards slamming her befuddled head against one of the rounder's rails. Pain bounced around inside her skull as she gripped the cold pipe rail. The warm metallic taste of blood momentarily cleared her senses. 'Stay conscious Scar, must stay cons...' She blacked out with visions of rainbow lights twinkling in Jace's vein as she fell across him.

Ryan pulled up in the police designated spot in the emergency bay of the Cairns District Hospital as they unloaded the unconscious girl. He knew she'd be his most reliable witness, and remembered his promise to Debra.

Inside the hospital, he sat beside the girl's bed with the curtains pulled and waited. Scarlet was coming in and out of consciousness, babbling words he could not decipher. Pulling out his notebook, he looked at his last entry.

- *D T? Black doctor's bag.*

- *He stared at the tiny stars on the emergency room curtain, making mental bullet points.*

- *Geezuz, Debra Turner.*

- *Why and how did Scarlet have her mother's bag?*

- *Did her mother know she had it?*

- *How well did Scarlet know the other deceased children?*

- *Why the rounder?*

This was getting him nowhere fast. He needed to get some answers, and fast. Turning to the nurse in the room checking the girl's vitals, he handed her a business card.

'Can you call me as soon as she wakes?'

'Certainly Sir.' She looked down at the card. 'Detective Jeffery Ryan.'

Ryan left for the station to interrogate the Cartel wife, Sonya Rodriguez.

'This interview is being recorded. Do you understand?'

The woman, cheeks stained with mascara, made no sound or movement.

'Do you understand?' He lent forward slapping the table.

Jumping in her seat, the woman nodded.

'I'm not after a confession here. I'm after the truth. Does this device belong to you or your husband Michael?' He pushed the tray holding the unusual glass Hookah machine towards the woman.

No answer.

'Why would your children be doing drugs in Pinto Park?'

No answer.

'How'd your children get their hands on it?'

The woman sat forward in her chair, elbows on the desk and stared daggers at him.

'You think I killed my own family. Fuck you.'

'No, just trying to get some straight answers.' He pointed to the device and said, 'It's got the Mexican Cartel insignia etched on the side.'

The woman's eyes grew as large as ping pong balls as she reached for the device. 'What? Why would they kill...'

He pulled it away from her and turned it so she could see the symbol. 'We tested each of the six compartments, and each one had a different drug, with the exact same genetic components your syndicate push.

'You have no proof of that.'

'Not hard proof, not yet!'

A smirk crossed the woman's face.

'We did find a single underlying trace substance in each of the six compartments. Can you enlighten us?' he said not wanting to give away the presence of what had looked like floating black berries.

'Look, it turned up at the front gates days ago and the CCTV was out. But I didn't touch it.' She sat back again, crossing her arms. 'It had those needle things, thought it was from that crazy Phlebotomist, Debra Turner, because of what happen to h...'

'Because of *what* happened. Care to elaborate?'

'Nothing! I want my lawyer.'

'One more question. Again. Why was your child in Pinto Park, on the rounder?'

'I WANT my lawyer,' the woman growled through clenched teeth.

And he flipped off the recorder.

Standing, he walked towards the interview room's exit.

Addressing the constable at the door, 'She's lawyered up,' he said, knowing he'd get no more from her.

'Wait.' The woman stood up.

Ryan turned back.

'I'll give you your brother's killer if you find out who killed my family.'

A ruse, he thought, but said, 'Deal.' He knew this was a pact he'd never keep.

Ryan flipped open his notebook again.

- *Why would Debra do it?*
- *Why would she try to kill her own daughter?*
- *What happened to Debra? Was it Cartel related?*
- *Yorks Knob precinct files re: Debra Turner.*

Ryan's phone rang. 'Doc Carol.'

'Atropa *belladonna*.'

'What?' he said.

'The berry from the device. Its Atropa *belladonna*.' Or, in laymen's terms, Night Shade, Devil's Berries or Death Cherries. They are one of Australia's most deadly perennial weeds.

Ryan's phone pinged as a photo of a purple bell-shaped flower and tiny black berries took up most of his screen.

'Be careful around this plant. It kills quick.' She emphasised. 'A single leaf or twenty berries would be fatal to an adult. And the plants just pop up in people's gardens. They look pretty, so people leave them until it's too late.

Ping.

'I just sent you the genome for this little killer. Gotta go.'

Ryan looked at his phone. *She's so abrupt sometimes*, tapped on the information and decided to read it later. He had more pressing matters.

Turning to the admin constable, he said, 'Can you pull up any files on Debra Turner?'

'One moment Detective.'

Ping.

The computer screen lit up with an extensive investigation file, including hospital records, toxicology reports, private documents, and the victim's statement.

'May I?' He indicated to the constable's chair.

'Certainty Sir.'

'Thank you.' He sat, hand on the mouse as he scanned the document.

DEBRA TURNER, 15 – Rape, Pinto Park – Rounder – Yorks Knob.

Date: 2nd June 2006

Suspects:

- Michael Rodriguez
- Chad Rodriguez
- Markus Rodriguez

Hospital records show, Miss Debra Turner had extensive bruising of the genital area with evidence of forced intercourse. She claims the suspects gave her alcohol. She took this willingly. All three suspects were known to her and from her high school. Miss Turner then states the alcohol had been drugged, and had incapacitated her. Miss Turner said she had been fully awake but could not move. Drug and alcohol tests confirm, along with a small amount of alcohol, there were large quantities of the drug Rohypnol in her system. She recounts each of the suspects then raped her in the order of suspects listed and left her, naked from the waist down on the Pinto Park Rounder. No samples were taken from the male suspects as lawyers intervened. The suspects were released due to being minors and no hard evidence.

'Those bastards!' The words *raped* and *Michael Rodriguez*, leapt out at him as he slammed his fist on the desk making a coffee cup jump splashing the desk. He wiped the file with his sleeve as he read through the file again.

'Geezuz.' The date shot towards him like a bullet. It was the same night he'd seen her at the park, the same night he'd decided to leave, the same night they'd...

Ryan placed a hand on Debra's shoulder, startling her.

'It's alright D.' He sat in the hospital chair next to her, gathering up both of her hands. 'I know everything. I've read your file at the precinct.'

'Why'd you leave Jeff?' She searched his eyes. 'Those bastards hurt me.'

'I know that now D,' and rubbed her hands with his thumbs. 'I'm so sorry you went through that.' Tears threatened, as he cupped her face gently, turning her towards him. 'I followed you that night. You'd left your precious jacket, and well, I wanted to make sure you got home ok. But I saw you walk arm and arm with that Cartel kid Michael. I couldn't control the rage crashing through me, it was like red-hot fire. I wanted to kill him right there, right then. I wanted to crush his corrupt family so badly for killing my brother. And it hurt, standing there watching you with him. I couldn't take it. I couldn't watch a minute longer. I had to leave, and I knew then, forever.'

Her sad eyes bored into his sole.

'If only I'd called out. If only I'd just made sure.'

'Oh Jeff, it's all such a mess.' She tore her eyes away to look at her unconscious daughter.

He followed her gaze and said what he'd been thinking since he sat down.

'Is she mi...?'

'I don't know. You, them, it all happened on the same night.'

'Mum?' Scarlet said groggily, opening her piercing green eyes.

'Oh sweetheart.' Debra jumped up to hug her daughter.

Days later, the trio drove to Debra's bungalow in silence. All of the news had affected each one of them profoundly. Pulling up, Ryan opened the car door for Scarlet.

'Let me,' he took the small overnight bag from the girl. He stared into the exact same inquisitive green eyes he saw in the shave mirror every day. He smiled, and silently followed Debra and Scarlet, the child he never thought he'd have.

By the front door of the veranda, the bag he was caring bumped hard into a large black pot plant, and dropped the bag. Bending to pick it up he squinted, dangling right in front of his eye were the same tiny black berries he'd seen floating in the device at the crime scene. The bush, sitting in a large pot, was lush and healthy, and covered in the distinctive bell-shaped purple flowers Doc Carol had told him about.

His step faltered, and he saw Debra look back to where he'd been staring. Their eyes locked, and she turned back around to enter her bungalow, pain etched on her face.

He knew then, the device had been a perfect means for revenge for the perpetrators who had gang rapped and left her for dead as a teen. He had already deduced that the device was meant for the cartel as five of the victims were Australian cartel relatives. He'd even had Debra on his mental suspect list, but took her off almost immediately, as her daughter had been one of the victims.

He understood her need for retaliation. The sinking memories of his own brother's death crashed through him. His career was on the line, but he knew then he'd do what was needed, whatever the consequences. He ripped out the crime scene pages from his notebook intending to rewrite them and destroy the others.

Besides, they'd been riding that same rounder for way too long, their lives circling the truth.

It was time to step off.

CROSSINGS

GINA PINTO

Author's Note.

When a stranger and a journalist become the story...

... you step into their journeys as you would a newspaper – one column at a time.

CRUZAMENTO
CARLOS CRUZ

*L*ike the water from El Alamein fountain, their conversation pours out onto the street.

'Told you to deal with the broad!'

'Boss, I'll fit her with concrete slippers and drop off the cliff at Nielsen.'

CROSSED JOAN
WATSON

*O*n a raw July morning, the wind howls a voiced forecast. It sweeps through the streets of the Cross, rushing at the running text, shaking the front page, roaring my inconceivable headline.

Crossed by Evil

After a hard night's work cleaning filth, it's one thing to hear men speak of murder, it's another to know them.

The smell of Brilhiantina drifts my way as Senhor Duke combs his hair.

'Set up a meeting with the bloody journalist.'

In my country, people say, 'It's not the bullet that kills you, it's fate.' And I know I'm invisible to these men... until I cross them.

Below the surface of the nineteen-word lede rustles the fate of those who enter this place.

There is still no trace of the missing woman. Police searched the vicinity of the nightclub, where she was last seen.

There is only one way out of the Cross.

THE MILE OF SIN

In Australia, they call me 'dago'. There are worse names. I was baptised Carlos Cruz in a village where names matter. Today I want to be incógnito.

I follow the two men. Cars stop when Senhor Duke crosses Darlinghurst Road. Ned walks like a thief, hands in pocket, head down.

They go into Duke's other nightclub, Copa, on the corner

THE GOLDEN MILE

As Joan Watson, a reporter at The Daily, my high point is to uncover foul play till my boss turns it into muckraking stories.

I work for Ken Parker. His motto is: 'There's a little whore in us all, so do what it takes to get the story.'

A mugshot of the missing prostitute flies across Parker's desk.

of Roslyn Street.

Not all clubs stink the same. This one, it's Brilhiantina, cigars, and rats. I wait outside.

The lights slice through the dawn rain to show the Cross never sleeps.

I walk like a man in jail. Back and forth. The puddles on the footpath bleed through the holes in my shoes. The smell of stale cigarettes rises from the gutter. Men like me, should see, hear, and do nada.

As I walk away, the two men exit Copa. They look at me like I'm part of the trash spilling onto the Mile of Sin.

Car doors slam. A red Dodge speeds around the bend on Darlinghurst Road. What I do next is like a car in a one-way street.

'What now?'

'Parker, you know what this is.'

'Stick to thumb sucking. Just cover the petty crimes.'

'I've got leads. This is Page One.'

'What leads? You heard some Cross whispers. So, what!'

'It's more than whispers.'

'Let the big boys handle this. A good-looking sheila like you shouldn't be sniffing in bins at the Cross. Don't get your hands dirty, or worse, break a nail.'

'I can bust this case wide open.'

Parker doesn't answer.

'I'm offering you... the King of the Cross.'

'Are we done here?'

A BROAD, BULLET, & BLOOD

Four weeks ago, at Priscilla's, my life took a turn. Parked

PROSTITUTES, PAYOFFS, & POLICE

Three weeks earlier, Parker had me cover a robbery.

outside the nightclub was a yellow Ford Falcon.

When ordered to clean the basement, my mistake was to arrive too early. A man, like Capone, stood in the middle of the room. Gold cufflinks sparkled beneath his suit sleeves. Opposite him, a woman, on her knees, her ringed fingers laced together. She begged. Her eyes down, she didn't see me in the shadows. I didn't see the gun.

My eardrums exploded with the shot. Her body dropped like a bag of cement. Her underwear peaked below the miniskirt, legs twisted beneath her body. The blood flowed towards his patent-leather shoes.

The man with the Capone hat controlled the silence until his words fired like the rat-tat-tat of a machine gun, 'One less whore-snitch on the streets.'

Repeat offender. Rumour had it he once scored an Heirloom-opal ring. This time the safeblower, on arrest, screamed about his missing girlfriend, an opal-wearing prostitute from the Cross.

I wrote the ten-line robbery article, handed it to Parker, and sniffed around the Cross for this missing woman.

The travails of the human condition reign in this place, and I was there to exhume its underbelly.

A street-girl, dense with makeup and bruises, solicited away from the glare of the new Coca-Cola neon. The only one willing to talk, she vented about the cold, and her johns. Her rouge lips flapped with a warning, 'Darl, life's like da Cross. Dirty and flippin' dangerous.'

'What's your name?'

'Charlie, like da perfume, darl. Ya not goin' ta write 'bout

Like a coward I hid. When the sound of his steps and the dragging stopped, I entered the room. The mop, red as a bullfighter's cape, absorbed what was left of this woman.

Except for one small item.

POLICE VS. PEOPLE

At Darlinghurst station, a policeman barks at a thief sitting with handcuffs.

'There's the right way, the wrong way, and the 'Darlo Way', mate.'

He looks from the thief to me and says, 'Behold what the wind blew in. What can I do for ya on this lousy day?'

'I have a crime to report.'

'You speaka the Queens's English I see. Crime ya say, and what might that be?'

'Two men want to kill a woman jornalista.'

'Is that so? And pray-tell when is this event takin' place?'

me, are ya? People like me get fed to da sharks. Know what I mean!'

Her scent, gardenia, hid the stink of the Cross. Her whisper gave me a name.

POLICE VS. JOURNALIST

The missing prostitute intersected with a dangerous cesspit of corruption. She knew names, was ready to spill, and was last seen outside Priscilla's.

Fred Krane, a man who knows more than he's saying, clenches his jaw. Like many of the detectives, he sports a fedora, and a lousy disposition.

I'm at the precinct to find out about 'the Laugh' - bribe money from the Cross prostitutes to detectives at CIB. A profitable arrangement for those in on the joke. Investigating corruption is not for the faint hearted. It's one

'This I do not know.'

'Who's going to commit this crime?'

'Men from Copa nightclub.'

'Who's this woman?'

I shake my head.

I didn't help the woman in the basement. I am failing again with the jornalista.

'I tell you what fella, if you walk out of here quietly, I won't kick ya up the rear for wasting my time.'

The policeman pulls out his baton, slams it hard on the desk, and yells, 'Capeesh?'

THE SIGN OF
THE CROSS

In my Sunday suit, moustache trimmed, looking mafioso, I go to where sirens scream and prostitutas shout. I call this the Cross melodias. Inside Copa's, there's the silence of the lobos' den.

'Boa noite Senhorita Lyn.'

thing to deal with mobsters, it's another to expose bent cops.

Krane, like a meat-eater, devours anyone in his path. I'm no exception.

'A girl can lose her sense of smell poking her nose where it doesn't belong,' says Krane as he tugs at his monogrammed cufflinks.

'The festering rot of corruption is there for those willing to take a sniff.'

'This is beyond any filth you ever wanna smell.' And like that, I got the One-Time Warning.

BEWARE THE
RUSSIAN CROSS

I never back out of a crusade. But they've seen me prowling their turf. I can handle the rats in the sewers of the Cross, the anonymous late-night calls, but I've become a target. I suspect the threats are from Mikha'el Alexandrovich, aka Duke. He doesn't take too well

'Bona noychay handsome. What's with the fancy clobber?'

'Can I ask you some questions?'

'Course.'

'Boss is meeting a woman jornalista. What's her name?'

'My name is all ya need, luv.'

'It's importante. Please.'

'You sure 'bout this?'

'I am positivo.'

The jewel I slide to Lyn helps persuade her.

'The dame's name is Joan Watson. Works in town at The Daily.'

Wearing the ring, Lyn makes a gun out of her fingers and shoots the words, 'These kinda questions can get ya killed luv. BAM!'

to my chats with his street-girls and the cops.

And my auto-da-fé headlines don't help.

Tapping into Organised Crime
Crime Doesn't Pay,
But Prostitutes Do

I'm beleaguered at the paper for my obsession with Duke. But I'm onto a scoop. I can expose the top dog.

The Rise and Fall of
the Cross Boss

I don't leave a trail his hounds can follow, but I have become visible. My peripheral vision catches a shape. When I turn to look, it disappears. But dogging me like my own shadow, won't stop me.

DENIED ENTRY

I run up William Street, past the cathedral and through

QUICK EXIT

A degree of stupidity, a pinch of courage, and journalistic tenacity

Hyde Park. Before I enter, I catch my breath leaning on the massive granite façade.

I ask the receptionist, with Colgate teeth, 'I need to see Miss Joan Watson.'

'Do you have an appointment sir?'

'It's very importante I speak to her.'

She stares at my forehead. I wipe the sweat away.

'Without an appointment, my hands are tied.'

'Assassinato.'

My word has no impact.

Her stare slides from me to the Security Guard at the door. He is the size of a train and speeds in my direction.

'This woman is in danger.' I yell.

I know that acting nervous in the Cross attracts attention, and not the kind you want. It's no different here.

The guard grabs my collar and throws me onto the street.

compels me to keep the meeting organised by Ned Trent on behalf of his boss. I know it's a ploy to get me to the nightclub, but it's the scoop of a lifetime.

Running late may have been the first warning sign. This is the second — as I pull out of the office carpark, I almost hit Parker with my Porsche 356. The tires squeal to a halt.

'Where you off to in such a hurry? There's no story worth dying for!'

'You'll get a bullet between those defiant eyes if you move another muscle.'

I adjust the rearview mirror. Parker stands there, hands on his hips. Without turning around, I yell out of my coupé, 'I have the story of a lifetime.'

Both his hands bracket as if he's posting breaking news and yells back, 'I can see the headline now: Dying to Tell a Story, Crazy Sheila Wraps Porsche Around Lamppost.'

I consider going back in when a car backfires.

I turn.

A woman in a sportscar races down Elizabeth Street.

Foot to the pedal, I speed off. The roar of the engine and the rasp of tyres on the basement-level carpark drown Parker's last words to me.

Later, the police examine the marks left by the tyres and interrogate Parker on my state of mind.

DOUBLE-CROSSED

The carpet at Copa is red for a reason.

I've seen men thrown out with their noses on the other side of their faces. Bones sticking out from their arms when they shield their heads.

The motto at Copa is, 'Don't shit where you eat.' The real dirty work happens at Priscilla's.

'Not a good time handsome. Boss is in a meeting.' says Lyn.

'With the jornalista!'

'Ya way ova ya head luv.'

Her eyes go to the door.

As Ned enters the room, he tugs at both his sleeves. I

CROSS-EXAMINED

Outside Copa nightclub, a spruiker, hands behind his back, calls out, 'Hey fellas come see them beautiful gals.' Ned Trent is next to him, a fag hangs from his thin mouth. He has a sallow complexion, known around Kings Cross as a 'nightclub tan'.

Without looking, he says, 'Upstairs.'

Lyn Collins types as she eyeballs me. I'd heard stories about this transvestite. In her youth she performed at Copa's all-male show. Now the blonde bombshell works behind a desk.

expect a gun to drop out.

His eyes dare me to say the wrong word.

'Little birdie tells me you've become a curious man.'

I look at Lyn.

'Cat got your tongue!'

'Put da piece away, Ned,' says Lyn.

I see irritation run through his stick-thin body. Skin like ash, teeth ready to bite, he says, 'What's worse than asking questions?'

He moves closer and growls.

'It's getting answers!'

'You're that reporter, aren't ya luv?'

I nod.

'Don't catch many of your type 'round here. Duke can scare the fleas off a dog!'

I follow Ned into the VIP Lounge. I smell a fruity scent of Brilliantine. In the corner, back turned, Duke smokes, and gestures with his cigar to sit.

'You're the sheila sniffing up my arse.'

'I'm here to set the record straight.'

'We both know it ain't happening.'

'What's this about then?'

'When you dig in my front yard, be prepared for a hole.'

SINNERS & SAINTS

Ned breaks my nose. There's worse that can happen to a man in this city.

As I leave, I hear a woman say, 'This is not the last you'll hear from me.'

THE JOURNALIST & THE DEVIL

I reach for my lipstick and remind myself why I am doing this. I wasn't expecting a confession. But the prick made a threat! And bloody

The jornalista, wearing a coat, and bell-bottom pants, is taller than I imagined. Her dark brown hair is pulled up and adds inches to her elegant figure.

'I'm not finished with you dago.'

I've heard enough barking from Senhor Duke's guard dog, and I chase the jornalista outside.

Her trembling hand applies red lipstick on her pale lips. I press a handkerchief to stop my nosebleed.

She looks my way.

How can a man like me, a cleaner from the Cross, a stranger, explain my behaviour to a woman like her? How do I tell her my boss, Senhor Duke, wants her dead?

Without warning, the yellow Ford Falcon stops in front of her.

SINFUL SYDNEY

There are places in a city where sin grows. A prostituta is too underestimated me.

It didn't escape my attention Lyn wearing an Heirloom-opal ring. The same one the safeblower stole and gave his missing girlfriend. There are no coincidences in the Cross.

When you meet the Devil, you learn when to ask questions and when to shut up.

As I stand by the curb, a striking European man runs out of Copa with a bleeding nose.

I never forget a face.

Especially one sporting a Burt Reynolds moustache being thrown out of my office building. And here he is again.

This is no coincidence.

As I turn to confront him, a car screeches to a halt. The driver jumps out, makes his way towards me. He stands so close I smell the rot within him.

CITY OF CRIMS

The steel shoved against my back directs me down the

young to be on the streets, a needle is left on a playground, and a policeman commits the sins of criminals. I didn't need to see his eyes that morning to feel the force of evil behind them.

My letter to the newspaper will explain how Lyn got the opal ring and what happened to the prostituta.

This time I see the gun in the hand of the man wearing the Capone hat, and the police badge on his belt. He pokes her back to get the jornalista to cross Darlinghurst Road and into Priscilla's.

There's a public phone by the laundromat. I can call triple zero.

I grab the handset.

What do I say? A man like me has no voice in this city of loud noises, dangerous voices, and evil men.

There's no time.

Fate, dealt from the bottom of the deck, carves my path.

steps of the nightclub into the basement.

'What are we doing here?'

'Get down on your knees.'

The coldness of the concrete floor rises up my body.

'We can come to an agreement.'

'The only agreement I want is the same I dished that whistleblowing street whore.'

Krane's face, shaped like a rock, twitches in anger.

'You will never tell this story. No one will ever hear your voice.'

'You'll have your whole squad looking for me.'

'Cops won't look for bullet holes once the sharks finish with you.'

My watch, heedless of my predicament, ticks on.

Krane holds the gun, but I know who whispered in his ear. Charlie's own whisper warned me of Krane.

I run into Priscilla's thinking, You don't get a saint to catch a sinner.

BELOW THE CROSS

Like last time, his back is turned away from the entrance to the basement and the woman is on her knees. This time, the woman sees me. It's for an instant, but it makes the man spin.

Like a boxer, I put my fists up. The Capone man stares at my worn shirt cuffs and laughs once. Before he points the gun at me, he touches his gold cufflinks, and says, 'You're a fuckin' nobody.'

'I am Carlos Cruz, and you need to pay for your sins.'

He watches with the calm of a wolf. Without taking his eyes from me, he spits to the side.

In a moment of hatred, I lunge. My fist crashes into his face once, twice. Each knuckle has his flesh, his blood. His

Head held high I fix my eyes on his gun until I see movement in the shadows.

BENEATH THE HEADLINE

A front row seat is every journo's dream. The quest for answers leads down here and to the man within. Kneeling I face the underbelly of the Cross. In this place, there are men who creep out of the shadows. Others hide waiting for the right moment to act. Crossed by good, I am gifted a stranger. I see the words in my head like I'm in the newsroom. He becomes the lede sentence to my headline.

A young immigrant, on a mission to save, arms himself with his fists and fate, and heads to the lawlessness of the Cross to hunt evil.

The back wall where Krane stands is crossed with cigarette-

reaction is slow. The type a corrupt cop gets when he shoots kneeling targets.

Just as he hits the back wall, his hand with the gun flies up.

I see a glint and the dark barrel of the pistola pointed at me.

The explosion drowns her scream. My hands rush to my chest. His look cold as the ground I lie on, the blood hot as fever. Her velvet eyes rest upon me and I become visible.

sized holes embedded with crushed bullets. My heart hitches so hard it turns his every move into slow motion.

It halts with the hissing of the bullet.

My body doubles onto itself. Head bowed, my shallow breaths inhale the stench of this concrete dungeon.

My head springs up as Krane turns to face me. I move to stand.

'You'll get a bullet between those defiant eyes if you move another muscle.'

CROSSED BY EVIL

As I face the devil, a last breath exits, a bullet awaits in the chamber, thoughts become actions.

I leap from the floor and charge. Krane, not surprised by the move, is quick to react. He clutches my neck and pushes me onto the bullet-ridden wall. Feet dangle in the air. A knee to the groin makes Krane loosen his hold, lose his footing, and reel back. We tussle.

I run towards the exit. He yanks me back with a claw-like grip, swings me around. A coward's punch across my jaw radiates a pain deep inside my head and knocks me to my knees. Clenched within my hand, a monogrammed gold cufflink.

My name is Joan Watson and I write for The Daily.

The scoop and the silenced voices meant everything. Now, a calm, like a warm breeze, envelops my body.

I don't flinch as he presses the muzzle of the gun to my temple and says, 'Any last words?'

THE JUGGLE

EMMA RENNISON

My stomach flips as the aroma wafts up and makes my nostrils contract. I close my eyes and visualise the scene again. Multiple stab wounds between the breasts and across the stomach. Just like the last six.

'Mummy?'

I spring back to reality, the knife in my hand coated in thick brown spread. Nausea sits in my throat. I don't remember morning sickness lasting this long with Ellie. A lot has happened in the last three years.

My daughter turns. Kneeling, her feet kicked out underneath her. So close to the 65-inch screen she has to twist her head side to side to see the whole image. Her flame hair glows in the midday sun filtering through the kitchen window. A short fiery halo around her face. My heart throbs. I want to squeeze her till she pops.

'Mummy, is my Vegemite toast ready?' she asks, the bright colours of her favourite lunchtime programme flickering blues, reds and yellows in her eyes.

I scrape against the dry toast. A jumping line of darkened crumbs appears with each new drag.

'You're a little close, sweetheart. Sit on the couch.' I nibble on a dry cracker and deliver the pink plastic plate of soldiers. I'm so tired. I could sit for a bit more. There's no rush today.

Another song begins. Ellie's head whips around, her question forgotten.

My phone lights up and shudders across the kitchen counter. Work.

'Anna,' I announce to the caller.

'Anna, it's Ben. Sorry to call you.'

'It's fine. What can I do for you?'

'We got the go-ahead on the warrant. Are you okay for us to progress without you?'

I screw my face up. I hate it when approvals go through on my day off. I glance at Ellie. She's winding her hands around, forwards then backwards, following the onscreen routine. I could drop her at nursery. Race in. Just for a few hours.

'No. I mean yes. Go ahead without me.' I bite the inside of my cheek. I can't do that to her. The last time I made it home for bedtime was weeks ago. It's been so long since we had any proper time together.

I grab my file from the high shelf and flick through images of the six female victims like a flipbook animation. None of them change. All pale, naked and defaced. Eyes closed in a peaceful slumber despite their violent deaths.

'Good call. I'll keep you posted,' Ben says.

'Hey, Ben. Before you go...' This is hard to say. '...my phone will be on, but try not to overuse it.'

'Yes, Boss,' he replies. His voice formal and deep.

'I'll see you tomorrow.'

I end the call, turn the phone facedown and slide it away from me. My shoulders rise and fall as I breathe hard out of my nose. I shove in the rest of the cracker, churning it around in my mouth to make it soft. I shrug. Today will be the day they'll find him.

'Look, Mummy! You're on TV!' Ellie points, her eyes ablaze.

And there I am.

I place one hand under my stomach, the other swings me around the breakfast bar towards the television.

'I've heard you have an eyewitness, Detective?'

'That's right. And today we're releasing an artist's impression of our main suspect.'

I freeze, with my hand still on my belly, and marvel again at the black-and-white sketch as it flashes up on the screen.

Caucasian. Twenty to thirty. A mop of overhanging dark hair that stops where his brows start, each spiralling towards the centre so they almost meet. Large deep-set eyes framed by long black lashes. Thick bottom lip that juts out like a lonely schoolboy. Clean-shaven with a dimple on the left side, apparent when he talks as well as when he smiles. It's a strong description. We have to find him. Before he reaches number seven. Before I get to eight months and my maternity leave begins.

'Mummy,' Ellie says, clutching her favourite teddy so his arms wrap around her neck. Her eyes glued to the ones on the screen. 'He looks a bit funny.'

'Hmm? He does, doesn't he? Have you seen the remote?'

I scrabble around, lift random objects. A sippy cup, Ellie's plate, a half-eaten piece of soggy toast smeared across the table. It's never where it should be. I throw the scatter cushions on the floor, slide my fingers between the cracks in the couch. A plastic dinosaur, crumbs, a sticky lolly wrapper. No remote.

'And what can you tell us about the victims?'

'Female. All between twenty and twenty-five.'

'And is it true they all have red hair?'

'Yes, that is true.'

'And he cuts off the hair once he's stabbed them?'

I press my lips together. *Why do they put this on during the day?*

'Come on, you. Let's go and get ready for our day out.' I pull my face into a forced smile and reach for her hand.

'Yeah!' Ellie skips towards her bedroom, her little hand in mine. 'Can Bear-bear come?'

'Absolutely! We need his help to find a friend for this little one,' I reply and pat my tummy, willing the news to move on to the weather report. It doesn't. I'm still there. My giant face. Too large for this room. The shadows under my eyes hang halfway down my cheeks. New grey hairs straggle up and away from my signature neat work bun. Aged by the juggling act of the last few years. The case. Motherhood. Life.

My giant mirror image moistens her lips and waits for further questions. Please cut here. Go to the next segment.

'And what can you tell us about the victims' teeth, Detective. There's a rumour he likes to take them too.'

Ellie clambers into her car seat, dragging Bear-bear behind her. Every journey she holds his bobbled felt paw and strokes his pointy stitched nose and down-turned mouth. The routine - strap Ellie in, strap Bear-bear in - always makes us late. But it's not worth the red-faced screams to fight it.

The phone vibrates in my pocket. It stops and restarts as if on constant redial.

'I'm busy!' I tell it. Ellie's brows draw together. 'Silly Mummy talking to her phone.'

I slam the door shut. Work has called three times. I drum the top of the car with my fingers, swing open the driver's door and ease in, chucking the phone on the passenger seat. *It's just one day.*

The radio begins its chatter just before the engine comes to life.

'What can you tell us about the victims?'

'Really?!'

I jab at the button until Ellie's music comes on. Stretch my neck to catch her reflection in the rear-view mirror. She's already singing along. *Breathe. Forget everything else.*

'Are you ready, sweetpea?'

The red curls framing her face bounce in an overstated nod.

'And Bear-bear too?'

'Yes, Mummy!'

The bear's head wobbles as we leave the smooth driveway and bump over the curb. His old-fashioned body loose now from the last three years of endless cuddles.

'Come on Mummy!' Ellie pulls my arm away from our parked car, desperate to lead the way.

I hesitate. *We are so close. It wouldn't hurt to take another look.* I tug back in the opposite direction.

'It's this way,' I tell her.

Our arms stretch until the jolt forces her to follow. In between skipping and singing she points out every tram as they ting past. Oblivious to my detour.

It's just a few blocks. Then we'll go. Ellie flaps a hand to mimic the song actions. *What harm will it do?*

When we arrive, my feet anchor at the entrance of the graffitied laneway. The place where we found the last victim's tooth.

'Mummy! We have to go!'

Ellie leans back to make me follow her. Desperate to keep moving. To get to the place I'd promised. Her purple Mary Janes dragging across the concrete pavement.

'Just a minute,' I answer and pull on her tiny arm as I step into the narrow alley. The killing ground now covered with overflowing rubbish.

I still can't get my head around this one. So open. So fearless.

The black shiny plastic of one bag has split. Clawed or pecked by an opportunistic raven. A tapered trail of rotten meat, stripped chicken bones, grey and gristly, points to the perimeter of what was the crime scene. I take another step, my arm held back by my reclining daughter. The sour tangy scent punches me. My throat swells, as it did the morning we found her, dumped like the leftovers.

'It smells.' Ellie pinches her nose and loosens her grip. 'I don't like it.'

I take a short breath, swallow a mixture of hot acidic bile and death. *Now is not the time to be here.*

'Again, Mummy!' Ellie skips through the art deco archway into the old Arcade.

'Don't you know this story already?' I grin.

Work stopped calling. My attention belongs to her.

'I've forgotten,' she says, blinking.

'Oh really?' I chuckle. 'When you were a tiny baby in my tummy...'

'Like baby now?' She points at my stomach.

'Yes, but much smaller,' I answer. 'I found a special toyshop where Bear-bear was living all by himself.'

'And then what happened?' Ellie's eyes widen and the corners of her mouth twitch.

'Well, as soon as I saw him, I knew he wanted to be your best friend. And I asked the nice lady in the shop if I could buy him.'

'Yes.' Ellie's little face tilts up, her smile broadens.

'The lady asked a thousand questions about you, climbed a ladder and brought him down. I cuddled him against my tummy and you did a little kick. As if to say "hello".'

Ellie lets go of my hand and spins with her teddy. Her skirt flows around her.

I want to pause this moment, save it. I remind myself again that I must be more present.

'Mummy? Is this it?'

I smile and nod as she presses her face into the shop window. Her breath bellows a foggy damp cloud between her hands, as the tip of her nose flattens against the glass. She pauses on the collection of tiny porcelain animal ornaments lined up. Penguins, snails, koalas, frogs. All no bigger than a marble.

'Can I get one, Mummy? Please?' Ellie begs.

'We'll see.' An answer echoed from my childhood.

I push the door. The bell above jingles. The shopkeeper raises her head. Her glasses perched on the end of her nose.

I smile, hoping she remembers me, and whisper to Ellie not to touch anything.

Ellie's eyes dart from one toy to another. Her mouth an open pout to match the collection of china dolls and their painted red lips. Wooden trains wobble past each other and ballerinas dance in delicate lace skirts inside music boxes. Goggled pilots circle aeroplanes above her, their scarves flying out behind them. A red and white big top surrounded by circus creatures bob to the tinkling tune of *Send in the Clowns*.

As Ellie's little body turns to take it all in, the shopkeeper watches, her mouth pursing into a small 'oh'.

The noise catches Ellie's attention, her gaze snaps up to see the woman stare, wide-eyed, at her teddy. She steps towards the counter and holds him around his worn-down tummy. His head flops forward.

'This is Bear-bear,' she tells her.

'Hello, Bear-bear.' The shopkeeper leans across the counter to shake his paw. 'How are you today?'

Ellie laughs, which makes the shopkeeper laugh too.

'Is there anything, in particular, I can help you with?' She directs her question to my daughter.

'Yes!' she replies. 'Mummy has a baby in her tummy and the baby would like a Bear-bear like mine.'

The shopkeeper smiles at me.

'We can help you with that.' She side-steps from behind the small counter, brushing past my stomach. 'These are our bears. All made here in the shop. Do you know if the baby is a boy or a girl?'

'It's a surprise!' Ellie says with shiny crescent eyes.

'Well, we have lots of options for surprises. Is there anyone Bear-bear thinks would make a good friend?'

'That one up there with the big fat tummy.' Ellie points to a dark brown teddy with a long nose and fluffy ears.

'Excellent choice, Bear-bear.' The shopkeeper congratulates him as she lifts the stuffed toy down. 'This one will make a perfect companion.'

Ellie shakes Bear-bear in front of the furry grizzly and his head rocks from side to side.

'He's excited!'

'I can see he is. Have I met Bear-bear before?' She focuses on me with her head twisted to the side and her eyes squinted.

'Yes, you have,' I say with a smile. 'I bought Bear-bear from you when I was pregnant with this little one.'

'I thought I recognised you!' The shopkeeper ruffles his furless stomach. 'He's been well-loved.'

Ellie squeezes her face to his and kisses him. Her lips pucker like a little fish.

'*Very* well-loved.' I grin.

A door latch above us catches, followed by rhythmic steps bouncing down carpeted stairs. A curtain next to the counter twitches and a young man's face appears.

'What's for lunch, Mum? I'm starving.'

'I'm with customers, dear,' the shopkeeper says to him, her eyes remain on me.

'Oh. Sorry. Sorry, Mum,' he replies in a small voice. His gaze flicks to me, hovers for a moment before dropping to my little girl. He has the same face as his mother. Heart-shaped. I feel for her. He's a little old to have lunch made for him. Must be at least twenty, twenty-five. The shadow of a beard and thick dark hair not cut in a while.

'We bought a new Bear-bear!' Ellie tells him. He half-smiles, and a small dimple appears.

I reach forward and wrap my arm around my daughter's chest, pulling her into me. The movement returns his gaze to me. The contact jolts me, my heart quickens. The eyes. The hair. *The dimple.*

'Is there anything else you'd like?' The shopkeeper raises her brows and pushes her head forward to bring my attention back to her.

'No. No thank you.' I shake my head and offer my credit card. Keen to get away. Make a phone call. I steal another glance. He straightens the line of bears so they are neat and tidy. Looks back at me, grins, and steps forward to open the door.

What am I thinking? Stop it. Just stop it. This isn't him at all! You're desperate. He only fits the description because you want him to. You can't let go of work for even one whole day to be with your daughter. And now you're pinning this horrendous crime on this poor man. This lady's son. Her boy.

'Thank you so much.' A sudden rush of exhaustion and nausea floods through me. I need to get home. I need to rest.

'See you again soon,' he says.

I nod and guide Ellie out as I stoop under his raised arm holding the door open.

My legs ache as if set in concrete hardening with every step. Ellie comments on everything that bothers her. She's too tired to walk. She's hungry. She's thirsty. She wants to go in this shop. No, that shop. My head throbs as each whine carves a deeper slice of pain.

'I want something to eat.' Ellie snivels as I strap her in. 'And I want the new Bear-bear.'

'You can't have food and the new Bear-bear, Ellie. You'll get mess all over him.'

'No, I won't.'

'You will.'

'No, I won't!'

'Okay, okay. You won't. But you still can't have both. Here. Have some animal biscuits and have *your* Bear-bear. He'll be sad if you cuddle the new one on the way home.'

Give it five minutes and she'll be asleep anyway, half a bag of biscuits left and Bear-bear on the floor.

She scowls as if I am to blame for the failure of her whole world before taking the packet and pulling Bear-bear onto her lap, making it even harder for me to reach the buckle.

I get in the driver's seat, slump back and tilt my head against the rest.

The phone vibrates. *It's been a few hours. I'm allowed to answer.* I turn Bluetooth on, set to drive and reverse out of the spot.

'Anna,' I answer. 'I'm on speakerphone.'

'Hi, Boss. We found another one,' Ben says, careful with his words.

'Another one? Where?' I grip the steering wheel and lean forward as if I'll see the body, stabbed, shaved and toothless, right through my windscreen.

'Mummy! My biscuits are on the floor!'

'Wait a minute, Ellie.' I direct my voice over my shoulder, keeping my eyes ahead as I take the tight corner to the multistorey ground level.

'McLean Alley. Near Queen,' Ben tells me.

'Mummy!' Ellie's voice gets louder.

I lift my finger to my lips and 'shhh', hoping she'll follow the instruction.

'Mummy! My biscuits! I'm hungry!' Ellie starts to wail.

'Just a minute, Ellie! Mummy's on the phone!'

'Sorry, Boss. Thought you should know.'

'Email me the details. I'll be home in forty minutes,' I say. 'Sure it's our guy?'

'Mum! Bear-bear! Bear-bear's got a hole!'

'Yep. All the same trophies.'

'Look, Mummy! Look!' Ellie's shrieking and kicking the back of my seat as I wait for the car park barrier to lift.

'Ellie! Stop! Give him here!' I twist to reach round. One hand holds the wheel steady, the other to grab the bear.

'Careful Mummy! He's broken! He's broken!' Ellie screams.

'He's fine! Just stop it! Give him to me!' My voice loud and sharp as my hand flails around in the air behind my seat.

My fingers latch around a furry arm and I yank him towards me. Ellie grips harder and releases an ear-piercing scream. I tighten my hold. Give another hard tug. A rip growls as the fabric tears. He flies towards me, split and gaping, and showers us in a perfectly soft homemade stuffing of red matted human hair and blood-stained teeth.

UNSOLVED

MEGAN STEELE

Seven deaths in the last five days.
Cause of death – unknown.

All were carefully placed, surrounded by glass.
But how did they die? The doctors are stumped.
Who, or what, is to blame? Nobody knows.

Blinded with grief. It just isn't fair.
I need to know how? Why?
Will it happen again?

Wading through data, looking for clues...
I've been here before, but this time it's harder.
I've done everything right! What more can I do?

Don't give up, everyone says.

But hope is a breeze on a sweltering day.
It comes and goes but does not stay.

I am the detective in this story.
A story that may have an end I'd never imagined,
a nightmare in which the mystery does not get solved.

The crime scene is a laboratory.
The victims, seven young lives – ended before they began.
Along with the future we had dreamt.

Would they have had my eyes, his smile?
Will anyone – ever?

THE COLNE SYNDICATE

HOLLY SYDELLE

The stale scent of sweat hit Detective Olive Moore as she entered the crime scene. Before her, a woman lay slumped on the carpet, her skirt splayed out like the petals of an Easter lily. The blood beneath her hadn't dried yet, the carpet as slick and shiny as a bed of velvet. The only obvious mark on her body was a circular gunshot wound to the left clavicle.

Officer Kaia Coleman of the LAPD Forensic Science Division was photographing evidence as Moore approached. 'What have we got?'

'John Miller's back at the precinct. He's not talking, but has been swabbed for gunshot residue.'

Moore frowned. 'Mr. Miller is the husband?'

Kaia nodded. 'Neighbours called it in. Noise complaint. He was detained on the premises.'

'And the female victim?'

'Mrs Anne-Marie Miller.'

Moore took slow, deliberate steps around the scene, twisting the loose latex of her glove between her fingertips. She squatted next to the body and studied the woman's hands. The fingers were devoid of jewellery, but a pale outline on the ring finger suggested a wedding band had recently been removed.

The detective leaned forwards to study the woman's face. Her eyelids were dusted with gold, and black kohl traced her lash line. Foundation was streaked along her cheekbone, marking the track of tears.

Noticing nothing of interest in the living room, Moore left Kaia to bag the Glock 22 sitting directly across from the body, adding it to their stocktake of evidence.

The detective strode through the narrow hallway into the house, stepping over uneven piles of papers and a basket of laundry, before reaching the entrance to the single bathroom. The countertop was clear, save a cup holding two toothbrushes, the bristles worn thin.

With a gloved hand, she nudged the bathroom cabinet open, revealing only a paracetamol bottle and a cannister of cotton buds. *Where were the victim's cosmetics?*

Stepping back out of the bathroom, Moore moved on to the nearby bedroom. Switching on the light, she saw nothing out of place. The bed was unmade, a quilted blanket strewn across the sheets, with a few hardcover novels scattered across the bedside tables.

Moore reached the closet and slid open the mirrored door. Gliding her hand over the delicate fabrics, the detective drew the clothes aside, revealing a black duffel bag tucked into the back corner.

She zipped open the bag, stuffed with what looked like Mrs Miller's clothes and toiletry bag. 'Kaia, come look at this!'

Footsteps padded down the hallway. Kaia entered the bedroom, clutching her camera. She knelt beside Moore. 'What's this?'

The detective smiled. 'This Kaia, is our motive.'

Moore was back at the precinct, writing up her case report on the homicide of Anne-Marie Miller. A freshly removed wedding ring and a getaway bag suggested Anne-Marie recently discovered a reason worth ending her marriage over, leading to a deadly confrontation with her husband. It hadn't taken much investigative work to learn John Miller was having an affair with his assistant. Ample motive. How clichéd.

Lab analysis confirmed gunshot residue present on John Miller's hands, the gun was registered in his name, Anne-Marie's blood was on his shirt, and he was found at the residence minutes after the neighbours heard gun fire. Easy solve. Case closed.

'Detective?' Kaia rounded the corner, clutching a pile of papers. 'You might want to see this.' Kaia handed Moore the papers, tapping her toe as she waited for her superior to scan their contents.

Moore took in the information. 'A second set of DNA was found on the murder weapon?'

'We don't have a name, but the DNA is from a woman, European descent.'

'Suggesting an accomplice?'

'The gun was wiped to remove prints, but we found a skin cell scraping on the firearm's magazine. The person had recent contact with the weapon.'

The detective flipped through the pages again, double checking the results.

'That's not the craziest thing,' said Kaia. She leaned in towards Moore and dropped her voice to a whisper. 'We found a match to the DNA on the system. There was a hit with a DNA profile lifted from the crime scene of a two-million-dollar diamond heist in Switzerland two days ago.'

'Two days ago?'

'Less than 24 hours after Mrs Miller's time of death.'

The detective rubbed her temple, her pulse thudding under the soft skin. 'It takes about 11 hours to fly from California to Zurich. That only gives a ten-hour leeway for this woman to leave our crime scene, hop on an international flight, and stage a two-million-dollar heist.'

Kaia bounced on the balls of her feet, enthralled by the mystery. Their last five cases had been easy-solves. 'And what would John Miller, a man with no priors, who's evidence suggests he reacted in the heat of the moment, have to do with an international jewel thief?'

Moore tilted her head. 'I think we should ask John Miller.'

The next day, Moore arrived early at the precinct, the air thick and soupy with humidity. With a quick detour to the bathroom, she slicked down the soft flyaway hairs at her crown. Running a hand under the faucet, she trickled cold water down the nape of her neck and wiped away the sweat.

Walking into the interrogation room, she found John Miller slouched in his seat, waiting. His face was stern, but a slight muscle twitch in his jaw gave away his discomfort.

With a detached smile, Moore took a chair across from her suspect. Miller's lawyer sat next to his client, beads of sweat collecting on his balding forehead. The name on her file was Laurence Franklin. She hadn't encountered him before. Noting his lack of eye contact and permanent grimace, she decided that might be a good thing.

Looking away from the lawyer, she placed a stack of photographs on the table, catching John Miller's attention. 'Please state your name for the record.'

Miller took in a long breath. 'John Henry Miller.'

Moore splayed the photographs across the desk, an image of the Glock 22 sat atop the rest. 'This is your gun, correct, Mr Miller?'

'I've already answered your blasted questions about the gun.'

Moore pressed her lips into a tight smile. 'Please Mr Miller, this won't take long.'

He looked down at the image and shrugged his shoulders.

'Have you always kept it locked in the family safe?'

Miller brought his eyes up to meet hers and nodded. 'That's right.'

'Until you killed your wife.'

He refused to confirm the statement.

'Mr Miller, we have forensic evidence which proves someone else was part of this. Their DNA was on the gun. Who helped you?'

Eyes wide, Miller sat back in his seat.

'You're going away for a very long time, Mr Miller. You must know that by now. Why protect this person and be the only one to take the fall?'

Miller ran a hand over his face, deep lines etched the corners of his mouth.

Moore sat in silence, waiting for him to articulate his thoughts into words.

'...They pulled the trigger.'

Pen poised, Moore grabbed her notebook. 'Who are they, Mr Miller?'

'It... it was all a blur. I never wanted my wife dead, Detective. You have to believe me.'

Moore looked up from her notebook, face blank. 'Why was this other person in your house?'

'I... I dunno. It all happened so fast.'

'How did you know them, Mr Miller?'

The Adam's apple on Miller's throat was pronounced as he swallowed. He leaned over and whispered to his lawyer.

Franklin nodded, scribbled in his own notepad, then turned to Moore. 'Before this conversation goes any further, I think we need to talk about a deal for my client.'

'In exchange for providing information about his accomplice?' Moore raised her eyebrows.

Before Franklin could respond, Kaia knocked on the door, giving her superior a pointed look.

With a sharp glance at Miller, Moore swept up the papers and followed Kaia into the hallway. 'Have you got an update on the case?' asked Moore, re-tucking flyaway strands of hair behind her ears.

'I don't know.' Kaia shook her head as she passed Moore a sheet of paper.

Moore scanned it, silent.

'Our mystery woman has been linked to another case.'

Moore nodded. 'A car theft in Auckland.'

'Only two hours after Anne-Marie's death,' said Kaia, fingers pressed against her lip as she gauged Moore's expression.

'That's impossible.'

'I know.'

Kaia followed Moore, who marched back to her office. She cleared a space on her desk to spread the documents from the three cases.

Kaia took a seat on the other side of the desk, watching Moore's gaze shift between the different files. 'Did you get anything from the suspect?'

Moore nodded. 'He confirmed the presence of a third party but wants to cut a deal.'

'Damn,' muttered Kaia. 'Are you considering it?'

'I think we might have to if we want any chance of catching her.'

'Or catching *them*.' Kaia beamed, thrilled by their conundrum. She walked to the whiteboard at the side of the room and scrawled a timeline. 'According to this, there were at least two, but more likely three of them to make it to each of the crime scenes.'

Moore clasped her hands together to rest her chin, squinting at the whiteboard as though it helped her see an answer. 'Three separate people on three separate continents, with the same set of DNA. Christ, have we stumbled onto some sort of crime syndicate of clones?'

Kaia plopped back into her seat and unpeeled a tab of gum, smiling. 'God, I hope so. Homicide and Organised Crime. Bam. I hear the sweet sounds of a promotion.'

Moore smiled at Kaia's enthusiasm, then gestured at the pile of papers. 'Let me look through these for any new clues as to her whereabouts. It's as a good a place as any to start.'

Kaia rose, ready to leave the room, when the seed of a new idea shone in her eyes. 'I may have a lead. I'll need to work with our sister lab in Santa Cruz.' She rushed from the room.

'Wait! Kaia, what lead?'

'More forensic genetics. Let me see if it works and I'll get back to you!'

Moore slumped in front of her files, flicking through the endless pages. 'I need some coffee.'

With a soft thud, Kaia dropped a tall latté onto Moore's desk, jolting her awake. Moore shot upright, her forehead indented from sleeping on the stack of documents. Kaia, opposite her boss, sipped her own coffee. 'Moore, the sun's gone down. Why aren't you home? Don't tell me you've been going through those case files for the last three days.'

Rubbing her eyes, Moore relished the caffeine. 'You shouldn't be here either.'

Kaia smiled. 'I know, but this is my best shot at that promotion.'

Moore put down her coffee. 'Did you find a break in the case?'

'Yes ma'am, I have a lead.' Kaia leaned forward and handed Moore a sheet of paper. On the page was a digital rendering of a woman's face. She was middle-aged, with brown eyes, chestnut hair, a long, slim nose, and a round face.

'Who is this, Kaia?'

'Our mystery clone.'

Moore held the image up to the light. 'Did you find a witness?'

Kaia smiled. 'No, but I knew Adele Ridley from the lab at Santa Cruz had worked on a DNA phenotyping project, where you use genetic markers to identify the body shape and facial features of a suspect, right down to the freckles on their nose, just from their DNA. We may not have this woman's name, but we have her face.'

'A DNA mugshot,' whispered Moore, in awe. 'How have we never used this before?'

'The program is still in its infancy. The science is pretty good, but for some traits like hair colour, we're only reaching an accuracy of 70%.'

'By and large, this is what our suspect looks like?' Moore traced the rendering's soft eyes, they were less menacing than expected.

'Yep, that's her.'

'I'll put out an APB for this woman. With this detailed sketch, we might be able to actually find her.'

'At least one of them,' mused Kaia, glancing at their impossible timeline.

Moore sighed. 'One mystery at a time.'

Two months later, Moore and Kaia sat in an empty meeting room staring at the LED screen. Within minutes, the camera connected, and a man's angled, slim face filled the screen.

'Detective, it's great to meet with you, even virtually,' smiled Moore. 'I am Detective Olivia Moore, and this is my colleague, Officer Kaia Coleman.'

Scotland Yard Detective Ian Taylor nodded in greeting. 'Your contacts at the FBI said I might be able to help with your investigation?'

'You reported a sighting in the U.K. that matched our sketch?'

Taylor ran a hand over his salt-and-pepper stubble and nodded. 'We had two separate workers at a Xurac warehouse in London identify the woman in your image as a previous employee. Greta. Neither could remember her last name. The company recently went through tech issues that wiped all information of their past employees.'

'But we have a name,' whispered Moore, feeling so much closer to solving their case. 'Could you send through some images of the plant? It might give us a sense of the scene.'

'Sure.'

Moore opened a file of images and clicked through different angles of an old plant facility, lined with steel counter tops and cold lighting.

'Stop.' Kaia jumped out of her seat, pointing towards the top of the image on the screen. 'Enhance that section of the photo.'

Heart beating, unsure what Kaia saw, Moore increased the magnification.

'There, that sign,' pointed Kaia again. She turned to Taylor on the other side of the screen. 'Does that say U.V. irradiation?'

Taylor squinted at the image, then checked the case file notes in front of him. 'Yes, that's the sterilisation room. The last phase of production for the cotton swabs manufactured at the plant.'

Kaia's heart dropped to her stomach in realisation. She turned to Taylor. 'You said this is a Xurac plant?'

Taylor's brow furrowed. 'Yes, does that mean something to you?'

'Xurac ship their cotton swabs internationally,' breathed Kaia. 'To places like the U.S., New Zealand, and Western Europe.'

'I know,' responded Taylor. 'We use them in our precinct too.'

'Why didn't I see this sooner?' whispered Kaia. 'They must have falsified certification of their products for DNA testing. This is a criminal breach of standards.'

'Why, what does that mean for the case?' asked Moore.

'Their sterilisation process only kills bacteria and viruses; it doesn't destroy DNA. No one in a forensic lab would touch U.V. irradiation as a decontamination technique.'

Moore slowly inhaled, taking in the gravity of Kaia's words. 'So, the woman in our photo did nothing but breathe and shed skin cells on the cotton swabs as she packaged them in the factory, and forensic teams shipped her DNA into crime scenes around the world.'

Taylor balked. 'There is no international killer? Just a lab mistake?'

'Yes,' said Moore, cheeks aflush with mortification.

'Xurac should be liable for the misdirection of criminal investigations globally,' stated Taylor. He leaned forward and pinched the bridge of his nose. 'Let's just keep this between us for now.'

Moore imagined the embarrassment of her office finding out about her suspect being nothing more than a phantom. She nodded. It couldn't hurt to clean this mess up quietly.

'I'd better go,' said Taylor, bundling the papers in front of him. 'I need to get my team back to Xurac and re-process the scene.' He gave a quick wave of the hand in gesture of goodbye, then ended the connection.

The two women sat for a moment in silence, until Kaia exhaled loudly. 'I guess that could have gone better.'

Moore turned to face her. 'Coffee?'

Kaia nodded.

Kaia and Moore sipped their expressos in the police carpark. Kaia sighed. 'So, there's no evil cloning mastermind.'

'I guess not.'

'Shame,' muttered Kaia, taking a long swig of her coffee.

'At least I don't have to cut a deal with the devil,' mused Moore.

Kaia raised her eyebrows.

'Miller had no accomplice. He almost swindled his way out of a life sentence. We can sleep easy now, knowing we got the guy who did it.'

Kaia shrugged her shoulders. 'Another easy solve.'

'I wouldn't call this easy. We've been on a wild goose chase, and the only reason we didn't waste years chasing our tails is because of your pick-up.'

Kaia smiled at the praise, then her face dropped a little. That promotion would be far off the cards for now, and it was hard to know how likely a case would stick against an international company like Xurac.

Their work was far from over.

ICE QUEEN

JC LESLEY

I took a shallow breath and glanced over my shoulder, ever worried he'd suddenly appear. My masterpiece only lacked the finishing touch. My modus operandi, as they said on American cop shows, was infallible. They'd never know how it was done. I slithered my finger down the sleek chill of my ice sculpture and smiled. It was almost perfect.

The trick I'd learned, thanks to tips on the internet, was to use boiled rainwater, and freeze it slowly. I had to keep adjusting the fridge so it lowered the temperature in small increments. He yelled at me when ice formed in his beer. I'd solved that problem by popping his cans of Carlton Draught into an esky bag in the fridge a few hours before he arrived home each day.

While he was at work I needed to keep up a strict schedule of housework. He'd yell and backhand me across the face if it wasn't done to perfection. In between rushing to clean and iron I'd spent time freezing a perfect slab of ice. As it set I needed to regularly agitate it to get the bubbles out. This made it freeze clear and hard. That was the secret to flawless ice used in sculptures, how to make it denser and slower to melt. This technique forced gases from the solution via crystal formations.

Once I'd produced the basic form in my slab of ice, I needed to turn it over and mist it with water. My sculpture had been built up layer by layer until it was a magnificent clear ice form, so dense it was harder than steel. After innumerable failures, today I would unveil my masterpiece. Pay day. I ran my tongue over my broken teeth and split lip and gently touched the bruise on my cheek. No more abuse. No more being told I was a stupid fat whore. No more being forbidden to visit the doctor or dentist. No more explaining why it took me a minute longer shopping than his timer allowed.

At the local supermarket I worked night-filling shelves. It paid poorly, but what else could I do? I needed to escape the house. I needed a job where I could hide my bruises. Every box of cereal I stacked denigrated my university degree. I could never apply for skilled jobs while I was stuck with this bastard. 'He-man' would never allow me to get a better job than his. I was his house slave, forced to do all the cooking, cleaning, laundry and shopping.

When I met him at a party he came across as charming and sensitive. We'd gone out to dinner and then the cinema. He'd had quite a bit to drink, apologised he couldn't drive me home, and convinced me to come back to his place. Seemingly a gentleman, he left me to sleep peacefully in his spare room. But I was in the middle of hunting for a new room to rent while finishing my studies, and he offered his spare room. I accepted. He wined and dined me for the first few weeks until I gave into having sex with him. It wasn't even good sex. Over time he stopped me from seeing my friends, shut my social media accounts and monitored my phone calls, emails and internet.

The first time I tried to visit my mother he held a knife to my throat. He told me if I ever visited her he'd kill her, and make it look like I'd done it. I knew he would. My friendships had disintegrated. There was nobody I could turn to for help.

Every Friday he played the pokies and drank away his entire weekly earnings. I paid the rent, utilities, bought the groceries and his beer. Exhausted I needed an out. At a car service the mechanic found tracking devices on my car. I snapped.

That's when I'd come up with my plan. Tonight, when he arrived home penniless and drunk again, he'd get his real payday.

I relied on his routine being the same as normal: his arrival home at 9pm, demanding more beer, and passing out within thirty minutes. And I'd leave for work at 9:45pm.

My ice sculpture lay ready in the freezer. The silicon cake form I'd used was scrunched up in my bag ready to throw out in a random bin on the way to work. What had I forgotten? I went through the checklist in my head. I sprayed a mist of Coco Chanel between my breasts. He liked that.

Right on schedule I heard his boots on the stairs.

'Bitch! Open this frigging door!'

I lowered my head and obeyed, purposely not locking the security door once he pushed past me.

'Where's my beer? What is that stink?'

I ignored him and went into the fridge and grabbed the esky bag.

'Where's my hamburger!'

'But you asked for steak for dinner.' I muttered.

'No I didn't. Stupid bitch. Can't you remember anything? You've got it wrong again. Imbecile. You are so lucky I put up with you. Nobody else would.'

I bit my lip. I'd used the computer at work. I'd researched. I knew this was called coercive control.

He never ate what I cooked on Friday night; always too drunk, and passed out before the first bite. I had to go through the motions. One time I'd done nothing, and he'd come into the kitchen, pushed me to the floor, and made me lick it. Besides, the scene needed to look right: his uneaten hamburger part of the picture.

At 9:20, I placed the hamburger next to him. He was sitting in his recliner, with a beer in his hand. The football was blaring on the TV. His eyes were half open. He was in his boxers, his shirt and jeans in a mangled ball on the couch.

I picked up his clothes and left the room. Was there anything else I still needed to do? Was he going to pass out in the next twenty-five minutes?

I washed the dishes and brought my bag to the table. I was fidgety, my hands twitched. Could I go through with this?

It was 9:40. If I was going to do it, now was the time. I went to the doorway of the lounge room and announced, 'I'm off then.'

His head was slumped forward on his chest. He sounded like a chainsaw.

'I'll be back around 2:30am.'

He didn't stir.

I walked back into the kitchen, pulled on a dishwashing glove to protect my fingers from the cold, opened the freezer and reached in. The magnificent ice dagger glinted in my hand. *You can do it. You can do it,* I recited in my head.

If I crept into the lounge he'd probably wake up, triggered by something out of the ordinary. I tried to take normal steps across the room. I stopped in front of him and examined once more the glistening ice dagger in my hand. My intention was to stab him in the heart. From all I'd read on the internet at work, I knew stabbing him in the abdomen wouldn't kill him, and trying to jag his femoral artery was difficult. For that reason I'd made the dagger long enough to pierce his heart on an angle from just below his ribcage.

Before I lost my nerve, I thrust the dagger in an underarm motion into the flesh below his ribs. Oh my god. It was like puncturing denim with scissors, harder than I imagined. My dagger was sharp. It penetrated up to the hilt.

First time killers normally pull the knife out and thrust it in again, getting drops of blood all over them and everywhere else. Had I hit his heart or a major vessel? So far there was no blood spatter, but I'd read the dagger plugged the hole tight so very little blood escaped. I fled to the lounge room doorway, waiting for him to die.

He suddenly rolled his head up and glared at me. He looked down at his chest and grabbed the ice handle and tried to pull it out.

'You stupid fucking bitch. What have you done? You'll pay for this.'

I grabbed my bag and ran out the back door. He would use the knife on me if given the chance. If I stayed I might get blood spatter on me. That wasn't part of the plan.

As promised I arrived home at 2:30am. I walked in through the kitchen and peeked into the lounge. A warm rusty smell assaulted my nostrils. There was blood spatter up the walls, congealed in the security screen, sprayed across the timber floor, and in a dot painting on his recliner chair. He was lying face down on the floor. I bent over and vomited. Oh crap, I'd contaminated the crime scene.

My hands shook. What had I done? I was elated yet sickened. I dialed triple zero.

The detective rested his hip on the kitchen table. I was sitting in the same chair I'd collapsed into and was still shaking. Part of me wanted to jump for joy that I'd killed the bastard, and the other part was horrified that I could kill a person. I wiped my sweaty palms down my trousers.

'You don't remember if the front security door was locked before you left for work?'

'No. But, he's very particular about everything being locked. I'm sure he would have locked it when he came home.'

'How'd you get the bruise on your cheek?'

With one finger I lightly touched the painful lump. 'Fell. I'm very clumsy.'

'Did he have any enemies?'

'I don't know. He never introduced me to his friends.'

'His family?'

'I don't know. I never met them. He never talked about them.'

'Do you have a friend you can stay with tonight?'

'No. Yes. Maybe.' I nervously twisted the ring on my finger, as I pondered on the right answer to give.

'You can't stay here, this is a crime scene.'

'Oh. Yes. Maybe I could stay in a hotel?'

'After a traumatic event like this, it would be better if you had a family member or friend to stay with.'

'I can't stay with my friends.'

These questions were making me break out in a sweat.

'Did he stop you from having friends?'

'I'm just a bit of a loner.' Was I giving them the fuel they required to look at me as a perpetrator?

'You're obviously tired and upset. We'll need you to come in tomorrow for more questions. I'll let you go now. We'll see you get into a hotel for the night.'

'Can I get my toothbrush and some clothes?'

'Yes, but one of our female officers will accompany you. We still haven't found the murder weapon. We need to thoroughly check the premises.'

I glanced around the kitchen. My eyes rested on the empty knife block. They'd bagged all my knives and every other sharp kitchen utensil. Had I forgotten any detail? I didn't look towards the lounge as that gory mess still made me want to retch. Some killer I turned out to be.

'One thing before you go.'

I turned back to the detective. My fingernails dug hard into my palms.

'There is a hamburger on the table beside the chair.'

'Yes. I made it for him for dinner before I left for work.'

'It's not been touched.'

'No. When he comes home dru... from work on Friday, he often isn't hungry.'

'One other question. There's a puddle of water on the floor. Did you give him water with his burger?'

My head whipped around. My eyes skittered across the lounge room floor racing to find the puddle. My heart was hammering in my chest. There it was, right beside the coffee table. That's what I'd forgotten! I'd meant to leave a near-empty glass of water near his dinner so it looked like he'd spilled it.

.

IT'S ALL CHEKOV'S FAULT

ALEXIA LEIGH

'The reader might not know who the killer is but the author always knows.'

Silva's sharp voice grates against the headache forming at the base of your skull. You reach up and massage the nape of your neck, the muscles rigid beneath your fingertips. It's three hours into the workshop and already your shoulders ache, you're hungry and your butt's gone to sleep.

You fidget in your chair trying to awaken your sleeping rump without drawing too much attention. Then you reach forward and scoop up a handful of the signature single wrapped Mentos from the white bowl in the middle of your table. *Why does every workshop have these?*

At the front of the room Silva moves over to the whiteboard, the heels of her red pumps tap against the aged floorboards. The hall is nothing flash, just four brick walls and a wooden floor. There is a stage, it even has a long scarlet curtain, but it's been bleached into stripes of pink by sun and age. The one saving grace are the windows.

The stained glass tints the light, casting lapis shadows across the scuffed floor, as a silent choreography is performed by dust motes in sunbeams. But fill this tired relic with plastic fold-out tables, a whiteboard and some truly uncomfortable chairs and what do you have? The Highlands Writers Retreat.

'And that is how you become a best-selling author.' Silva concludes. She opens her arms, as if to encompass the room. Her Pandora-laden wrists jingle.

A cacophony of claps fills the room. The loudest, of course, comes from Janice. You glance over at her table at the back of the room. Her thick thighs bump the table as she shoots upright. She stumbles and you smile, a flush of concern comes over you, followed immediately by the sting of betrayal.

You don't clap. Rather you rest your clammy palms face down on the polyester tablecloth. It's not that it was bad workshop, Silva has always had a way with words, crowds, other people's husbands. You draw a deep breath and taut muscles draw your shoulders up around your ears.

Janice struggles to weave her way through the crowd. Writers sit three to a table, a collective of caffeinated zombies blocking her path. As Janice pulls herself past the front row and onto the tiny stage, her bust brushes the whiteboard; her staff lapel angled just right to catch between the metal frame and the board itself.

'Thank you so much, Silva.' Janice turns herself towards the audience as she wrestles with the caught lapel. Silva reaches forward, her pristine French manicure reminiscent of claws, and yanks at Janice's lapel. There's a loud crack.

Janice reddens, nods and steps forward. 'Again, thank you Silva, your presentation was amazing as always.' Her hands tug at the hem of her shirt: she's modelling the retreat's latest merchandise, a black polo with #retreater scrawled across her chest.

'It's always a pleasure.' Silva faces the audience, absorbing a second round of adulation. Her cherry red lips spread into a wide smile. Her perfect white teeth shine, but her eyes don't seem to be smiling at all and they're fixed on you.

'Well, that's it for now, guys. Lunch has been provided in the foyer.' Janice announces. 'And don't forget to head across the street to check out the Writer's Retreat pop up store. We have shirts, pens, bookmarks and as always first editions from our very own retreaters, see you back here at 2pm sharp.'

The room erupts with noise as the attendees push back their chairs and stretch sleepy muscles. You settle back in your seat and inspect the crowd. There are so many new faces, but you note a few old faithfuls. Susan Crest with her crooked smile and pencil eyebrows, James Francis who always carries two things, his leather satchel and the smell of tobacco, and Doug Hass who appears perfect in every way, except his ability to be faithful.

Doug weaves between the tables towards you, his grey pin-striped suit a sharp contrast to the surroundings. 'Sarah, we need to talk.' He says, his hands pressed against your table.

'Not this weekend.' You rise and push the chair out behind you, it catches on a broken floorboard and tumbles over.

'I just want us to fix this.'

Your chest tightens, your heart races. 'Not here, not now. We'll discuss it after the weekend.'

Doug huffs, his chiselled jaw juts forward. You turn away to retrieve the fallen chair. As you do there's a familiar tap, tap, tap of red pumps on wooden floorboards.

'Doug darling, how are you?' You turn back to see Silva's French manicure wrapping around Doug's bicep. *Claws.*

Suddenly you're back in your living room in Chestnut Bay. The lace curtains drift in the breeze that weaves through the open window, your fist clenched around the handle of your carry-on luggage.

Doug's leather recliner is covered with women's clothing; a cream silk shirt and lace unmentionables. A pile of Pandora bracelets litter the mahogany coffee table you'd bought on your Balinese honeymoon. You never go upstairs. Rather, you leave, the salt of your tears on your lips.

Doug pulls his arm free from Silva's clutches and looks at you intently, 'I'll call you.' He turns and walks away. Janice stands at Silva's elbow, her honey brown eyes wide, she tugs at the hem of her shirt.

Silva turns towards you. 'It's been so long Sarah. I thought you were still in America.'

'No, got back to Aus, last week.'

'And you thought to join us, how nice. I must admit I was surprised to see you here, after all I knew Doug was coming. I thought...'

'We're working through it.' You say between gritted teeth. You steer the conversation into safer waters and force a smile, 'The new retreat shirt looks good.' Janice opens her mouth to answer but Silva cuts her off.

'Hmmm, yes. I think we'd sell more if we had a less 'voluptuous' model.' Silva replies.

Janice reddens, her eyes glazing with tears.

'Perhaps, you will sell lots. After all most people these days accept beauty in all shapes and sizes. It's nice to have a real-sized model for once.'

Janice shoots you a grateful smile. Silva sneers, turns and saunters out of the room.

You turn to Janice. 'She can be such a cow. You ok?'

'Yeah.' She blinks a few times and nods. 'It's been ages... six months right?'

'Yeah, it's nice to be back home.'

'I missed having you around in the writers group.' She smiles again, more genuine this time. Silence hangs between you and Janice starts to fidget, twisting the ends of her auburn hair between her fingertips. *Ah here's the awkward question.* 'You and Doug are ok now?'

'Oh, these things are never simple.'

'It feels like only a moment ago we were all together. It was more fun before you both resigned.'

'It's feels like ninety seconds?' A cheeky smile tugs at your lips.

'What?'

'A moment is exactly 90 seconds long.'

'Truly? Nah!' She pulls her phone out of her back pocket and brings up the search engine. 'Oh, no way! It is too.'

'Yep, just be super careful when you write that one. For example, 'I glanced into her eyes for a moment.' You fix Janice with a stare until she laughs. 'Hun, that was only 20 seconds, you'd never last a moment.'

'Oh, I've missed you.' Janice laughs. 'You always did give the best workshops.'

'Thanks.' You say. 'Now, I've heard a rumour about some prize for this weekend you had specially made...?'

'The Golden Gun award? Come let me show you.' Janice leads you to the front of the empty room. She reaches behind the whiteboard and draws out the trophy. A model golden Derringer pistol, mounted on a wooden plaque.

'Nice. Is this Chekhov's gun?'

'What's that?' Janice asks. 'Be kind to us amateur writers please.'

'Google it.' You answer with a wink.

You lift the soggy ham and cheese sandwich out of the plastic wrap and sniff it. The retreat-provided lunches have certainly gone downhill since you stopped being treasurer. You rewrap the sandwich and drop it back in your lap. You decided to steal some privacy during your lunch and chose a quiet park near the hall, while your fellow retreaters crowd into the pop-up bookshop.

You lean back into the aged wood of the park bench and allow the gentle aroma of eucalyptus and wattle to wash over you. The cool air tickles your nostrils. There's something special about the air here. It's like every breath is filled with untold possibilities. As if you really could achieve anything, anything you could imagine.

Silva's frustrated screech pulls you from your reverie. You lean forward and watch her try to cross the spongy soil in her pumps. Eventually she throws herself down on the wooden bench beside you.

'I've been looking for you.' She puffs, her cheeks red.

'And you've found me.'

'Look, about before... I realise I may have been too harsh on Janice.'

You raise an eyebrow. 'Janice? You're here to talk to me about Janice?'

'Well of course.' She removes one of her shoes and inspects the impacted dirt and grass around the heel. 'I know I shouldn't have said what I said. It's just she's been really pushing me lately. You know she's planning to leave the club.'

'So? She's entitled to her own life, Silva. I left.'

'Yes and you nearly destroyed us. I always thought you were rather selfish. Running off to secure your little book deal and leaving behind the ones who helped you get there. I mean, did I leave when I began my voice acting career? No! I record the books right here.'

The muscles in your jaw tighten, pain shoots up your neck towards your fledging headache. 'Silva, my marriage was failing thanks to...'

'Look, that's not the point.' Silva waves a hand as if to dismiss the subject. 'Janice is going to start her own retreat. In direct competition. I'll... We'll be ruined.'

You've had enough of Silva and her first-world problems, you collect your soggy sandwich and your handbag, and get up from the bench. You take a step to leave, but then you pause, your fist clenches and you turn back to Silva.

'She signed a non-compete.' You almost whisper.

'What?'

'When she joined the club, she signed a non-compete, we all did.'

Silva's jaw slackens, her cherry-red lips agape. You turn and walk away.

That night, despite a heater beside the bed, the cold seeps in through every crack and cranny. You pull the feather doona over you and settle against the cream pillowcase but your toes quickly lose their sensitivity and you can't feel your nose. You flex your fingers and reach for your mobile. Maeve James gave the final workshop for the day, and your phone now sports an illegal voice recording. You select the file, snuggle down into the pillows and switch off the bedside lamp.

The recording is poor quality, Maeve is too far from the microphone and you can't hear her speaking. Frustrated by the static, you decide to end the recording but your numb fingers tap the wrong point, and it jumps to the end. Two voices scream from the phone's tiny speakers.

'It's a bad plan.'

'No, it's the perfect plan,' the second voice replies. You pause the recording, you must have left the phone running after the session, when you'd gone to buy some first editions in the giftshop.

This is someone's private conversation. You pause over the play button then shrug. *After all, aren't writer's connoisseurs of human folly?* Tap.

'You'll never get away with it.' A husky male voice speaks. *European maybe?*

A female voice replies, it's almost sultry. 'Really? At a writer's retreat? None of them will believe they're watching a real murder. I'll use the oldest trope in the book, I'll turn off the lights. No one will see anything and there'll be over sixty neurotic introverts to take the fall for me. Silva Charming is going to die.'

The recording cuts out and after a pause of silent shock, and simmering anger at the neurotic introvert dig, you think you recognise the voices. You tap the screen to replay the message only to watch in horror as your numb fingers slip and delete the file.

You lie in the dark, desperately trying to process what you've just heard, amid a flutter of thoughts and questions one idea keeps returning. *Would it be so bad if Silva did die?*

You flick on the bedside lamp, find your thickest socks, drag on your boots and grab your jacket from the room's solitary recliner. You wrap your scarf around your neck and over your numb nose. When you pull open the wooden door, the cold smashes against you like a wall.

You park, rest your forearms on the steering wheel and squint through the dull light of the streetlamps at the hall. You reach for your phone, open the photo gallery and click the folder 'Do not open.'

Your Nokia reminds you daily it's low on memory. Every day you delete more but never these, even though you want to. After sliding through old wedding pictures and adventures you stop on a photo of the five of you. You stand with Doug on the left, his arm wrapped around your waist. You're smiling, sunshine lights up your raven curls. To the right are Silva and Janice, arm in arm. Both beam at the camera. Janice's ex-husband stands slightly behind her, his eyes fixed on Silva. In the background is a retreater villa. The very first Highlands Writers Retreat.

You swipe once, the next photo is of Janice and her ex. They pose before the camera, copying a stance from some recent spy flick. Janice is holding her anniversary present: an antique golden Derringer.

You run your thumb against the power button to lock the phone screen, but it lights up with a message. It's from Doug, 'My little detective, please don't give up on us.' A small smile jumps to your lips, inside your chest rages, a battle of love and pain.

'My little detective.' He's called you that ever since you started writing your children's mystery series. It's what he'd called you last month when you met for coffee, when you finally learnt the truth of that fateful Saturday.

It's midnight when you open the car door, as you step out of the car, a flash of copper tumbles from your pants pocket and rolls into the gravel drive. It shimmers beneath the moonlight and you scoop it up before you follow the twisting pathway around the back of the hall. There's a single light inside.

You turn the door handle. It's unlocked. Janice sits at a table at the front of the room and you startle her as you enter.

'Oh, Sarah it's just you. Why are you sneaking around at this time of night?'

You weave through the rows towards her.

Janice is organising novelty pins for the gift shop, pinning them to business cards and inserting them into tiny pouches.

'Why are you still working?' You wave your hands at the packages in front of her.

Janice shrugs. 'Silva wants them ready for tomorrow. Why are you here?'

'I think we need to talk.'

'Okay?' Janice puts down the pin she's holding and looks up at you with her patient, brown Labrador eyes.

'I know about the gun, Janice.'

Janice's eyes widen and she tugs at the hem of her shirt. 'I don't know what you mean.'

'So, if I go here...' You head to the whiteboard. 'And check this trophy...' You retrieve the golden gun award. 'I'm not going to find that this is a real gun?'

Janice bursts into tears. Trophy in hand you walk over and sit beside her. Cradling the trophy in your lap, you reach out and squeeze her wrists. 'It's okay.' You say gently.

'No, it's not!' Janice gulps air between her tears. 'She stole Jake, you know.'

'What?'

'Jake, my Jake, she slept with him! And I thought, Oh Sarah! I've been the worst friend. Silva never slept with Doug, I told her you were coming home early. It was all a setup, Doug wasn't even at the house when you came home. I'm so, so sorry. ' She trembles as she speaks, rivers of tears pour down her face and drip off the end of her chin. 'Silva wanted him and I thought if she got Doug then maybe she'd leave Jake alone. I'm... so pathetic and so sorry.'

You reel back, shocked by the confession, shocked by Janice's repentance. Part of you wants to slap her across her round, endearing face. But you don't, instead you hug her. You whisper softly in her ear. Janice rests her head against your shoulder and sobs.

'Who did you tell about your plan?'

Janice pulls back, she shakes her head. 'No one.'

'You didn't talk to someone last night, here in this room?'

'No.'

From behind the scarlet curtain comes the tap, tap of red pumps on wooden floorboards, your hand slips into your coat pocket, tap. You both turn towards the sound as Silva emerges.

Janice jumps up, pulls the trophy from your lap and points it at Silva. She pauses, weighs the trophy in her hand and examines the weapon. 'This isn't my gun.'

'No.' Silva answers. 'This is.' She pulls a small golden handgun from her purse and fires directly into Janice's head. You flinch, as the crack of the tiny weapon echoes around the room.

Janice's blood freckles your forearms. You glance briefly at her fallen corpse but a chilling wave of nausea forces you to look away. You don't want to know, you don't want that image forever, yet there it is.

Silva turns to you, double-barrel raised. 'Stupid girl thought I wouldn't notice if the plastic model suddenly became a real gun. She wasn't even subtle about it. Came straight in here after she read the non-compete. Idiot.' She walks over and spits on Janice's corpse.

Your hands shake as you get up from your seat.

'Now what about you?' Silva says with a smile.

You step back. 'I had nothing to do with this.'

'No, not at all.' Silva's voice changes becoming low, masculine, and with an accent. European. Then she shifts character again, her voice feminine, almost sultry. 'You were trying to save me.'

'The voices on the recording. It was you! But why?'

'Because Doug won't move on while you're still breathing. I thought you abandoning him would be enough, but it wasn't. On and on he droned about his lost love, his little detective.'

Silva steps towards you. Her eyes narrow, her lips curling into wide smile.

'So, I let you play detective, but only the author knows who the killer is.' She aims the golden pistol directly between your eyes. 'And honey, I'm the author.' She pulls the trigger of the tiny golden weapon.

Your mind reels backwards. It's a month ago, you're sitting in a café in Melbourne with Doug. He's crying, his hazel eyes red-rimmed, his shoulders heave beneath his blue suit jacket. 'I never slept with her.' You'd found out that day, the truth of their betrayal.

The next memory from today, you followed Janice at afternoon tea. You'd watched her from behind the curtain. Watched her google Chekhov's gun. Saw her remove the model from the wooden panel and replace it.

And your final memory is hugging Janice, whispering three simple words. 'I already knew.'

The Derringer clicks but doesn't fire. Silva pulls the trigger again. Click. You reach into the pocket of your pants.

Silva's mouth forms a perfect cherry red O as you raise your hands. Between the forefinger and thumb of your left hand, you hold up a copper-tipped bullet, with your right hand you show her your phone screen, triple zero typed across the face. The call is active. You carefully tap mute, deactivating your microphone.

'How wonderfully simple, two traitors, one bullet.' Your lips spread into a sneer. 'You were never a good author Silva, a good author does her research. A Derringer can only hold two bullets and I took one.' You let the bullet fall to the ground as the sound of sirens fills the hall.

'You aren't the author, Silva. I am.'

THE WATERY GRAVE

ZZ ANDERS

I would have screamed if I could.

The cold crept over my body, as the water slowly soaked into my recently purchased Hugo Boss suit my mother called overpriced. The rhythm as it lapped and retreated against me would have been soothing if not for the cold temperature and oh, the fact that I had just been kidnapped.

Drip, plonk, plunk!

Three separate distinct beats of entering water, loudly announced my future demise in the otherwise quiet dark space. Well dark, except for the small amount of dull light seeping in behind me. My shiny two-day-old Detective badge, attached to my pristine black leather belt meant nothing, as I struggled to drag in air. The ostentatious gag was so large, it had ridden up to also cover my nose. My heart raced as I silently begged all and sundry for a miracle.

I wasn't ready to die.

My muscles burned as water seeped into the ropes making my bindings tighter. The ability to straighten my legs would have been welcomed in the small, cramped space. The worst aspect of my slow death was the time to think—my mother was right—I should have bought the mustard-coloured Range Rover with the extra boot space. Not that she cared about the colour or the size of the boot, she cared that Range Rovers were supposedly safe, hardy vehicles. And safety was a huge factor when it came to her only gay son who had chosen a macho male-orientated career. In my mother's opinion, it was wasteful to spend good money on great looking clothes, but it was an entirely different story to spend a ridiculous amount on a safe, 'manly' vehicle. If I somehow survived this, I would suffer the words no twenty-four-year-old independent male wanted to hear from their mother. 'I told you so!'

Two days ago, I was excited and anxious to start my first day as a detective. Excited because I had worked hard and achieved my goal a full year earlier than planned. Anxious because I was partnered with the most egotistical cop in the state. His name was whispered when spoken about, as much in awe as disdain. As a new transfer to the station, he had certainly lived up to his reputation in the two days I'd been with him.

Solomon by name. Solo Man by nature—his catch phrase, not mine. He'd made it clear he preferred to work alone. I would be nothing but a hindrance on the drug case that we now shared. Even though, he had worked it by himself for months and yet the Botanist—so named by others in the department—had eluded him.

I was banking on my sparkling, some would say snarky, personality to win the old fart over; well, he was at least ten years my senior. The black leather jacket, white T-shirt over denim jeans, so out of fashion but in stark contrast to his trademark flowery scents which did nothing to disguise the underlying smell of cigars. We were a mismatch in style, but my brains would surely provide the fresh look our case needed. I would solve the case and prove myself, even as I endeavoured to learn all I could from his vast experience. Now, I'd likely never get the chance.

Drip, plonk, plunk, tinkle!

Okay, maybe I needed to pee...

Four distinct beats, the sound of the water entering the space in different locations a form of torture all its own.

The water took its time, leaking in through crevices and gaps. Even with the small amount of light seeping in, it was hard to see. Time was likely distorted as this panicked tirade reverberated through my head. The water was still only a centimetre or so high. If I wanted to give up, I could face plant the floor and drown myself on my terms instead of waiting for nature to take me.

Was it ironic that pink was my favourite colour?

I was taking in the pink splendour of the Salt Lake waiting for my Criminal Informant, CI for short, to turn up. I couldn't have imagined that minutes later, I'd be overpowered, bound, gagged, and coffined in my own boot before my car plunged into the very lake I'd been admiring.

Drip, plonk, plunk, splat!

Okay, that one landed on my face. Great! Now I get to suffer through Chinese Water Torture, one splat at a time. Or I could just shuffle over a bit, I guess. Yeah, maybe I'll do that. And before you ask—yes, I've been called a drama queen before. But seriously, the longer this goes on without the water significantly rising, the calmer I get. My heart isn't beating as fast, my breathing feels less laboured. Maybe I'm slipping into unconsciousness.

Wait.

Yeah okay, the gag slipped from covering my nose when I shuffled over. I guess I should have thought to rub my nose on the carpet to move the gag out of the way. It was hard to think straight as I slowly drowned.

The thing is, I didn't see who attacked me. There was an overpowering scent of lavender before everything went dark as a dowdy hessian bag was pulled over my head. Before I could react, I was grabbed from behind and forced to the ground. The next thing I knew, I was bound and being gagged as the hessian bag was lifted high enough to expose my mouth. I was left for a moment before I heard what sounded like doors being opened and closed. Suddenly I was lifted and unceremoniously dumped onto what felt like carpet to my restrained fingers. The hessian bag was removed, I was in my boot—I knew it was my car because my Louis Vuitton shopping bags were in my line of sight—the outside light narrowed as the hatch descended. I should have turned and tried to get a look at my captor. But instead, the closing sound behind me, an announcement of my pending demise. CLICK. I was shut in.

Who did this to me?

Was it my CI?

The man had contacted me out of the blue with promises of information for my ears only. The small titbits he had offered up over the phone were enough to get me out here on my own, salivating at the thought I could close this case. Thus, ensuring I would win the respect of my partner.

Was it the drug dealer we were looking for?

Did he know I was close to catching him? Did he know I had an informant and my own leads? How did he know I was working solo without my partner? Who by the way, didn't trust my instincts when I said we were looking in the wrong direction!

Maybe it was my partner?

The man who wore overpowering flowery scents and hated me at first sight. The man who wanted to work alone and made sure I knew it.

Did it matter if I was going to die here in my watery grave?

This was not how I imagined it would be like to be in a car that plunged into a body of water. I thought the splash would be loud, the impact would feel like smashing into concrete. I assumed the water would rush in and overpower me. There'd be no time to wonder what happened, let alone form a plan to escape. Instead ...

Drip, plonk, plunk, splat!

The splat had moved again, I needed to shuffle onto my back. All my years of yoga would come in handy. All I needed to do was thread my body through my arms. It was harder than I thought— usually when I did yoga, I didn't have my gun holstered to my side.

Wait.

My gun.

Seriously?

I could shoot off my bindings, then the lock of the boot before making a mad dash for the top of the lake.

Wait.

That was panic talking.

If he left my gun, maybe he left my knife, the one my partner insisted I wear even though knives weren't allocated to police.

Right ankle, check.

What an idiot!

Why would my attacker leave me with my gun and knife? Surely, he knew I would be armed, wouldn't a respectable criminal check for weapons?

This didn't make sense, maybe it was a clue.

I needed to get my head in the game.

I removed the knife from its sheath, the move difficult with my hands bound but easier than I expected. I cut through the rope binding my ankles, for some reason they had been tied tighter than my wrists. The release sent instant pins and needles through my feet. The hands were harder, I needed to grip the handle between my knees and saw back and forth like cutting through stringy calamari. Hmmm, calamari, I digress.

One—back and forth. Two—back and forth. Three—back and forth. Four—back and SUCCESS!

I was free.

Well, sort of ...

Now to escape the boot. I sheathed my knife before taking out my gun. I just had to shoot out the lock on the boot, take a deep breath and swim for it.

I could do this.

Although, shooting in this tight space wouldn't exactly be safe and my ears would not thank me. Did I have another choice?

Wait.

This was my car, which wasn't the important part. The car was old, but still manufactured after 2002. That was the crucial element. My mother still reminded me of its age and demanded I replace this piece of crap—her words, not mine—every chance she could. Most cars built after 2002 had boot release switches. I just had to find it and release the switch to open the boot. No shooting required.

Okay, focus. It had to be here somewhere, near the rear lights made sense.

Found it.

Now, to take a deep breath, hit the switch, open the boot and swim to safety.

Wait.

What would happen if I got to the surface and my attacker was waiting for me?

Wouldn't it be safer to work out who did this to me before I escaped? It's not like the water was rushing in or anything, I had time, lots of time. It didn't feel like I was sinking so the car must have settled. I was free from my bindings so I wasn't really trapped, I could be out in seconds if the water, for some reason started to pour in.

So, who was the attacker?

I had three suspects...

The CI. The Drug Dealer. My Partner.

The CI smelt like lavender. The drug dealer was named the Botanist. My partner always wore flowery cologne.

It could have been any of them.

That was it.

The answer was right in front of me.

I needed to escape and report to my sergeant.

A few shallow breaths.

Wait, I should take the gag off first. Better!

Why the hell hadn't I realised I was still gagged?

Moron.

A few deeper breaths, my heart slowed as my finger rested on the release switch.

Ready.

Drip, plonk, plunk!

Go!

I pressed the button, the boot popped open, I clambered awkwardly to my knees, mindful not to hit my head. The water didn't completely swamp me as I had assumed it would.

It took me a moment to steady myself. I looked down. I was kneeling in the boot of my car. My car was sitting in the pink Salt Lake, but it wasn't fully submerged. The lake wasn't deep enough. The car was nose first on a slight angle. Most of the boot rested in line with the water level. In fact, apart from one corner, the water only pushed high enough to cover the rest of the boot as the lake rippled rhythmically in the wind. With the boot open, the water had entered fast to fill that one corner, but the rest was still just a slow, steady procession.

I was free from my watery grave, but I wouldn't have died. Well, maybe after a few days without food and water.

On the bank, my attacker stood smirking.

I would have yelled at him, pulled my gun, but it would have to wait. He was not alone.

My attacker—the traitor—stood next to my mother, my sergeant, and the rest of the station all watching me with smiles on their faces.

I was right!

I had concluded my suspects, the CI, the Drug Dealer, and my partner were all guilty.

In fact, they were all the same person.

My partner!

There was no drug dealer, no CI.

My face heated as I trudged through the water towards the bank where they all stood grinning like lobotomised goofs. Some had even started clapping.

Arseholes.

I reworked the summation of my near-death experience because the brand-new mustard-coloured Range Rover parked next to them, sported a big pink bow on the roof. Across the windscreen, the message in large white writing on a big pink banner:

CONGRATULATIONS ON YOUR PROMOTION!

I'd been had.

I thought initiations were a thing of the past, but despite all this I learned my lesson—mother would always get what she wanted, no matter what she had to do to get it.

PADDY O'MALLY'S WAKE

ROBIN MARTIN THOMAS

Sure, there's nothing so entertaining as an Irish wake, especially one in Newfoundland, where they're more Irish than the Irish themselves, even though it's on the other side of the Atlantic. But, Paddy O'Malley's wake wasn't just entertaining, it was downright sensational.

It started with all the basic requirements for a wake — plenty of alcohol, relatives, a priest, and of course, a corpse. Paddy O'Malley, sixty-one, when he passed, hadn't long retired from the St John's Penitentiary, where he was a prison guard. Lots of people liked him (or so they said) but not everyone. Still, everyone went to the wake. I was no exception. I'd been his solicitor, but I was also his friend. And there was something about his sudden death which didn't sit easy with me.

We were gathered in the front room of Paddy's small house where he lay in state in his Sunday best with the Knights of Columbus badge on his lapel. Chairs were pushed against the wall to make space for his casket and in the corner a rickety table was laden with beer bottles and casks of wine.

'He's a beautiful corpse,' Mary Donahue said, lifting her Kleenex to wipe a tear from her eye. 'You'd hardly think Uncle Paddy was dead. Such a shame we couldn't visit him at a nice funeral parlour.'

'A good old-fashioned wake at home with family and friends was what he wanted,' I said. Pad-dy's instructions about this had been specific, and I'd followed them to the letter.

'Yes b'y, and nuthin' wrong with that, even though he was taken so suddenly,' Charlie Green said, raising a glass of whiskey towards the coffin. 'We miss him down at the prison. Old Joey was only asking after him a while back. Said he was going to visit when he got out.'

Colin sniffed. 'Don't think Dad would've wanted to mix with the likes of him.'

Mary gave him a look. 'How would you know? You hardly ever visited him. I saw him nearly every day towards the end.

'Colin's grey eyes narrowed. 'Careful there, Mary. Someone might think you had an ulterior motive. If I'd known he was so close to the end, I would've been round in a flash.'

'Why? To make sure you were in the will?' Mary said out loud what was on everyone's mind. Colin scowled at her.

There was an uncomfortable silence in the room. I felt all eyes on me. Paddy had won a sub-stantial amount of money last year from the Lotto, which was why he'd been able to retire. Despite my advice, he hadn't made a will. That would set the cat among the pigeons — yet another worry.

Mary sat beside Paddy's youngest son, Danny, who was nursing a beer. Next to him his tanned Aussie friend, Jake, shook his sun-bleached hair. At least this was one person who wouldn't try to prise information from me about the nonexistent will. I sat on the other side of him.

The door burst open. Maggie O'Malley, dressed in black from head to toe, swept into the room. Black stilettos clicked on the linoleum as she headed for the coffin.

'Holy mother of God, my poor darling Paddy!' she cried, clutching her suit jacket. 'You were taken from us too soon.'

Danny gave an audible sigh, and Colin dropped his face in his palm. Father Bill Cleary, moved forward and, patted her on the back. 'Now, Maggie, you know Paddy wouldn't like you to suffer so.'

She raised tear stained eyes to him. 'I know, Father. Never was there a kinder, more generous soul than my Paddy.'

'That must be why she divorced him,' Sylvia, Charlie's wife, said in a loud whisper, which most of us tried to ignore, but I heard the sniggers behind me. Satisfied she'd made her point, she added, 'I could do with another drink.'

The Aussie got up and took her wine glass. 'I'll get it.'

Sylvia gave him a smile, her scarlet lips bright.

'You're a darlin'. What's your name again?'

'Jake. Wine?'

Thick, black eyelashes fluttered at him. 'Red. Not the cask stuff, mind. The bottle. Colin put it at the back.'

'No worries.' He sauntered away, holding the attention of the ladies in the room.

Maggie allowed herself to be guided to a chair by Father Cleary. 'You know, Father, we were on the verge of reconciliation. We found our way back to each other, though in the eyes of God, we were still man and wife.'

'Though not in the eyes of the law,' Mary said loudly. 'Five years, isn't it, that you've been di-vorced.'

'Never having been married yourself, Mary dear, you don't quite understand how strong the bonds between a husband and wife are, even when they've been apart.'

Mary flushed.

'How did he die?' Jake asked, sweeping his eyes around the room.

My lips tightened. Only a foreigner would be so insensitive. Yet, it was a question I'd asked myself. Was it just a heart attack? Or was it something more?

Charlie said, 'He was the finest kind a few weeks ago when Sylvie and I went out for a fish'n chips with him.'

'Such a lovely man.' Sylvia sighed. 'So thoughtful too, especially in all those little things, ...' Her voice trailed off and a wistful look came into her eyes.

Charlie frowned at her. 'You were very chummy with him.'

'Of course, m'darlin', he was one of your oldest friends.' Sylvia flashed him a smile, but Char-lie's scowl only deepened.

The silence hung heavy in the air.

Mary dropped her voice to a whisper, 'I knew his time was close when he asked us to get in touch with Danny.'

Colin looked over at his younger brother, still slouched in the chair.

'For God's sake, sit up, Danny, show some respect. You haven't been home in over two years. You might at least pretend you care something for Dad.'

Danny's dark eyes filled with disgust. 'Seriously, Col, did you ever wonder why? You did eve-rything you could to poison him against me. You acted the golden boy, but you were never much of a brother to me. Mom was missing in action most of the time, finding herself, or whatever the hell she was doing the last few years. In the end it was easier to stay away.'

'You made it easy for Dad to disapprove of you. You haven't had a steady job in your life.'

Danny lifted his chin. 'I'm a musician.'

'Is that what you call yourself? Where did you even get the money to come home? You proba-bly had to borrow it.'

Danny stood up, the chair falling behind him. Face red, he moved towards his brother, raising clenched fists. 'You want to say that again?'

Jake grabbed his arm, 'Don't, Danny. Not here.' The Aussie turned to Colin, 'Steady on there, mate.'

Colin stared back at him. 'Stay out of this, mate. This is none of your concern. I don't even know why you're here.'

Danny dropped his hands and threw an arm around Jake. 'Jake's a part of this family too, now. We're together.' He smiled up at him.

'Danny, I'm so sorry I haven't been there for you,' Maggie went over to him and gave him a hug. She looked up at Jake and smiled. 'Welcome to the family, Jake.'

'It's okay, Mom. I know you had stuff on your plate,' Danny said, as he gave her an awkward pat on the back.

127

Sylvia sighed. 'Paddy did too. He was full of plans for his trip in his new motorhome this sum-mer. We were that excited about it...' She stopped.

'WE?' Charlie's voice rose.

'Did I say we? I meant he, of course.' She forced out a laugh. 'Silly me.'

'I knew it. You were seeing Paddy behind my back. You were having an affair.' Charlie's voice shook.

'Charlie, how can you say such a thing!'

Maggie stood up, and pointed a shaky finger at Sylvia. 'You were trying to get Paddy away from me. He was sick of you always calling or texting him.'

'That's a lie. Paddy... cared for me. He said he'd look after me.'

Charlie's eyes darkened, and the veins in his forehead looked ready to pop.

'You sleeveen, you.' Maggie lifted her glass and threw its contents at Sylvia. Red wine splashed against her face, making her mascara run. Sylvia stepped forward, but Mary stepped between them.

'Come on Sylvia, let's go upstairs where you can fix yourself up.' She dragged her out of the room. Maggie collapsed in her seat, shaking with anger. There was an awkward silence, then people began to talk again.

Jake came over to me. 'How you going, mate?'

I raised an eyebrow. 'Considering I'm at a wake, could be better.'

Jake shrugged. 'At least you're not family. You're his solicitor, right?'

'Yes, but I've known Paddy for a while.'

'Friends, eh? Didn't you help him with a few investments last year when he won all that mon-ey?'

I said in a tone I hoped would put him in his place, 'I'm a solicitor, not an accountant. He might've asked my advice about a few things, because we were friends. No harm in that.'

'If you say so.' Jake looked over at the coffin. 'Wakes and weddings, seem to bring out the worst and the best in people.' He looked back at me, as if he was trying to work out which category I fell into.

Where did Danny pick up this beach bum? I was the one who should be asking the questions, not him.

I moved away.

Sylvia, returned with reddened eyes and sat in a corner.

Mary got up. 'Everyone listen, please. Uncle Paddy had one last request before he died.'

A hush fell over the room.

'Uncle Paddy wanted each of you to say a few words. Speak your truth about him, and say your good-byes.'

This should be interesting, I thought.

Maggie, looking daggers at Sylvia, went to the coffin, placing one hand on her chest. 'I still feel our two hearts beat as one.' She gave a loud keening wail, and was about to put her other hand on Paddy's chest, when Father Cleary jumped up and pulled her back.

'You're distraught, my dear. Let me do the blessing over him while you settle yourself.'

Moving to the casket, he reached in his pocket, probably to take out his rosary beads.

'Let's close our eyes in silent prayer for a few moments.' Everyone did as he asked, except me — and the Aussie.

Father bent over Paddy.

'Not so fast, Father.' Jake rushed towards him, grabbing his hand.

Father Cleary tried to pull away from Jake's tight grip. There was a scuffle and a clatter on the floor, as a syringe fell out of Father's hand.

'Get it before someone steps on it,' Jake said, holding the still struggling Father Cleary.

Swooping down, I picked up the syringe with my handkerchief and slipped it in my pocket, still having no idea what was going on. But evidence was evidence.

'God damn you. What do you think you're doing?' Cleary said, trying to break free. But, he was no match for the muscle-bound Aussie.

'William Cleary, I'm arresting you for the attempted murder of Patrick O'Malley,' Jake said. 'You were about to give Paddy an injection and I'm betting the lab results will show it would've been lethal.'

'That's ridiculous. Dad's dead,' Colin said.

'Well now, that's a matter of opinion,' said a voice from inside the coffin.

It creaked as Paddy sat up.

It was a toss-up over who screamed the loudest, but at the end of it two bodies were on the floor, Maggie and Sylvia.

'What the...' said Danny.

'Dad, is that really you?' Colin's face was white.

'Who else would it be? Will someone help me out of this box?'

By now Sylvia and Maggie, since no one was paying them any attention, got themselves off the floor and into chairs, looking for once as old as they really were.

Danny opened the bottom half of the coffin, helped Paddy out, and guided him to the nearest chair.

'Thanks son. I got awful stiff lying in that box.'

Stretching his legs out, Paddy shook his head at the priest, held by the Aussie on one side and Charlie Green on the other. 'I'm disappointed in you Bill. I never said a word to anyone about your gambling, or your jail time.'

'I was in trouble, Pat. They were after me when I couldn't pay up. I was desperate.'

'Desperate enough to murder. That's why I laid the trap, not just for you, Bill, but for everyone here.'

For everyone? I'd thought something was up, which was why I was watching everyone like a hawk. But why would Paddy lay a trap for me? I'd thought we were friends.

'What trap?' Mary asked, her voice unsteady.

'Only Jake and Bill knew.'

'Jake?' Danny said. 'What's he got to do with it?' He looked over at him. Jake reddened.

'Jake's a detective. I hired him from an agency in Australia to keep an eye on you. Colin said you were into drugs and I didn't want you to get in trouble. But then, I had another job for him, so I asked him to come home with you.'

'Jake?' Danny's voice broke.

'Sorry, Danny, I did come to care for you. It wasn't all fake. But, initially, I was being paid by your dad, and I had to do my job.'

Danny turned away, his eyes moist.

'Just what was that job, besides looking after Danny and keeping him out of trouble?' I asked, still puzzled. I knew there was something off about the Aussie. I just hadn't realised he was working for Paddy.

'I asked him to help me fake my death, partly so I could find out what you really thought of me. He was to watch you all.'

Swear words filtered through the gasps in the room.

Paddy continued. 'I knew Bill was trying to get hold of my money. I first met him in prison. I thought he'd reformed when he joined the church. Then I won the Lotto. After that, he was at me all the time for money for the church. Gave him some, at first. But I suspected all of it went to Bill Cleary, not the church. Finally, I said, 'Father, I'll leave you some money in my will.' It was a joke to get him off my back, but it was a mistake. From that moment he was out to get me, so I came up with a plan.'

'To cause your family pain and grief?' My tone was scornful.

Paddy sighed. 'I was worried for my life. I had to do something.'

Jake nodded. 'Pat told Bill he was going to fake his death and I was going to help him with a new drug I'd found on the internet. It slows the heartbeat and mimics death.'

Paddy continued, 'I told Bill if he went along with it and presided over my 'funeral' I'd pay him a hefty fee along with the money I was leaving the Church. I said I wanted to find out what my family really thought of me so I'd know who to leave my money to. I wanted to catch Bill out too.' Paddy shook his head. 'But when he nearly stuck me with the needle, I thought I was done for. I'd gone too far. Jake stopped him just in time. Now all he'll get is more jail time.'

Bill roared and lunged forward, but Jake pulled him back.

Paddy added, 'When the sedative wore off, I could hear what everyone said about me — and about each other.' He sighed.

'How could you do this to us?' Maggie cried.

'It was a mean trick to play, Dad,' Colin said.

'I never thought you'd put a spy on me,' Danny said. He looked over at Jake.

Jake hung his head, but he never let go of Father Cleary.

'So what did you learn from all this, Uncle,' Mary said quietly.

He took her hand in his. 'I'm truly sorry for the pain I've caused. But, you see, money is a terri-ble thing, for those who have it and those who want it. It changed me from someone who loved his family, to not trusting anyone. It changed some of you too. I occasionally wish I'd never won it at all. What have I learnt? That I'm a foolish old man.'

He turned to face his family. 'For all your flaws and faults, you're still my family. I'm not so lily white myself. I should have thought more about loving you than what you thought of me. I'm think-ing I'll give you all some money now, so you won't have to wait until I'm dead.' He looked over at me. 'Instead of drawing up that will, you've been bugging me about, maybe you could help me di-vide some of my assets, including something for yourself. You've been a good friend to me over the years.'

I nodded, a lump forming in my throat.

The tension in the air softened. Perhaps Paddy might be forgiven after all.

The doorbell rang.

'That'll be the police,' Jake said. 'Where's that syringe?'

I took it out of my pocket as Mary went to get the door. Two burly constables came in.

'So what's this all about then?' said one of them. 'Where's the victim?'

'That's me,' Paddy said.

The other one looked over at the coffin, 'Hang on, where's the corpse?'

'That's me too.' Paddy said.

The cops looked at him, one shaking his head in disbelief and the other raising an eyebrow.

'Why don't you boys handcuff Bill and put him in the paddy waggon? Then I'll tell you the whole story. While we're at it, let's have a drink. After all, I've got some celebrating to do. It might be my wake but, I've had a resurrection.'

UNDETECTED

CHRISTINE BETTS AND KATE KELSEN

*I*know more secrets than any woman alive. Boss used to say I could spot bad guys around corners. I'd sniff the dirty bastards out. After thirty years of it, it's who I am. Can't escape it. Standing in line at the supermarket, I see the ones who can't afford the groceries they're holding and the ones who are praying no one checks under the nappy bag.

It's easy when you use the self-service checkouts. I see the plump middle-class boys who call their leafy suburb 'the ghetto' as if they know what the word means. The little buggers know the store detective can't search them. I watch them saunter out through the in-gate with packets of gum and crisps and whatever else in their pockets. I see them, but they don't see me.

I had a grasser once, ex-prossie. She knew more than I ever will. Dania knew far more than any woman should. She's dead now. Hepatitis. Her sister was grateful for the flowers at the service. There were a few other coppers there. Good stick, Dania.

Closest thing I ever had to a friend. Dania's smile could open doors. I told her that once and she'd said, in that cold-war era accent, 'What's between my legs used to open wallets and where did that get me?' And then her wheezy laugh.

They buried her on one of those days in December when the rain won't let up. I wanted to crawl into bed after, but the Job doesn't stop. The B&Es might slow down; no one wants to carry a telly out to their van in the rain, but the wife-beaters and the vilest of the vile don't stop because it's raining.

I try to remember Dania's smile when I see the people in the supermarket who can't afford their groceries. I help where I can. I never felt bad for the scum I'd lock up, but I feel for the little kiddies at home, hoping they get some dinner. Paid for more than one kid's dinner in my time. I think of those kids, and Dania, and I remember that bad things can happen to good people.

I try to smile when I see the big, mouthy lads at the gym, the ones who only know who I am now, not who I used to be. They just see a woman, and one with grey hair, into the bargain. I see them with their little baggies and their brown-paper packages. Sometimes I stare at myself in the mirror just to make sure I'm really there.

The women I work with now, they know nothing. No, that's not fair. They know where to go to get their nails done. They don't know what goes on after dark, when they're tucked up safe and sound in their homes behind security gates and cameras. They don't see that world, but it is going on around them all the time. Their fake eyelashes blind them to it, and they can't see past their puffy lips that enter the room five minutes before they do.

Sometimes, they remind me of Dania, the way they fluff themselves up on the outside, hoping to impress people. Just like Dania, they get paid for their services, but they get paid in credit cards instead of cash. They think they're different to Dania and her kind. Think they're above all that.

I needed this job after I retired. Needed the money. Needed to do something. But they don't need the work; their lives are cushy. They want for nothing. The call-centre is small change for them. An extracurricular activity. A social event. To get out of the house away from older, retired husbands. Yet it doesn't seem to be enough for some. I've seen them in the boutiques, burying their hands out of sight in the racks of clothing, removing tags, slipping past the clerk at the counter. On a first name basis with every other shopgirl in the mall.

'Nothing today, sweetie.'

They smile, saccharine sweet.

'Just browsing, darling.' The rings on their fingers twinkle.

Standing in the queue at the supermarket, I see one of them, Sharnee. The ringleader. Meanest, mean girl at Johnson Security. I see her slip her hand into the tote bag of the woman in front. Small hands, ever so quick. She pulls out a purse, or is it a phone? Shiny blue case. She slips it in her own bag. She glances round and I look away. She's smiling and chewing gum, but I'm sweating. Can't say anything. Wouldn't be worth the drama at work.

There are a couple of Uniforms talking to the Store Detective. Too young, I think. Babies. I look at them and raise my eyebrows. I'm sending them mental messages, willing them to nick Sharnee.

I run scenarios in my head.

Sharnee, hey, yes, Denise from work. I saw you, you know. I saw you put your hand in that lady's tote and take... What was it? A phone? Yeah, I notice things. Used to be a Detective.

In this scenario, the young Uniforms approach and thank me for my diligence and take Sharnee away.

Then I remember I'm invisible to them, too. My old colleagues. People I thought I'd always call friends. A few sent invitations to social gatherings in the year after I retired. I'll admit it was awkward. People acknowledged me, but now I'm outside their circle.

It's not like I wanted to retire. Turned sixty and I'm out on my ear.

After a while, even the ones who invited me to their birthday drinks stopped calling. I thought about contacting them and inviting them to catch up. It's not all up to them.

The woman in front of Sharnee is paying for her groceries. Her face drops. She can't find her phone. She pays with her card and leaves, still patting her pockets and rifling through her tote.

Sharnee puts her groceries on the moving belt and chats and chews gum and calls the girl behind the register 'darling.' The Uniforms have moved to the supermarket door. I get my hopes up, but Sharnee sails through, already pulling the other woman's shiny blue phone from her bag. She doesn't even try to hide it.

Like I always did on the Job, I put my rage into making calls. My arrest stats were the best four years running. Now, I'm the best on this floor, but they overlook me all the time. Of course, an ex-copper knows how to sell home security.

Sharnee isn't a good person. I know all about her. Did some digging. Shacked up with her mother's ex, apparently. All class. Amazing what people put on social media for anyone to read.

Overheard the Floor Manager on the phone. Talking to "Higher Up" about some anomalies with the takings. A few complaints. Elderly people getting ripped off.

I dug a bit more; used an old ID to log into the databases. Sharnee's got quite a history with the Boys and Girls in Blue. I made sure that paper trail got to the Floor Manager's desk. Slipped it into her mail. No need to get my nose dirty in the process. After all, I'm an expert at going undetected.

Another long day on the phones. I'm on the street outside work, waiting patiently for the bus. Sharnee is in front of me, yapping away on her 'new' blue phone, voice louder than is socially acceptable, even outdoors. Why do some people feel the need to fill every inch of space around them? To be noticed by everyone, even if it's irritated glances from people looking for the source of the awful noise.

I look at Sharnee's slim back. Somewhere between the staffroom and the street, she's removed the unflattering pale blue shirt and grey skirt we all wear. The Floor Manager says the uniform makes us feel like a team, but it'll take more than that to make that lot care about anyone but themselves. I'll admit it looks better on Sharnee and the rest of them than it does on me. I liked my old uniform. At least it got me a bit of respect.

Sharnee's activewear is tight and new looking. Her nails, freshly done, are the same shiny blue as the phone. She's talking to her mother. She keeps saying 'Mum' but the way she's speaking to her mother is not the way I'd speak to mine if she was still alive, but then I never shagged my mum's boyfriend. Sharnee raises her voice. People look over, annoyed. I should tell her to pipe down. I lean forward, my hand out.

The sound is sickening but not surprising. I've heard a body go under a bus before. More than once. I've bloody seen everything. People come running. Sharnee is wedged beneath the bus tyre. The bright red activewear matches her blood on the road. Someone is screaming and a woman phones for help. Concerned citizens mill around, hands to chest, hands to mouths. In minutes, Uniforms clear the area while the Paramedics work to free her small, broken body. They cover it, her, with a white sheet.

Onlookers comfort the Bus Driver. He's sitting on the curb. People are talking to the Uniforms and television crews are setting up. Vultures.

What happened?

Everyone is asking the same question. A young constable is taking statements. She rests her hand on the arm of the distraught girl beside me.

'She just stepped out into the street?'

The woman nods, her face awash with tears.

'Did you see anyone bump into her?'

The woman shakes her head.

'No. She was talking to her mum on the phone. The bus came. So sad. It all happened so fast.'

A replacement bus arrives to collect the passengers. I board with the others, barely notice as I tap my transit card to the machine. I take a seat. The city and suburbs pass, but for the first time I don't take them in. I'm seeing, but I've stopped really seeing. Instinct snaps me out of my daze. I press the button to get off. For once, I don't call out thanks to the Driver. I look around but I've got no idea where I am. I almost drop my phone as I try to remember how to call an Uber.

At home, I fumble in my bag for keys and hurry to the door. I close it behind me, exhaling a huge sigh of relief. I collapse onto the couch, sinking into its softness. Slipping my arms under the cushion, I rest my weary head. I lie there, staring into nothingness, until well after dark. The thoughts roll over and over in my head; after a while, they become so blurred I can barely make sense of them.

One less mean girl in the world, I tell myself before getting up and putting the kettle on.

I watch telly for half the night. In every show, there's a killer and they always get what's coming to them. That was my job. I caught the bad guys. Well, some of them. Most of them either got away with it because they were clever or because we turned a blind eye for a bit of information here and there. Only busted Dania that one time.

I wake on the couch. It's cold. I make a cuppa, but I can't drink it. I'm numb.

'Everything is going to change,' I say to the mirror with my toothbrush hanging out of my mouth. I don't know if this is a good thing or a bad thing.

I get on the bus. It's the same bloody Driver, the replacement one, not the one who skittled Sharnee. I swallow hard. What are the chances, in a city this big? I say hello and he's pleasant, but he doesn't look at me.

The office is quiet. Half the girls aren't there; took the opportunity for a day off. The rest sit at their desks in a daze, but the Floor Manager comes in around ten with take-away coffees and donuts. She talks about Sharnee and a few of the girls cry. One goes to the toilet and doesn't come back.

The funeral isn't a fancy affair, but there are some flowers. Sharnee's mum and sister get up and say a few words. Then her fella gets up. Says he buried her favourite purse with her. Bet he took all the money out of it.

The sun is shining. It's not a sad funeral, not like Dania's. I see two women taking selfies with the coffin. People from work sit in the back rows. We're all wearing our pale blue shirt and grey skirt. Floor Manager's orders. Must go back to the phones afterwards. Must sell that home security.

Sharnee's mum and fella, walking hand in hand, go around talking to people. When my taxi arrives, the one I'm sharing with Glenda, Ramona, and Josie, we see the mum and the fella standing around the back of the chapel, snogging.

The only one I feel sorry for is the Bus Driver.

Back at work, Josie stops by my desk for a chat on her way back from the loo.

'You see the mum and Sharn's Pete behind the Chapel?'

I nod.

'No shame,' Ramona chimes in.

'Coming for lunch again today, Denise?' Glenda's looking over the top of her cubicle at me.

I nod again. I'm smiling.

'I'll show you the best place to get your nails done.'

She's whispering, but still smiling, she disappears into her cubicle.

From the corner of my eye, I see the Floor Manager walking towards me. She rang me last night. Her name's Harper, we're on first name basis now. She stops next to my desk, taps on her coffee mug with a Bic, and clears her throat.

'Attention please, ladies. I'd like to announce our top salesperson for this month. Denise.'

I stand and smile at Glenda over the top of the cubicle. She seems genuinely happy for me, but I know some things about her, too.

IDA AND SQUIZZY

FRANK PREM

et to items performed by Ms Ida Pender and the girls of Miss Lillias Smith's annual pupil's display, as reported in the Malvern Standard, Saturday, 2nd August, 1919

Item 1: Ballet – 'Irish Scene'

twenty-four girls
all
a-giggle

miss lillias' pupils
in performance

taffeta
and tulle
and rustling skirts

ninon
or
plainer stuff . . .

I don't know

but
the hazel-eyed
young ida –
her mother's *babe* –
is just fourteen years

and already
she is
the dancer

Item 2: Ballet - 'Gipsies'

the little jazzer

that's
what they call her

she sneaks from home
at night

finds the way
to lose herself
at the *palais*

de dance

ooh la la

all sorts
call
to visit the *palais*
at night

and
sixteen-and-a-half
years of age
is not a fact
to stand in the road
of that underworld prince
leslie –
squizzy –
taylor

ooh la la

ooh la la

Item 3: Ballet – 'Vive. La France.'

no
detective

my leslie

was not afraid
for his life
that morning

no

he did not carry
a gun

no

he wouldn't
do that

no
detective
no

leslie
had no intention
to kill that man

snowy cutmore
was from
the fitzroy mob
that awful 'push'

they are a bad gang

of spivs

and of villains

my leslie
is richmond
through
and through

he would never go . . .

never do . . .

somebody else
must have . . .

detective
I do not know

I
cannot tell you

all I know
is that both of them
are dead

please
leave me alone

now

I feel
I would like
to dance

Item 4: Song and Dance – 'My Belgian Rose.'
jazz . . .

the jazz baby
she used
to be

green-brown eyes
and red-gold
hair . . .

they called her
beautiful

squizzy
picked her up
when she was sixteen
and looked
twenty-six

married
stole and robbed and ran

and hid

squizzy
and babe
all over the newspapers
and
through the courts

then he got shot

it was murder
but she knew
nothing . . .

nothing

and
just so
she testified

the coppers
had to let
her go

and watch
as her slight frame
danced past them
and years went by

dance . . .

as if
jazz
was all she'd
ever known

dancing now
with a new name
the crowd
bestowed

babe
the jazzer
is now
the angel

young ida
favorite
of the fast crowd

now
babe

angel
of death. <end>

DEATH LIST

VICTORIA VANSTONE

Cass stopped what she was doing and took in the dilapidated bar. The decor hadn't been updated in years. Faded photos of baseball players hung on the walls. A velvet covered couch with a lopsided arm rest sat like a rotting carcass next to a glass table covered in dirty ring marks. Shiny beer taps folded over a mahogany bar top that swept the length of the room, leading the eye towards the blue felt of a pool table.

A storm was bearing down outside. Rain lashed against the windows. The building shook. Thunder threatened from afar. 'Sweet Home Alabama' finished playing on the jukebox in the corner. Silence allowed for a pause in the bloodshed. Cass noticed a whisky bottle on the bar within reach. She grabbed it and took a long swig. A warmth spread from her neck, down her body, into her stomach. Cass let the whiskey drown out her mood and her day melted away. All that was left was to decide is the man should live.

He moaned.

Cass looked down at the mess squashed under her foot. He was on his side, hands bound with a zip tie behind his back. His knees were bent, black tape wound around his ankles. He wriggled like an eel. His nose was compressed, bent to one side from the pressure of her hold. There was an open wound on his forehead, surrounded by dark, congealed blood.

'Not so fucking cocky now, are you Marty, eh?'

'Look at me you piece of shit. Look. At. Me.'

Cass wanted to see the fear in his eyes.

He turned and looked at her through his swollen and bloodied eyes and she thought about her mother screaming for help....

Cass had managed to lure Marty into staying past last orders with a promise of a business deal. Marty's eyes had lit up when she said, 'I just wanted to have a chat with you about some girls I know that need a quick pay day.'

Marty rubbed his hands together. It made her stomach turn. This wretch was everything she hated about the world. A weak and selfish man, like all the other lowlifes that gathered at the run-down Irish bar where she'd been working undercover.

For three months she had stood polishing glasses, pulling pints of sour smelling ale, and flirting with toothless ruffians. The men that frequented the ramshackle establishment dribbled into their whisky tumblers when she turned around and bent over to scoop ice from the machine. They sat in a row along the bar alternating between shots of strong liquor and green bottles of Heineken. With each empty vessel, the men slumped and slurred. Their behavior becoming more aggressive and obtuse as the night wore on. By the end of the night each man made her the target of his affection, pulling her in close as he handed over measly tips. She could smell rancid breath and a faint stench of urine. After each shift her feet ached and her throat was sore from the cigarette smoke. Cass spent an hour in the shower scrubbing away any remnants of the belligerent imbeciles. Dealing with reprobates was what Cass did, so she sucked it up in the hope that every casual conversation, each revolting flirtation and warm smile would help her gain a deeper insight to the men on her hit list.

'Get deep into the underground scene Cass. That's all. We just need intel on what these guys are up to.' Chief said when giving her a rundown.

Chief West knew Marty and his gang were responsible for most of the petty crime on the East Side but had never managed to bring him in for anything big. There were rumors swirlling around that Marty had something to do with the recent flood of overdoses being bought into the Brentwood ER. They needed more evidence; all this circumstantial crap wasn't enough to lock him up, so Cass had been bought in to get deeper into the scene.

'Just get them to like and trust you Cass. That's it.'

She liked Chief West, he was one of the good guys, Cass wanted to be a good cop, get the job done. But as soon as Cass saw Marty's car outside the high school the case had jumped from work to being highly personal.

It was a Friday and she arrived early to pick up her girls from Brentwood High. There was still 15 minutes until her girls finished so she sat in her car and turned on the radio. When she saw him pull up the blood drained from Cass's cheeks. There was no doubt it was him in this clapped-out 80's Cortina with a crappy go-faster stripe down the side, alloys and lowered fender. Tacky, furry dice hung from the rear-view mirror and mindless techno vibrated from a set of speakers in his boot. Marty wound-down his window, flicked a cigarette butt onto the road and looked around to see if anyone was watching him. Cass saw his features as he turned towards her. He had a gaunt, sallow face and looked troubled, damaged in some way. The deep lines etched on his skin told her his story and for a second, as she stared at him, a stab of sympathy pierced her heart.

Cass had been a Police officer in the National Crime Agency for ten years now so she knew he was up to no good. Her instinct told her to hang back and watch him for a while and it didn't take long for her sympathy for him to dwindle.

After three minutes, a blue school bag flew over the high wall that ran down the side of the playground. Cass then saw a girl, not older than 14, swing her legs over the top of the wall, her feet land on the pavement just near Marty's car. The girl put the strap of her satchel over her head, pulled open the car door and jumped into the passenger seat. Just before the door closed, she caught a glimpse of the young girl kissing the much older man in a way that confirmed her suspicions.

From that day on Cass made a point of finding out everything she could about Mr Dent.

Back at the station she bought up his file. His rap sheet wasn't pretty. A life starting with petty crime that grew more serious with each passing year. His latest arrest was for possession, which made sense and could link him to the overdoses.

Chief said that some of the bodies that were dumped on the sidewalk outside the hospital were all in some way connected to Dent. They'd either brought drugs from him in the past or been in a relationship with him. Most were over 18 when they disappeared from their families so there hadn't been much the police could do. The Chief was pretty sure Marty was forcefully injecting them with heroin and he was getting greedy too, the girls were getting younger.

'The girls need money to support a habit. It's a trick as old as the game itself,' Said the Chief. 'Some bad dope means bodies are starting to pile up and somebody needs to go down for it Detective Colt. I'm handing the case over to you.'

Cass took copies of everything in Marty's file, she pinned photos to a wall in her living room of every girl that had overdosed, and stuck Marty's Mug shot in the middle. Over the few months of working in the bar she managed to connect every woman back with a line of red string to Marty's sallow face. At that point, with the evidence all in order Cass could have done what the chief wanted but then Marty crossed the line.

One afternoon her daughter Lexi came home in tears. A man had tried to grab her, pull her into his car.

'He was trying to kiss me Mum. I was so scared.'

Cass held her daughter as she sobbed.

'What did he look like sweetie?'

Cass deciphered the perp's description through her daughter's tears. She knew who it was straight away. Dent.

That's what had led to the list. Every member of the gang was on there and Dent sat right at the top.

And now, here he was, snivelling under her shoe, begging for his life.

'Please, I was helpin' the girls. They wanted the money, and the drugs were just a bit of fun. I was just givin' them what they wanted.'

'Are you telling me Marty that these young girls liked being taken from their homes and forced into drugs and prostitution? Are you trying to fucking tell me they had a choice?'

Cass pushed her shoe down onto his face again. He let out a deep guttural groan.

'They're all the same' she thought. 'Selfish, greedy perverts.'

She poured some whisky over Marty's broken body. The amber liquor made a satisfying glugging sound as it exited the bottle. It reminded her of home.

Her father used to stand in the kitchen and pour himself a whisky after work. Cass watched from the hallway as his glass repeatedly tipped upside down until it was empty.

'What are you looking at?' He yelled at her.

The young Cassandra Colt grew up watching her mother defend herself against the man she called Daddy. Her mum had become timid in his presence over the years. He blamed Cass's Mum for everything. If the house was a mess, or his fish dinner wasn't on the table by 7pm on a Friday, he paced the house looking calling her name.

'Where's my fucking dinner?' His constant state of anger meant Cassie grew up in a house stifled in fear. She spent most of her childhood hiding in the pantry where her mother shoved her as soon as the arguments started. She sat on the cold tiled floor, amongst the condiments, jam jars and crackly packets, reading the food labels aloud to herself to drown out the sound of her mum's head being banged against the kitchen counter.

'Tomato sauce'

'Nutritional information. Serving per package. Sugar content.'

'Tin of peas'

'Carbohydrate 5.3gms, Sodium 103 mg'

She read those labels until the front gate slammed shut and her mum stopped crying. Then, before long, the pantry door opened, and her mum's soft hand would take hold of hers.

'Don't look at me Cassie. Don't look at Mummy. It's time for bed now.'

Cass was too afraid and too young to help, to stand up and fight him.

Then, when Cass was 14, the screaming ended. She sat in the pantry and waited for her mothers hand to reach for hers but that night she didn't come. The pantry door was opened by a police lady and everything changed.

Cass moved in with her grandmother and was told to 'get on with it.' No-one talked about what happened. Cass decided to never talk about it either and buried her head in books. She didn't want people to see how broken she was. But memories of her mother stayed with Cass, she thought about her all the time... and right there, in the carnage with Marty reacing out for help, she felt her mum's presence.

Cass got her lighter out of her pocket and thought of her daughters, about Lexi crying and she heard her mums' gentle voice.

'Don't look at Mummy Cass. Just remember how much I love you.'

Cass knew her job was to bring this pathetic excuse for a human back to the station. She had to process him, take his prints, get a mugshot, do the paperwork. But something had changed in recent months. Cass's most recent relationship had ended. She'd caught her latest boyfriend staring at her eldest daughter in a way that made her uncomfortable. She knew that lustful glare and it made her skin crawl. Cass drew her weapon on him and he left. It was much quicker than a heart to heart. He was just another betrayal, another reason.

Even though she'd been told on numerous occasions by the chief to 'Not take it personal' her personal life was lurking near this case like a sneaky stalker.

She saw her father in these men. In Marty. The snide expression, the lack of concern for anyone but himself. She knew what Marty was capable of and it made a fire burn so fiercely in her gut she was incapable of thinking straight.

Cass inhaled. The strong oaky smell of whiskey filled her nose.

As her thumb turned the little metal cog of her lighter, a small flame appeared.

'Men like you Marty, only bring pain into this world. I'm here to end that pain, for you, for mum and for all those innocent girls.'

Cass moved the flame onto the collar of his blood-stained shirt. She heard him whimper a last attempt to get out of this; but it was too late. Her mind was made up. She wanted to rid the world of this scourge, men that knowingly demolish lives.

Cass leant down and whispered in his ear.

'It's too late Marty.'

A tentative smile built as the silence of his death sunk in. The moans and screams ended when the fire tightened around his neck. She didn't turn away from him. Instead, she watched. His body twitched and jolted. His skin turned black and charred.

As she stood over him, Cass took hold of the locket that hung around her neck on a silver chain. Inside was the only photograph left of her beloved mum.

'I love you' She whispered.

As the fire smoldered Cass walked around the bar to the sink. She washed the blood from her knuckles and splashed some cold water on her face. After she dried her hands on a towel she dug in her pocket for the list. She pulled it out and read the names out,

'Marty Dent.

Steve McCray

Jim Shultz

Dillon Jackson

Mack Davids

Lenny Peach....

One down, five to go.'

She grabbed a biro from a pint glass next to the cash register and scribbled out Marty's name. She picked up the bottle of Whiskey from the bar and poured the remaining liquid along the wooden countertop. Cass held a flame on the liquid until it caught.

As the flames licked the surface, she caught sight of her reflection in the mirror behind the upturned bottles. Her eyes looked dark, angry, and for a moment Cass saw the face of her father looking back at her.

As the blaze took hold, Cassie made her way outside the run-down building into the dark night. Cool droplets of rain ran down her face and washed away the any scent of death.

As Cass walked towards her car, she thought about her children again. Her beautiful girls. They seemed like a world away. She loved them with every pore of her body. This was for them. This was an act of love.

Cass got in and turned the key in the ignition. The engine of her sports car roared. Before she pressed her foot down on the accelerator her phone beeped.

A text message from an unknown number lit up the screen.

Cass looked down. Five words in bold type.

'I know what you did.'

What?

Her phone beeped again.

Cass could barely bring herself to glance at the screen.

'Don't worry Cass. Daddy can keep a secret.'

Her hands trembled. Her phone dropped to the floor.

Rain streamed down the windscreen.

And Cassie Colt drove into the storm.

WHO STOLE THE CHOOS?

DEBBIE KAHL

Okay, so I have a shoe fetish. But that's no reason for the police to treat me like an idiot. Honestly, you buy one pair of Jimmy Choos and the whole world thinks you've lost it.

And now, thanks to my obsession with Choos, I'm officially a victim of crime. Forced to sit on a sticky, plastic chair in the stinkiest little police station on earth, while trying my best not to melt into the cracked lino floor. But that's not my fault. It's not like I went out this morning and asked to be robbed.

And let's not even talk about the beads of sweat dripping into cracks of my body I'd rather not discuss. Honestly, how do people work in here? Where's the air-con? Can't they crank that thing up? I'm melting. Whoever thought a plastic fan mounted on the wall across the room is enough to cope with an Aussie summer needs their head read! Who ends up in a police station over a pair of stolen shoes anyway?

And yes, I understand they cost me a small fortune but lucky for me, I have Ben. Good, solid, reliable Ben Smith. He always makes sure I have everything I need. I fluked in when I married him. Unlimited access to our joint bank account for mini spending sprees and he never complains, or even notices, what I'm up to. Yes, I'm very lucky indeed.

Still, it's not every day you get robbed for your new shoes. *And* break your new phone fighting them off. Now I have no way to ring Ben, but that's not my fault. And the police won't let me use their phone because they're all too busy dealing with their so-called 'serious crimes'. I have no idea how I got myself into this situation. Really, I don't.

One minute I'm happily paying for my new season, fuchsia satin Jimmy Choo strappy stilettos with a diamante ankle strap. The next I'm being held up at gunpoint. I've seriously considered stealing shoes more times than I can count – but I never thought someone would actually do it. I don't know what I'm more offended about; that someone stole my idea or they stole my shoes. Who do they think they are?

Well, people may think I'm a bimbo but nobody steals from me. Especially not shoes. And if I have to sit in this disgusting excuse for a police station all day to get that thief locked up then that's what I'll do.

Not that I'm very helpful. Facing a pointed gun will kind of do that to a girl. I can describe the gun perfectly; black, round barrel, pointed in my direction but my description of the criminal was no help. And so much for CCTV footage. All it showed was a body not much taller than me, wearing sneakers, jeans and a hoodie. It could be anyone. A bored housewife in disguise who loves Choos as much as me, a wannabe influencer in their cheap, knock-off trackies, or even a crackhead ex-model who wants to sell them off for her next hit.

It could even be the guy sitting directly across from me. The one with the sneakers, jeans and hoodie sneering in my direction like he wants to eat me for lunch. Blergh. Thank goodness I have Ben waiting for me at home and not this doofus.

My vision is interrupted by another hoodie-clad criminal escorted past me in handcuffs. I can't see his face but my skin bristles in response to his familiarity. That's him. That's the guy! Well, I think that's him. I'm pretty sure that's the guy who held me up. It looks like him... well, his hoodie anyway. Give that man a gun and I'll know for sure. Actually, probably not the best idea with a room full of police but I'm not known for having good judgment.

Once I told the police about my shoes, all they did was laugh. Well, not about the gun part. They took that pretty seriously, but at spending a 'ridiculous' amount of money on shoes. I'll tell you what's ridiculous; that fashion-tragic female sergeant, clod-stomping with those boots on her feet. I'd die before wearing something like that in public. Tell me I'm ridiculous, after having a gun shoved in my face and my Choos stolen. Then force me to sit for hours on this crappy plastic chair, like I have nothing better to do with my day. Well, I'll tell you Princess Porkchop, my time is very precious and as it seems you've forgotten, I'm the victim here. The clenching of my fists has left little half-moon dents on my palms from my acrylic nails. Come to think of it, I need to get them refilled when I get a chance.

My grumbling is interrupted by the Adonis in a police uniform, walking towards me. Well hello officer, can I submit to the cavity search now? I smooth my hair for good measure and pat the sides of my eyes to check the Botox is still working. It doesn't matter though, he ignores my smile and walks right past me, without even so much as a glance in my direction. Honestly, if invisibility is all I have to look forward to in the future, perhaps I should've fought harder for the Choos and just let the robber shoot me.

I hear the cheap clod-stompers before I see them, and all too soon Princess Porkchop is back, the smirk on her face condescending.

'Mrs Smith,' she barks, jarring me to attention like a new cadet, 'it seems we've found your shoes.'

'My shoes?' I screech, louder than intended. People stop to look.

'Yes, your shoes,' she replies drawing out her words, as though my brain is the size of a marble. 'Follow me please.'

I skip down the hall behind her. I knew it was that guy with the hoodie in handcuffs. Not sure why he'd want to steal my Choos, I mean, he doesn't strike me as someone who knows about expensive shoes. But who cares, I'm beyond excited about getting them back. They found them, they actually found them! They're coming home to mama. The thought of it makes me dance on the spot.

Princess Porkchop opens the door to a small interrogation room and the happiness drains from my body. My Choos have been chewed. And not just nibbled on, they've been massacred! Who would do such a thing? My Choos. My beautiful Choos. They're ruined. I drop to my knees and scream. It's loud and it's bloodcurdling but I don't care. Why God why?

'C'mon Mrs Smith, take a seat,' Princess Porkchop says as she drags me up from the floor with one pudgy hand under my armpit. I swear I hear her mumble, 'Such a Barbie' but I can't be sure. I'm in too much shock – my $1200 Jimmy Choos are in pieces! I wipe my eyes in a poor attempt to redeem myself but get a mascara-stained hand instead. It's probably pointless anyway - the woman doesn't care about me or my Choos.

'Mrs Smith, are you okay?' Her tone is not at all sincere and I've had enough of her.

'I'm fine,' I spit back. 'How did you find my shoes?'

'They were delivered here about ten minutes ago.'

'From who?'

'Says his name is Ben Smith.'

'Ben?' I shriek, thoroughly confused by this new development. 'Why would he have my shoes? Where is he?'

'He's in Interrogation Room Two, we're questioning him about the robbery.'

'Sorry,' I stammer, 'You're saying my husband robbed me?'

'Well, that's what he claims. He said that he followed you to the shoe store today, put on a balaclava, pulled out his toy gun, stole your shoes and fed them to your new puppy.'

'But why?' I whisper, not quite believing what I'm hearing.

'Apparently he's had enough of you and your shoe fetish draining his bank account. He wants a divorce.'

167

SPICE

GEORGINA BALLANTINE

Alison's mobile pinged as she hurried through the shopping mall to work. She rolled her eyes at the message: I WARNED YOU. Last week she'd fired Penny, her assistant manager, for absenteeism. 'My dog's sick again,' was Penny's usual excuse. Alison doubted the animal existed.

'And now this...' Alison murmured. It wasn't the first of Penny's threatening texts, but she was all bark and no bite.

Scents of cumin, cinnamon, and chai tea enveloped her as she drew back the security screen outside Spice. Gleaming tubs lined the room, exotic flavours of the world captured in colourful blends. Fastening her linen apron, she froze when she noticed the open storeroom door.

She peered inside the narrow room but saw no sign of movement. Hurrying past the rows of boxes, her hands closed on a bulging sack of Seafood Masala Spice. She unclipped the neck, her palms sweating. Two fat bags of cocaine lay nestled inside, an investment towards her daughter's palliative care. Drug dealing was high risk, but Alison would gladly sell her own soul to give Abigail the best possible quality of life.

Sighing in relief, she tucked a strand of blonde hair behind her ear. She must have forgotten to lock the storeroom when she rushed home to relieve the carers the previous night.

Alison's day passed quickly after its unsettling start, a steady stream of customers requesting ingredients as diverse as saffron for dyeing hemp ribbons and tonka beans for flavouring pannacotta.

At closing time, two police officers entered the store. One remained near the entrance while the second approached the counter.

Alison's fingernails bit hard into her palms. She'd told no-one the location of her stash; their visit must be unrelated. But still her heart thumped against her chest.

'Alison Palmer? Detective Yang. I have a warrant to search your premises. Do you give me permission to search your store?'

'I, um... yes,' she spluttered.

The detective made straight for the storeroom. Should she make a break for it? No, too risky. Her stomach tightened at the sound of rustling plastic. Every nerve on edge, adrenaline flooding her body.

Detective Yang emerged in a cloud of curry-scented air, holding the bags of white powder. 'Do you recognise these?' he asked, removing a test kit from inside his jacket. When she shook her head, he scooped small amounts into two ampoules and shook the contents gently.

Alison held her breath, fixating on a splash of coffee staining the detective's lapel.

'No colour change,' he said, sniffing the bag. Tasting a pinch, his eyes widened. 'Vanilla sugar. Ms Palmer, someone's played a prank. I apologise for the intrusion.'

Alison grabbed the counter chair with trembling hands and sat heavily.

Sugar. Her daughter's care, her future, all gone.

Her phone pinged. Still shaking, she opened the message. Penny's face appeared onscreen, laughing, and pointing a finger at a sign: 'SCREW YOU'. At Penny's side, a bone-thin dog gazed mournfully up at her.

CALAMITY IN THE COMMUNITY

LEA SCOTT

Who's there?' Cynthia Myers held her breath, struggling to listen over the howling wind. Did she just hear a door bang?

No answer. Probably just the wind throwing branches against the windows. She wished she was at home looking out over her uninterrupted views all the way to the coast. Not in this cramped and cluttered community office in town. She loved living on the top of the ridge, ruler of her own kingdom, but it was a vulnerable spot when the southerlies blew up like they had today. The community Facebook forum had been running hot and she had to monitor the posts and make sure nobody was breaking her rules. The space-age NBN satellite dish on her roof was pitched as the way of the future for those out of town. What a joke! These strong winds not only took down trees, they also slowed her internet signal. At least the office still operated on ADSL technology, which was more reliable on windy days.

Cynthia had spent the morning scrolling through the community forum posts, smirking at the locals forced onto the

NBN and their complaints. The locals always had something to complain about – tourists' radical driving, local re-developments, or the 'gentry' invasion. She had a strict list of forum rules and with one click, she could block messages and delete members who did not obey. Most went to that *other* group to complain about her. Like that fruitcake conspiracy theorist Jules Vernon. *That had to be a fake name.* She had given him his final warning this week. One more of his rants about the evils of 5G and he was gone! Just like Clive Luddmuth. *Loudmouth,* as she referred to him, who took a swipe at everybody and everything. There was no place for trolls like him on her forum. The *other* group was welcome to him!

Bang!

Cynthia dropped the box she was carrying and old papers and photos scattered across the floor. She drew in a deep breath. The front door wasn't locked, there was never the need to. It was probably that dodgy catch. The reception door was wide open and dusk began to settle in. She slammed the door shut so the catch caught and headed back to the storeroom to clean up the mess.

She hadn't meant to stay so long. Around lunch time her obsession with clearing the storeroom of useless junk made her lose track of time. She cursed. Thanks to a slashed tyre the day before, she was without a car. It would be pitch black by the time she walked home. There was a drawn-out beep on the landline as she tried to call the local taxi driver. Her mobile phone was out too.

If she wandered across to the hotel, they might give her a lift home in the courtesy bus. They also wouldn't mind if she dropped the last box of rubbish in their skip. She'd already filled the wheelie bin. As she headed back toward the front door with the box in her arms, it swung open.

'Oh good, I was just–'

A hand reached for the light switch. The room turned dark.

Detective O'Reilly was woken from a deep slumber by the shrill ring of his phone. He was now out in the bitter wind, unshaven and hunched over the body of a woman at the bottom of the community centre stairs. The victim appeared to be in her early fifties. Well dressed, salon-coloured nails and hair in matching rose tones – marred only by the bloody halo around her face, glistening in the morning sun.

His second week on the job. Last thing he expected to investigate was a homicide case in this sleepy town. He'd noted the woman's neat office upstairs. The chaos at the front door. A half-crushed box. Papers strewn across the room and down the stairs. An overturned lamp. All indications of a struggle.

Sleepy town or not, there were always cracks under the surface and he intended to uncover them. Beginning by rounding up the rubber-neckers gawking at the crime scene.

'Right, you lot. Everyone inside!' He herded the bystanders into the downstairs hall.

One fidgety young fellow in blue overalls tried to duck away.

'Got somewhere to be this early in the morning, lad?'

'Um, yeah, got to get to work. I'm an apprentice at Jenkins' Mechanics just around the corner.'

'You can go first, then Mr?'

'Jenkins. It's my uncle's business.'

O'Reilly put his hand on the man's shoulder and turned him in the direction of the double doors.

'Everyone take a seat and we'll get through this as quickly as we can. I know you all have important places to be.' He glanced around the spacious hall at the motley crew made up of dreadlocked shoe-less hippies, one with a strange shiny hat, and grey-haired retirees in loafers. None of them seemed to have anywhere to be, but he wanted to keep them on side.

'Right. This way.' He beckoned Jenkins. 'Tell me everything that happened this morning, starting from the time you got into town.'

'I... I was just waiting for the pie shop to open. To grab some brekkie before work.'

'Uh-huh.'

'I swear, I didn't see anything. I caught sight of the crowd and just wandered up to see what was goin' on. She was just lying there. All that blood. Wish I'd minded my own business.'

O'Reilly watched the young man's face turn the colour of the hall's sickly yellow walls. He didn't fit the profile of a killer, but you never knew.

'Did you know the victim?' he pressed.

'Not really. Seen her around. She came into the shop yesterday for a tyre change. Looked like someone slashed her tyre.'

O'Reilly perked up. 'Why did you think that?'

'It was a clean slice, like from a knife or sharp piece of metal. Normally, if she'd run over something like that there would be some tearing.'

'Did she say who might have done it?'

'No, but the boys called her a Facebook Nazi. Always blocking people from some forum. I'm not on Facebook.'

'Well thank you for your time. If I need to talk to you again, I know where to find you. Jenkins' Mechanics, right?'

Jenkins nodded and scooted out the wide doors.

O'Reilly turned to the whispering group, who fell silent as he approached. 'Right, anyone got something to tell me?' Most looked down as if hoping they'd disappear through the cracks in the aged timber floor. His gaze landed on a woman in her later years. Grey hair in a neat coif, hands rested in her lap, eyes meeting his. He gestured for her to follow him.

He was beginning to wish he was still back in bed, nursing the morning coffee he had missed, watching the world news.

'Name for the record?'

'There's no need to be so gruff, Detective.'

He studied her soft wrinkled face and felt a little ashamed. 'My apologies, Ma'am. Tough morning. Let's start again. Would you mind telling me your name?'

'Penelope Werther. Like the caramels.' She shot him a smile just as sweet.

'Thank you, Mrs?'

'Ms.'

'Ms Werther. Can you tell me about what happened when you arrived in town?'

She pointed up toward the offices. 'I came in for my morning shift. I do quite a bit of volunteering in the community, and today was my day to help out on reception. You know, answer phones, greet visitors. But...' She swallowed hard.

'It's okay, take your time.'

'I came across Cynthia. Well, you saw.' She was silent a moment. 'I was just chatting with her online last night. It must have been just before–'

'Did you know the victim well?'

'We'd worked together for over a year. I'm a member of her community forum on Facebook. I help out with the admin. There are some awful people, just out to cause trouble. Sometimes, I'll take care of them for her when she's too busy.'

O'Reilly's chair squeaked as he leaned forward. 'What do you mean by take care of them?'

'You know, warn them, block them if they don't change their behaviour. Some of them get quite nasty and even threaten her.'

O'Reilly pondered her response. It matched up with what Jenkins had said about Cynthia's tyre being slashed. Maybe the culprit was right under his nose. He'd have to read some of these *nasty* comments. 'Have you ever had any threats made against you?'

'Oh no. Nobody knows that it's me. Cynthia gave me her own password.'

'So, you do the dirty work for Cynthia, and she takes the blame?'

Her voice took on an exasperated tone. 'Not always. She does some of her own dirty work, as you refer to it Detective. I'd rather consider it a *community* service.'

'Okay, well would you be willing to give me this password so I can find these people and talk to them?'

She looked across the room. 'Of course, but I don't need to give you the password to find the two main culprits. They're right here.'

178

His gaze followed hers. 'People who threatened Cynthia are here at the scene of the crime? Which two?

She shrugged and pointed them out. 'It's a small town, Detective. News travels fast.'

'All right, what more can you tell me about these threats?'

'Well, there's Clive Luddmuth, the fellow in the tweed coat.'

O'Reilly peered over her shoulder. The man sat alone under one of the large windows, a marked distance from anybody else. He held his head low under a matching tweed flat cap.

'*Loudmouth*, Cynthia called him. He was always antagonising someone. Cynthia blocked him last week. There's another forum that's set up in opposition to ours. Cynthia asked me to sign up to keep an eye on them, you know. Well, Clive Luddmuth, he posted: *That cow will get what's coming to her.*'

'Hmmm.' O'Reilly made a note to read that post.

'Then there's that crackpot Jules Vernon. We weren't even sure that's his real name. He's the one with the scruffy beard and foil bits on his hat. Thinks the world will end if we get 5G and is not afraid to set anyone straight who thinks otherwise. I booted him myself yesterday morning because he just wouldn't let up despite Cynthia's warnings. He went mouthing off to the other group about Cynthia being on their side – whoever he thinks they are.'

'Well thank you. Ms Werther. You've been very helpful.'

He stood and walked her to the door, where his team had set up at an antique timber desk. 'Just give your details to the Constable and you are free to leave.'

He turned. 'Right everyone, if you are, or have been a member of the community Facebook group run by the victim, please remain. Anyone else can leave, but please provide identification to the Constable at the door.

Jules Vernon stood. O'Reilly crossed his path and growled under his breath. 'Sit back down. Now.' Despite looking annoyed and glaring at Penelope Werther's departing back, the man obeyed the order.

One by one O'Reilly called the remaining bystanders forward, but none of them had anything worthy to add. Not even Clive Luddmuth, who in O'Reilly's experience seemed to be one of those loudmouth types who was all talk.

'I was volunteering all night at the RSL club,' he bellowed. 'Everyone there will vouch for me.'

He'd check it out, but it sounded like a pretty solid alibi. O'Reilly had left Jules Vernon until last, as punishment for trying to break his rule.

'Name for the record?'

'Julian Brown.'

O'Reilly raised an eyebrow. 'And is that the name you use online for your Facebook profile?'

'No. I use a pseudonym, but I don't need to tell you what it is. I have fulfilled my legal duty.'

'Fair enough.' He already had the information from Penelope Werther. 'So tell me about this morning, when you came into town.'

'Someone posted on another forum about Cynthia's... *misfortune*. I thought I'd come and see for myself if it was true.'

'Did you hope it was true?'

Brown glared at him. 'Of course not. She could be a right pain in the arse, but I didn't wish her dead if that's what you are insinuating.'

'Calm down Mr Brown. I'm not insinuating anything. I simply asked you a question. You seem a bit defensive.'

'You lot are all out to get innocent people and lock us away. I can see through your *questions*.'

O'Reilly ignored the man's outlandish comments. 'Tell me about what you were doing last night then?'

'I was up late, setting all those straight who think that 5G is the saviour of the world. Just because the telephone lines went down, doesn't mean we need to let the government introduce technology designed to infiltrate our minds.'

O'Reilly was beginning to see why Penelope Werther had called the man a crackpot. 'So, the telephone lines went down. When was that?'

Brown rolled his eyes. 'Didn't you try to make any calls last night?'

'No. I was watching that atrocious game they tried to pass off as rugby.'

'You're lucky the game was on free to air. The telephone lines were down from mid-afternoon until about 11pm, and since you're in town on ADSL, you would've lost your internet. They said it was something to do with an accident, but I'm not falling for that. It'll be happening more often, you mark my words. They are trying to convince people they need to approve that proposed 5G tower. Then they'll be able to tap into everyone's brains.'

'Hmmm. Is that right?' O'Reilly scratched his stubbled chin, his mind clicking over everything he had been told. He was pretty sure he knew who was responsible for the murder of Cynthia Myers, but he just had to look over those forums to establish a motive.

The wind had calmed by the next morning as O'Reilly stepped into the red brick station. *The calm before the storm he was about to whip up.*

O'Reilly opened the squeaky door to the interview room, where he had summoned Penelope Werther, Clive Luddmuth and Julian Brown. Luddmuth and Werther were standing in the middle of the room shouting at each other. Penelope, shaking her fist, was far from the shrinking violet of yesterday.

'Sit down!' O'Reilly demanded.

Luddmuth turned, attempting to stand over him. 'I demand to know what we are doing here!'

'I'd like to propose that one of you is a murderer.'

Brown stood up and started waving his finger around. 'I told you. Didn't I? Trying to pin it on the innocent.' The foil on his hat glinted in the fluorescent lights, nearly blinding everyone.

'Please sit down, Mr Brown. I have more questions. Since you seem so eager to speak, let's begin with you. Last night you posted that Ms Penelope Werther, the woman on your left here, is not who she seems to be. What did you mean by that?'

'Ask him,' he said, this time pointing at Luddmuth.

'But I'm asking you.'

Brown crossed his arms. 'I refuse to say anything more without a lawyer present. I know my rights.'

O'Reilly shook his head. 'Okay, have it your way.' He turned to Luddmuth.

'Mr Luddmuth. Why has Mr Brown suggested that I ask you this question?'

Luddmuth exchanged glances with Penelope Werther, who wore an intense scowl.

Turning away from her, he growled, 'Because I know her secret.'

Penelope stood up and pounced on Luddmuth, digging her fingers into his shoulders. O'Reilly tried to drag her away from him, but she resisted, much stronger than her slight frame implied. He pushed her back down into her chair. 'If you move again, I will use these.' He dangled a pair of handcuffs in front of her.

'Go ahead, Mr Luddmuth.'

'Penelope Werther would like us all to think that she is the pillar of the community. All that volunteering. Lapping up the praise. But the truth is that she was once in prison!'

O'Reilly glanced at Penelope, who was barely holding herself in her chair. 'Is this true?'

She didn't answer but he had already discovered this information overnight. Her scathing eyes were focused on Luddmuth. If looks could kill, he would be dead by now too.

'One more question, Mr Luddmuth. Did Cynthia Myers know this?'

Luddmuth nodded, flashing Penelope a smug grin. 'I told her.'

O'Reilly had suspected as much. He turned to Penelope Werther, handcuffs held out. 'Penelope Werther, you are under arrest for the murder of Cynthia Myers.' As he continued to read out her rights she remained seated, glaring at him.

'That proves nothing.'

'Maybe not, but it does give you a motive. Cynthia Myers had already cut your admin privileges, hadn't she? That's why she had to come into town to do the dirty work for herself.'

Penelope squirmed in her chair.

O'Reilly's pitch rose. 'She was going to expose you, wasn't she? Your place in the community would be ruined.'

Penelope jumped up to face him. 'You have no proof of that!'

'Maybe not but tell me again about the chat you had online with Cynthia the afternoon of her death.'

'It was just admin stuff.'

'Ms Werther, you could not have chatted with Cynthia online. Because the telephone lines, and therefore the ADSL, were down all afternoon. You wouldn't have known that as you are out of town on NBN. You are obviously lying to protect yourself!'

Penelope's face dropped. She sucked in ragged breaths. 'I was just... trying... to convince her... to keep my secret. You don't understand... how important one's reputation is in a town like this. They'd crucify me. I didn't mean to push-'

O'Reilly snapped the handcuffs tight around her wrists.

HIDE AND SEEK

DANIELLE HUGHES

I stared at the file in front of me, thumbing through the pages. I looked up in disbelief at Denny, my mentor and one of the Senior Detectives at Portland Police Station.

'Are you kidding me?' I asked, eyes wide, forehead crinkled in exasperation. 'Accidental suicide?'

Denny looked down at me sympathetically and shrugged before running his hand over his greying, close-cropped beard.

'I'm sorry, Tam, that's the final ruling.' Denny reached for the file in front of me but I placed my hand on it so he couldn't take it.

'You know this is bull.' I stabbed my finger at the file. 'Boyce and his guys just wanted it closed quickly, it's just another solved case to make them look good to the department. They barely spent an hour at the crime scene and only interviewed two people. Two people!' I slammed my fist down twice on the file.

'Tammy, please. I know this is hard for you to accept.' Denny leant on my desk, lowering his voice. 'Boyce has been on the force for a long time and he's in the Chief's back pocket. This is exactly why we couldn't be involved, it's too personal for you.' Denny looked at me sympathetically. 'Ash was family, it's natural for you to have some denial about how she died.'

My sister was dead. Now I had to deal with incompetency from within my own department. 'Don't give me that "personal" crap. Ash deserves better than this and you know it. Sure, she liked to party, but she wasn't stupid.' I glared up at Denny. 'Can you honestly tell me you agree with this? Look me in the eye and tell me you completely believe what is written here, and I'll let it go.' It was risky, but I knew deep down he thought something wasn't right. Eighteen-year-old girls don't just 'accidentally' lock themselves in a chest freezer and suffocate.

Denny considered me for a moment, before closing his eyes and taking a deep breath. 'Twenty-four hours. It's all I can give you. If you can bring me reasonable evidence that Ash's death wasn't an accident, I'll file an Investigatory Query.'

'Yes! Thank you. I know you feel it too; this couldn't have been suicide.' I restrain myself from jumping up and hugging him. 'Wait, you're not going to help me?'

'I'll send you a copy of the autopsy report and all the case notes but that's it. Boyce will have my badge if I go behind his back. If you want to look into this further, you're on your own, kiddo. At the very least, it might provide you some closure.' Denny patted me on the shoulder before walking back into his office. 'Also, there's this.' He came back carrying a white, sealed, plastic bag. 'Ash's belongings, everything found on her.' He handed me the bag, then turned away, tucking his shirt back in over his slight pot-belly. I glanced at my watch, my shift was almost over and tomorrow was my day off. Perfect. It would give me plenty of time to do my own inquiries.

Ash was always taking risks and getting into trouble. 'Why can't you be more like Tam?' our parents would say. It wasn't fair. Ash had a zest for fun and mischief. She'd hated school, not because she was dumb, but because she found it boring. She had a hunger for adventure. We didn't have the perfect sister bond, but I loved her more than anyone else. The truth was, I wished I could have been more like her. I'd joined the police force three years ago, straight after school, and was now in my second year of a criminology degree. Ash was always teasing me about letting my hair down and having more fun, but I just wasn't that sort of person. I wanted to help people, to save lives. It was too late to save Ash, but at least I could find out the truth.

I placed the plastic bag with Ash's belongings onto the passenger seat of my car. The first thing I wanted to do was go back to the scene where Ash's body was found: O'Grady's farm.

A month ago, Matt O'Grady had a massive end-of-term party on his parent's property to celebrate finishing exams. I wasn't sure Ash had gone to any of her exams, but she had definitely gone to that party. Her best friend, Beth, had come over to get ready as our parents were out. The girls left the bathroom covered in loose hair and bronzing powder, smelling like a mixture of alcohol, perfume and burnt hair from the over-used curling iron, before clomping down the staircase in their too-high shoes and too-short dresses.

'Shall I call Tim to pick us up?' Ash had asked, checking herself in the hall mirror. Tim was Ash's sometimes boyfriend, and already had a speeding ticket and two parking fines, even though he'd only had his licence for two months.

I offered to drive them. Ash gave me a grateful hug, but as she pulled away her blue topaz necklace fell to the floor.

'Again! I need to get the clasp fixed,' she said, scooping it up and fastening it back around her neck.

I saw Beth touch her own matching necklace as if in solidarity, a symbol of their BFF status. They'd been friends since kindergarten and I was often relieved that they had each other's back at parties.

The girls spent the entire drive texting and giggling in the back seat, treating me like their Uber driver. As we pulled into the long driveway of the farm, the O'Grady's ranch-style house was lit up with fairy lights. Thumping music vibrated through the car as I pulled up, and Beth opened the door, jumping out. She ran straight over to a group of guys, throwing her arms around Tim, clearly tipsy from the alcohol they'd already consumed. Ash paused for a second and I wondered if she minded Beth behaving that way with Tim, but she just gave me a kiss on the cheek. 'Thanks sis, love ya!'

'Call me later to pick you up. Do not get in the car with Tim!' I called as Ash waved, heading towards the crowd of party-goers. That was the last time I saw my sister alive.

The ranch looked different now in the fading daylight. Mr O'Grady had given me permission to look around the outside of the property while no one was home. He said his family hadn't been comfortable to go in the barn where Ash's body had been found, so it should be as Boyce's guys left it. According to the report, the kids at the party had been playing an epic game of 'Hide and Seek' when Ash went missing. Apparently, a common activity at their parties, providing an excuse for couples to hide and hook-up before being found. Anyone caught in the act had to scull beer. Ash was renowned for being a great hider, with or without Tim, so no one was surprised when she'd gone missing. Not even Tim or Beth.

My stomach knotted as I stopped the car and walked towards the barn. I pulled on some gloves, took a deep breath and heaved open the sliding barn door. It was dark inside and it took my eyes a few minutes to adjust to the dim light. I pulled out my torch and flashed it around. A few pieces of torn police tape flapped in the breeze from the open barn door. Nothing else looked unusual. My torchlight fell on the old, disconnected chest freezer at the back of the barn, the box where my sister had been found, dead. A wave of nausea hit me as I stepped towards it, tears threatening. I blinked them away.

The freezer had a latch welded on to it, where you could thread a padlock through, but no lock had been found. The latch was stiff and rusted as I forced it upwards to open the box. Strange, I thought. If Ash had climbed in here to hide, the latch couldn't have just dropped down and locked her in accidently, as per the report. I took a video of the latch and made a voice recording on my phone. I flashed my torch around the inside of the box. It was empty apart from some loose strands of hay. With its heavy lid, it was no wonder Ash ran out of air.

I turned back to the barn, shining my torch on the ground, kicking aside hay. A glint caught my eye and I bent down for a closer look. Brushing aside the hay, I found Ash's blue topaz necklace, the one with the broken clasp. I picked it up and gave it a squeeze. 'Oh Ash, what happened to you?' A cold wind from the open barn door caused goosebumps to prickle my skin.

My phone pinged to alert me to a new email: Denny had sent through the information he promised. I scanned through the autopsy notes quickly, hoping for a hint of evidence Boyce missed. My heart skipped a beat when I read the words 'semen found inside the victim indicates recent sexual intercourse with two different males.'

My heart started back up in overdrive. This was it. With shaking hands, I scrolled through the case notes until I found what I was looking for. No sign of sexual trauma, and DNA tests ruled one semen sample belonged to Tim, the other unknown. As much as I hated to admit it, chances were that Ash had been cheating on Tim. The question was, did he know? Did he catch them and in a fit of jealousy lock Ash in that box? I could almost guarantee Tim would deny my theory if I asked him, claiming he had no idea. But there was someone who would know. I dialled the number.

'Hey Tammy.'

'Hey Beth.'

'How are you going, Hun? Coping alright?'

'Sort of. I'm doing some extra investigating into Ash's case and need to ask you something. Be honest with me, though. It's really important. Can you do that?'

There was a slight pause before Beth answered, 'Sure. What's up?'

'Was Ash cheating on Tim? Could she have slept with someone at the party?'

Another pause. 'Tammy, you know what Ash was like, she didn't really like to be tied down.'

'Is that a yes, then?'

'Yeah, she had been sleeping with Corey Mason off and on.'

'Did Tim know? Or do you think he could have found out?'

'Probably. I mean, Tim knew exactly what he was getting into with Ash. Why are you asking all this? Do you think he hurt her?'

'I'm not sure. But I know something doesn't add up. They're ruling Ash's death an accidental suicide, but I just don't believe that's the case. I think someone locked her in that box.' There was a long silence. 'Beth?'

'Sorry, I'm just in shock.'

'It's okay, it's a lot to process.'

'It's not just that, I think there's something else you should know. Corey has a girlfriend too, Lucy Jones, and she's always hated Ash. If she found out Corey was sleeping with Ash she would be majorly pissed.'

'Enough to hurt Ash?'

'I can't say for sure, but I once saw her throw a drink on a girl and scratch her face at a party when she started dirty dancing with Corey.'

It was my turn to be silent. It seemed I had three potential suspects for people with a motive to hurt Ash. But were any of them a killer?

I spent the morning interviewing Corey and Lucy. Corey was at home and cried the whole time. He said he and Lucy had broken up two weeks before the party when she had found out that he'd been cheating on her. Corey admitted to sleeping with Ash at the party, in the barn, but said they re-joined the party afterwards, and the game of Hide and Seek hadn't even started. Lucy was working at a café in town and agreed to speak to me on her break. That night, she had been out for dinner until late with family, and never attended the party. She confirmed the break-up with Corey, saying she couldn't care less about Ash sleeping with him, she wasn't the only one he had been unfaithful with. I quizzed her about scratching a girl's face, she laughed and said she had been the one scratched by Beth when she accidently spilt a drink on her one night. She had the scar to prove it. I couldn't understand or work out why Beth would lie about the story. Did she think I would be mad at her, or that she would get in trouble?

I tracked Tim down at the gym. He was working out with some mates but readily came outside to speak with me. We sat on a bench seat while he drank Gatorade and wiped sweat off his face with a towel.

'How you holding up, Tam?'

'I'm okay, how are you?'

Tim gazed up towards the sky for a moment. 'I'm okay, I guess. I just can't believe she's gone. Life is so quiet and boring without her.' Tim squeezed his eyes tight and wiped his face again. 'Sorry.'

'It's okay. I wanted to ask you a few questions. Something just doesn't feel right about the way Ash died.'

'Yeah, I agree. There's no way Ash would have hidden in that box. She was too smart for that. She liked to hide where she could see what was going on. She liked to watch people looking for her so she could brag about it later.'

I studied Tim's face, searching for a sign he was hiding something. I decided being blunt might catch him off guard. 'Did you sleep with Ash the night of the party?'

Tim blushed. 'Yeah, we snuck off pretty much as soon she got there and hooked up in my car.'

'Did you know Ash had been sleeping with Corey? That she slept with him that night at the party too?'

'No, but I'm not surprised.'

'Really?'

'Yeah, Ash and I had an understanding. We weren't exclusive. It went both ways.'

'You were sleeping with other people too?'

Tim nodded. 'I'm not a bad guy, just trying to have some fun, you know?'

I looked Tim directly in the face, 'Not really. Who else had you been sleeping with?'

Tim avoided my gaze and looked at the ground. 'Beth.'

I sat in my car, confused. The answer was staring me in the face but I didn't want to accept it. I looked at Ash's necklace which I'd hung from my rear-vision mirror, the topaz catching the sunlight and glinting, sending rainbows sparkling around my car. I followed their light. It came to rest on my passenger seat, with the bag containing Ash's belongings. I opened it, pulling out her long-dead phone, clothes and shoes. A small item remained down the bottom of the bag and I reached in to fish it out. It was a clear, zip-lock bag containing a blue topaz necklace, exactly matching the one hanging from my mirror. A cold prickle ran down the back of my neck as my heart started to pound. I grabbed the autopsy report and my phone, and with shaking hands, dialled the number at the top of the page.

John, the forensic pathologist who performed my sister's autopsy answered the phone. I explained who I was and gave him the case number for my sister.

'Yes, I have the file in front of me. How can I help?' John asked.

'In the victim's belongings was a topaz necklace, I was wondering whereabouts on her body it was found?'

'I remember, it was found clutched in the victim's hand.'

As I hung up the phone everything suddenly became clear in my mind. Ash must have grabbed the necklace as Beth shoved her in that box. I couldn't be certain why Beth would want Ash dead, perhaps she was jealous and wanted Tim all to herself? But I had evidence she could be aggressive, and was present when Ash was in that box. I wasn't sure it would be enough to convict her. I called Denny and explained everything to him, what I had found, and my theory. He agreed we had enough to bring her in for questioning and said he would drive around to her house and arrest her himself.

I looked down at my phone, desperate to call Beth and scream at her. I wanted her to feel fear, the way my sister would have. I wondered what Ash would do if she were in my shoes. I grabbed Ash's phone and plugged it in to my charger.

I found Beth's name and sent her a text:

'Do you want to play a game of Hide and Seek?'

MONTY AND MORAN PRIVATE DETECTIVE AGENCY

PAUL SMITH

Everything changed in 1955 when his father finally did a good thing and died. The modest inheritance he left was just enough. Jake Monty used every cent to set up Monty and Moran Private Detective Agency with his childhood friend, Billy Moran. Monty did the leg work, while his partner looked after the administration and accounting. It suited them both. Monty had no patience for numbers and Billy's ability to gumshoe was restricted by the leg braces, a memento from the polio he'd suffered as a kid.

'Hey, Monty, know what day it is?'

Monty lowered the broadsheet. 'Well, I know it's not your birthday.'

Billy swung around to face Monty's desk. 'Tuesday. And you know what follows Tuesday?'

Monty dropped the newspaper. 'Yeah. Wednesday.' He sighed, 'Which means tomorrow is rent day.'

'You're going to have to call Mrs Adler.'

Monty cringed. The old bat was willing to give Monty work whenever he needed it, but damn, she was so handsy. But beggers couldn't be choosers, so he stood, took a few steps and reached for the telephone on Billy's desk.

It chimed and he drew his hand back as if he'd touched the stovetop.

Billy met Monty's eyes, shrugged and picked it up. After greeting the caller with, 'Monty and Moran, where you can consider it as good as done,' he scribbled down the details. Every now and then he'd interrupt.

Monty went back to his newspaper but his ears did pick up when he heard Billy more than double their usual fee.

Finally, the handset rested back down with a click.

'You are not going to have cosy up to Mrs Adler for a long time.' Billy was grinning ear to ear.

Monty let the heavy get the first couple of punches in. If boxing had taught him anything, it was how to take a hit. Once the big guy felt confident enough to let his guard down, Monty started swinging.

He'd had enough of checking reports and digging up the dirt. Mort Walters, media tycoon, may have been happy to pay two hundred dollars a day plus expenses, but time was running out. His daughter was missing and he received a ransom demand of $200,000 which was sent along with one of her fingers. The kidnappers promised to send her head if Walters contacted the police.

Monty knew the girl might already be dead, but Walters promised an enticing bonus if Monty and Morgan Private Detective Agency managed to bring her home. So here he was, going toe to toe with the heavy last seen talking to the girl.

At first, he refused to answer questions, so Monty beat it out of him. Three lost teeth and a nose that would forever more point left, the guy spilled the beans.

Damn. Vinnie Tomatso's gang. This was going to get ugly.

Tomatso was one bad son of a bitch, his father had immigrated from Sicily in 1918 and found his way into the Chicago mob. So, little Vinnie was born into the crime syndicate, he was Al Capone's Godson. By the time he was thirty he controlled the East side extortion and prostitution rackets.

He learned that Clara Walters was locked up in a room above Tomatso's establishment, The Chicago Jazz Club.

Stealth and finesse would not work in the scenario he would face. He had learned on the battlefield that even elite, well trained soldiers could freeze when attacked unexpectedly with a ferocity that was terrifying. When he told Billy of his plan his friend gave an astonished look and said, 'That's your grand plan? To single-handedly go up against god knows how many heavily armed thugs and rescue the damsel in distress? Jake, you're insane!'

Within the hour, they were pulled up out the front of the club.

'Stay in the car, Billy. If things go south, take off.'

'You don't need to worry about me, Monty.'

'Are you crazy? This Desoto is less than a year old. I don't want her caught in the crossfire.'

Monty kept his hat on and his head down. Manoeuvring his way through the club entrance, he kept one hand resting on his coat inside pocket. The doorman's large hand landed on his shoulder. It was time to act. Monty had a frenzy mode, a scar left on his soul from his days of enlistment. A shadow that followed him. It acted now.

Spurred on by fear and in truth a little bit of glee, Monty spun, grabbed and hurled the big doorman through the front pane glass of the window. He bull rushed forward, a one man tornado, the pistol in his huge paw like an exclamation mark.

The crowd screamed as two goons drew their guns but they were blasted into the next life by Monty's Colt 45.

The room cleared in his wake. He made it to the stairs and faced another two men. They raised their guns and fired. Several patrons went down and Monty copped one in the shoulder. It didn't stop him. One of the men was left gut shot, the other blown over the rail with a slug to the chest. Monty reached the landing only to be confronted by a fat man trying unsuccessfully to fire a Thompson machine gun in the hallway. After blasting three doors and shredding a section of ceiling, the gun jammed.

On came Monty like a fierce avenging angel, taking the man's throat out with two shots. The solid wooden door was locked until Monty's size 12 shoe kicked it off its hinges. Clara was handcuffed to a filthy single bed, she was guarded by a butt-ugly, painfully thin man. The hand that held a pistol was shaking uncontrollably and it fell to the floor along with his cigarette. A puddle appeared under him as his bladder let go, he sank to the floor and begged for his life. Monty wasn't in the mood for leniency he put a bullet through one of the thugs eyes, brains, bone and gore splattered the wall behind him.

Clara's fragile frame was bruised, cut, and by the state of her clothing, he knew Tomatso's men had taken her. Even her dishevelled state couldn't hide a stoic beauty. He wondered if she would have the strength to deal with the things they'd done to her. He'd seen many a young man crumble under dark memories from the war.

She met his gaze, held up her cuffed hands and calmly said, 'Get me out of this f... ing thing.'

She was strong.

He tore a piece of wire from the beds base and had her out of the handcuffs in a jiffy. By the time he helped her down the stairs, as she'd refused his offer to carry her, the place was empty. Empty if you didn't count the bodies.

The club was exceptionally busy for a Thursday night and Tomatso had been in a good mood. Since Walters hadn't paid the ransom, he was going to take great pleasure in sending him Clara's pretty head. The thought of her father breaking down when he received the grisly present made Tomatso excited. He had been on his way to the back room, two beauties from the dance line-up in tow, when the commotion broke out. H turned to see Luther, his doorman, thrown through the front window.

Tomatso may have been an imposing figure, three hundred pounds, six foot three frame, and a piece in his belt, but facing this maniac was definitely out of the question. For such a big man he moved incredibly fast and darted out of harm's way through the back door.

Earlier that year, the New York Chronicle published an article labelling Tomatso as a gangster and psychopath. The editor was hospitalised and the reporter dead, found in a dumpster. As he put his Cadillac in reverse, gun fire resonating from his club, he thought not about the men he'd lose, but the joy of carving through the Walters girl's neck and how that thrill had been stolen from him. Whoever this piece of work was, coming into his club, he'd be sorry.

Monty and Clara jumped in the back of the Desoto and Billy hit the gas. The echo of sirens left in their wake.

At the Walters manor, they were greeted with warm handshakes and a $5,000 bonus, plus the agreed rate.

When they celebrated over a shared bottle of scotch back in the office, Billy raised his glass, sloshing contents. 'To Mrs Adler, you are gone from our client list, but not forgotten.'

'Hey,' Monty injected with a wry smile, 'I might be in a good enough mood to give the old girl a call for free.'

With the adrenaline gone, the two men spent the evening recalling the good and the bad of the night, the war, even childhood.

Two weeks later, Billy was shot dead on his way to the bank and Monty received a telegram saying, 'You're next.'

Tomatso should have known better, Monty would come a hunting, with his close friend, Samuel Colt 45 automatic.

200

THE MOTIVE

MARIA PARENTI

*T*he blood, moist on his still hand, reflected off the crescent moon.

She sheathed the double-blade dagger.

Her fantasy knife, she called it, had plunged deep into his left ventricle.

Halfway through their clandestine meet, she had decided sex was not the motive.

Revenge!

Swift, sweet, savage for another two-timing louse.

While her body wanted one last fling,

her mind wanted death – His.

To slice. To stab. To extinguish another miserable life.

It was again one strike to the heart,

pressing in deep – slowly, silently - with intent.

Part of her knew she would not remember the night,
but a tear did slip her guard.
She pressed her slender hands to her breasts,
at another lost love.
His eyes bulged at her betrayal.
Like countless others,
his eyes slid closed
surrendering to his fate.

'Nurse Spinks.'
'Inspector Smith.'
As her delicate frame disappeared back down the narrow corridor,
the Inspector let slip a sigh.
Turning to Sergeant O'Reilly he spat under his breath.
'No Sergeant. She's not a serial killer.
She could hardly swing an axe let alone some blade.'
'But I just want to ask her a few...'
'No Sergeant!'

Sergeant O'Reilly had seen the signs —
classic atypical murderer, or murderess in this case.
Quiet. Unassuming.
Well-toned arms, legs, tight torso, and an arse to match.
And Nurse Laura Spinks knew bodies.
She was more than a suspect.
She was a murderer getting away with murder under the Serial
Crime Unit's very nose.
But why was the Inspector protecting her?

O'Reilly found being new to the crime unit was a crime in itself.
After a few days, he noted the filing cabinets were far too neat —
evidence, interviews, victims – all in order.
Pressing send on WhatsApp,¬¬
O'Reilly put down his drink and rubbed his German Shepard's
arthritic shoulder.
'Yep mate,
twelve bodies,
eighteen months,
no fingerprints,
no arrests,
no phones,
no IDs.
Strange. All victims were within a hundred-kilometre radius.'

His faithful sniffer dog, Gator, lay his head on O'Reilly's lap
as if he'd heard it all before.

Tap, tap on the coffee table.
Hmmm.
Twelve cases.
Nurse had an alibi.
Inspector dismissed her as a suspect far too quickly.
And four Sergeants had transferred out.
What the hell was going on?

'What'd you think partner?'
His mate whimpered.

'Damn getting old, ay buddy.'
O'Reilly rubbed Gator hip joint.

Later that night, O'Reilly returned to the shadows of the hospital carpark.
After every shift Nurse Spinks would walk to the car giggling, phone in hand.
After ten days straight, O'Reilly couldn't believe he'd got it so wrong.
His prime suspect. He stifled a yawn. *Boyfriend again.*

But this time Nurse Spinks almost stumbled.
'What do you mean you want to break it off?'
Her voice, angry, squeaked an octave.
'I'm high maintenance!
What?
I'm too *possessive!*
How?
You've what?'
She leaned back on her car.
Her right eye twitched.
She placed her hand over it to calm the movement.

Then a voice, smooth like liquid gold, replaced her hysterical tone.
'Actually, Roger darling, I must confess, I've been busy with others too.
Oh, Roger. Don't sound so shocked.

No, it's not Frank.
No. Not Andrew.
Of course it's not Jack!
Stop guessing. I'm not saying.
But I'm happy for one last tryst if you are.'

From his hideout, O'Reilly saw her lover's response was far too slow for her liking.
Nurse Spinks' knuckles whitened; her dainty nostrils flared.
She touched her hair loosening it from its tie.
She breathed in deep and sighed.
'Well, if you don't want to Roger darling, it's okay.
But I've been dying to try that special move.
Yes, that one.
But not tonight darling.
I need time to plan something special.'
She let a girly giggle escape.

'Oh Roger. You must remember our cardinal rule.
No evidence anywhere.
No notes, no dates, no correspondence.
And... only use WhatsApp because... that's right, it keeps our secrets... secret.
Tomorrow night my love at... .'

O'Reilly cursed under his breath at the stray cat
as she revealed their clandestine meet.
'Where the hell are you meeting tomorrow night?'

He shivered at Nurse Spinks' change in persona.

Nurse Spinks suppressed a laugh as she got into the car,
'You have no idea what you're in for! You two-timing prick!!'
She peered into the rear-view mirror,
let her smile slide and tightened her grip on the steering.
Ignoring the black cat staring into her headlights,
she accelerated the two-door down the illuminated white lines.

The next day O'Reilly arrived to work early.
Coffee in hand, he reviewed the eighteen-months of evidence.
It was almost too perfect he thought.
As familiar footsteps approached, he stilled the mug to his lips.

'What are you doing O'Reilly?'
'Looking through case files Inspector.'
'Why? Don't think our lot are as good as your high-flying Metro
boys?'
'Just following procedure Sir.'
'Are you questioning my evidence in this investigation?'
'No Sir. Been told I could learn a lot from you. Sir.'
'Have you? Well then, continue Sergeant.'
The Inspector glanced back, then closed the door.

Evidence.
Nothing obvious.
It niggled at O'Reilly.
It prodded him.

Goaded him to rethink his unlikely killer.

But, why dismiss the Nurse as a suspect?

As he re-checked the last victim's autopsy report,

something was amiss - the coroner's signature.

It had been forged.

The anomaly was the tissue sample.

He quietly dispatched the evidence via his Metro lab courier.

Under the cover of a moonless night, Laura paced the rendezvous point.

'What? No kiss, no peck on the cheek Roger?'

Her breath hitched. Then her fists clenched when she saw what he held.

'I'm... I'm returning some things,' he said.

Laura stood, stock still. Right eye twitching.

'I've decided it's not good for us to have one last fling.'

Her voice squeaked as her heart rate rose.

'Is that all you thought we were?' she spat. 'A fling!'

As quick as a taipan's strike, the *fantasy knife* caught him unawares.

'You don't decide, Roger!' A venomous voice flickered out.

'I decide. You witless two-timing weasel.'

The gleaming blade had struck his neck, deep into his right carotid artery.

His eyes bulged at her betrayal.

But, unlike the others, his eyes stared wide-open.

She closed his lids.

'How did you figure out our last victim O'Reilly?' asked his Commander from Metro Headquarters.

'Remorse. She left behind a partial fingerprint after closing his eyes. The stab to the neck was a deviation on her M.O. She has a major psychological disorder especially after witnessing her dramatic two personality shift. It unhinged her after Roger's rejection. As for the excessive blood splatter, far too difficult to clean - even for a nurse.'

'What about victim twelve when you couriered the tissue sample?' the Commander asked.

'An anomaly. A salted tear had dripped into the right ventricle.'

O'Reilly noted.

Nurse Spinks' basement – pristine, prim, precise.

Phone – suspiciously void of hidden photos of victims or rendezvouses.

But Gator sniffed something amiss behind the pantry's far back panel.

Found - neatly catalogued – twelve cereal packets with photos, phones, IDs of each of her first twelve kills. Minimal disinfectant meant Gator could pick it up.

So much for her cardinal rule of secrecy.

Nurse Laura Spinks was committed to a psychiatric ward for women prisoners.

The kills had given her ultimate control. She stated the dead would harm her no more.

Inspector Paul Smith, her older brother from a different father, was sentenced to life in prison. Guilt ridden at his teenage sister's abuse at the hands of his tyrannical father, he murdered his own father to protect her. However, he had failed to notice her in the shadows.

When the murders started, Inspector Smith noticed the modus operandi was similar to his - blade to the heart, no evidence at the scene.

As for O'Reilly...
His job was to investigate unsolved murders in undercover operations from powers far higher than you and I would have access to. O'Reilly, currently on leave – destination unknown.

As the full moon glistened off the waters, O'Reilly took his loyal friend for a final float in the lake to ease the arthritic pain. As Gator lay in his arms, O'Reilly whispered,

'Well partner,
thirteen murders,
eighteen months serial solved,
photos, phones, IDs all found,
and two arrests
thanks to you.'
thanks to you.'

THE NEXT WAVE

RAELENE PURTILL

While the story lines for her novels were usually well plotted, Olivia Kent's 'little jobs' for her iniquitous cousin, Tony Antonetti, were somewhat vague in their execution. She told herself this was because he always came to her at the last possible moment, and it was always 'urgent baby'. Then like the flying monkey she had become, and without forethought, she would obey. So here she was at the book launch of a fellow author, which had provided her cousin Tony the opportunity for more nefarious adventures.

In the pages of Angela Connolly's latest novel was a detailed description of the Barrett Necklace, and that desired piece of jewellery was on display for tonight's event. Tony's counterfeiters made a stunning duplicate, and Olivia arrived at the publishing house with it tucked in the shimmering clutch purse which matched her lamé dress. She'd had no time to plan how she would procure the necklace or how the switch would go down.

She circulated the party greeting the many people she knew and acknowledging the guest of honour, always on the lookout for the moment her task could be fulfilled.

A steward passed her with a tray of appetizers. Tragic little prunes wrapped in bacon and pierced together with a toothpick adorned the silver tray. Alongside sat green gherkins and pale cheese embracing on their cracker bed, and to top of the nonsense, were king prawns bowing in reverence to Lord Lettuce. As her literary eye surveyed the tray of delicacies, the waiter tripped over her foot. The moment she'd been waiting for not only arrived, but announced itself with squeals of surprise, peals of broken glass and the thud of an embarrassed waiter at her feet. Olivia dove at the cabinet. When her neck and the side of the cabinet connected, she thought she must have miscalculated but as she slid to the floor, switching the necklaces deftly through the shattered glass, she realised her fall had been caused by a prune that had escaped its bacon captor.

In the chaos that followed, her deed was not detected. The real necklace was now safe in her purse, but oh God, her neck hurt. She lay prone listening to the sounds of salvage and disarray around her.

'May I help you?' said a low voice from above. She rose to meet the soft concern on the face of a tanned, dark eyed man with salt and pepper hair wearing a tweed jacket. In his face, Olivia saw all the romantic heroes from her novels arrive to manifest before her. Instinctively, she tightened the grip on her racing heart and on her purse with the necklace, and allowed him to lead her out picking their way through the debris.

In the foyer, she excused herself and found a bathroom where she could assess her injury that had already started to bruise. Her rescuer was waiting when she re-emerged.

'Are you okay to get home?'

Olivia nodded slightly acutely aware of the pain the action caused.

'Jason Carpenter.'

'Olivia Kent,' she replied, hesitant to touch his hand lest it fall away into a dream.

'The novelist?'

'Yes.' She did not want to leave him the way she did, abandoned in her wake. On any other night she would have hesitated, endeavoured to make the night last longer, but her purse burned with its cargo and her neck and shoulders ached. 'I really must be on my way. Good evening and thank you for your concern.'

At North Quay, she deposited the contraband into the designated locker and caught a taxi home. Until now her life as a novelist and her other life trapped within the mob had remained entirely separate. Tonight, they had collided violently, and the secret was in danger of being revealed.

The next morning, she returned to her developmental notes on the fictional sleuth she had named Clementine Oxenborg. As she devised the mystery and adventure that would entangle Clementine, she knew her own situation would drive the obstacles set in this narrative.

It was her practice to cast her characters with relevant photos as she wrote their stories. The black and white film noir image she stared at now suited Clementine perfectly. Her wide, open face held a thin smile that Olivia imagined would erupt at any moment into ironic laughter. Her voice would be smooth and smart along with that ironic sense of humour, Olivia noted. Clementine wore a felt cloth hat decorated with a large dahlia. It would be lilac, she decided. Her chin was surrounded by the exuberant Atlantic Beaver fur of a mid-calf length coat. To finish the 1920's look, Clementine's gloved hands were clasped in front of her with an underarm clutch. Happy with her description, Olivia looked up from her screen to see Nick her adult nephew returning from his run on the beach. He shared her cottage in Rose Bay, and she could not love him more if he had been her own. But that was not to be, so there was Nick.

'Good morning, Aunt Lilly.' He strode into her office and applied a generous kiss to her cheek. When her response was a sharp intake of breath and a frown of pain, he stopped with concern.

'What's this?'

'It's nothing.'

'You're hurt. Let me see.'

She had tried to hide the deep purple bruise on her neck under a light scarf which Nick now removed.

'What on earth happened?'

'Couldn't sleep. Fell over in the dark.'

'No, you did not. I would have heard you.'

Olivia closed her eyes. *Please don't interrogate me Nick*, she thought. *I can't tell you what happened. You cannot know that part of my life.*

From the computer screen Clementine Oxenborg sat in judgement.

'Come with me,' said Nick.

He led her back through the house where he sat her down at the large kitchen table and proceeded to administer his own first aid. She winced at his ministrations but the resolve to keep her secret and not reveal the cause of her injuries must remained steady.

'Many on the beach?'

'Oh, the usual faithful,' he replied, 'and don't change to subject.'

'Subject? I wasn't aware we were discussing anything particular.'

'You know what I mean.'

Olivia sighed, replaced the scarf, and returned her dark hair to its usual bun at the nape of her now bandaged up neck.

'I need to get on with some writing, dear. Charles will be here later today.'

'That editor of yours...' Nick left the sentence undone and shook his head.

Olivia smiled. Nick was so protective of her. 'He's my boss,' she said with a shrug that brought a twinge down her shoulder.

'He doesn't only edit your stories. He's controlling your life.'

'Not as much as he thinks, Nick.'

There had always been animosity between Nick and Charles Baxter, owner, and editor of Baxter Publishing. Nick saw Charles as a leech of a man who had overstepped the boundaries in his role of Olivia's boss. He thought he could appear at the beach house any time of the day or night. Charles did not trust Nick. Nephew or not, he was an adult who should be doing something with the education for which his aunt had paid, and not still living in her home.

Olivia herself desired a carefree creative existence as a novelist, but instead she bled pages for Charles Baxter, and she could not get away from cousin Tony's demands. It was all getting too much. Something had to give.

She returned to her desk where Clementine's broad face sparked some more thoughts. She tapped at the keyboard thoughtfully until a rhythmic knock at the door interrupted her. Charles? He didn't usually knock. She pushed away from her desk and made her way to the door.

'Miss Kent?' A tall man in a track suit stood on the step with a golden Labrador on a lead panting beside him. Her rescuer from last night. He held up an ID card and said, 'Jason Carpenter, Sydney C.I.B.' Then he smiled and Olivia thought her heart would expose her whole double life of an existence to him. The dog moved toward her and nuzzled her knee.

'You are recovered I see.'

'Thank you, yes. You're a detective?'

'May I come in?'

'We can talk on the back veranda,' Olivia replied.

They settled into the white cane furniture overlooking the water and the dog lay at her feet. Detective Carpenter raised an eyebrow at that, but he continued his questions.

'Is there anything else you can tell me about last night?'

Olivia grinned. 'You were there too.' She looked at him sideways from under her lashes. 'I don't understand. It was an accident. Why the police?'

'There was a robbery.' He licked his lips and deliberately turned to his notebook.

'Oh.' Olivia reached down to stroke the fleshy neck of the dog so she would not have to look at him.

'His name is Pistol.'

'Perfect name for a policeman's dog.' She laughed and ruffled the dog's head ignoring the twinge at her neck and wondering what it would feel like to run her hand through Jason Carpenter's hair.

'I am sorry I crashed Angela Conolly's party, literally,' Olivia giggled. She returned to her seat and watched Jason Carpenter, taking notes in his well-used notebook. 'A robbery?'

'Yes, the real Barrett Necklace is now missing.'

'All I remember is falling into the cabinet when that waiter slipped near me.'

The detective's dark eyes were like truth-seeking darts, but his face remained stoic. He continued in a tone that said he was changing tack, and now it was all business, 'thank you.'

'I also have a Nicholas Kent listed at this address. Is he here?'

'He was.' She stepped around the corner of the veranda, but the driveway was empty of Nick's Ford Capri. 'No.' She shook her head. 'He's gone.'

'He is a person of interest in another case, but I shan't take any more of your time.' His fixed look landed on her and stayed there a long time. She opened her mouth to speak and then realised he was using the technique she had researched. During questioning, detectives use silence to intimidate their suspect to a confession. She made a note to include it in Clementine's toolbox. She was keen now to get back to her writing and away from Detective Carpenter's interrogation which was pulling at the seams of her secret.

'Well, all I can say is that Nick is a good boy. He is also an adult, and he doesn't tell me everything he does.' That was the truth at least, and it hurt just a little that he wasn't always open with her. She suspected he had secrets of his own. The way he came and went from the house lately made her curious, and he was not with her last night either which she thought unusual. But she said, 'Detective Carpenter, I really cannot help you any further.'

'Has Nick ever spoken of Tony Antonetti?'

Olivia grasped Pistol's collar for support and watched the waves down on the beach roll onto the wet sand, tumble over themselves and withdraw.

'What?' The question came out with more force than she intended. 'Isn't he that crime lord?' She took a breath. 'And you think Nick...?' She laughed with relief. 'Seriously, Nick? Really?'

She bit her lip. Did he suspect her as well? How would Clementine Oxenborg handle this tipping point moment?

She stood and offered her hand. 'If there is nothing else.'

Detective Carpenter did not shake her hand, but instead placed a printed business card in it. 'Thank you. If you remember anything more.' He paused and smiled, 'or if there is anything I can do for you...'

Oh, there was, but Olivia would reserve it all for her stories. Already she was inventing compromising possibilities for him within her unwritten pages.

'Can we get to the beach from here?' he asked.

Carpenter tucked his notebook away and his eyes lingered on her face again as though he were leaving her with a promise. Was it a promise he would find out the truth, or was it a promise he would see her again at a time that had nothing to do with being a detective? Olivia decided he did not suspect her of any misdoing and that it would be the latter. She smiled.

'Yes. Down those stairs.' She pointed and then watched them disappear through the gate at the bottom of her garden. The momentum of new ideas returned her to her office.

When Nick looked in on her that afternoon, Olivia, unaware of his presence, tapped away at her keyboard thoroughly. Silently, he stashed the knuckle-duster, gun, and balaclava in the worn sports bag beneath the floor of the entrance cupboard and retreated to his upstairs room without disturbing her.

HONEY

MICHAELA SANDERSON

Sergeant Johnson flipped open his notepad. 'The deceased is Mrs Margaret Cronin. Aged 65. Married, one daughter.' He looked up at the detectives. 'Her daughter says her mother's new husband poisoned her.'

'What do you think?' One detective asked.

'Possible. Married just six months.' The policeman closed his notepad. 'Come inside.'

The house was held together by paint and a prayer. Several stairs groaned and shuddered as the men made their way into the shade of the veranda. The door was open, the screen torn and dusty. Julius and Cameron walked inside, blinking in the darkness of the hallway. Wailing came from a room to their left.

'Please come this way, Detectives,' Sergeant Johnson said.

Cameron and Julius followed the policeman down the hallway, and stopped when he did, at the door to the loungeroom.

The body of an old woman sprawled beside an upturned coffee table, the smell of faeces and vomit heavy in the air.

Julius crouched beside Mrs Cronin. A bruise stained her forehead. Dried vomit caked her mouth, chin, and faded blouse. Her thin grey cardigan was open, one edge sodden from the contents of the teacup beside her. A plate had rolled from the coffee table and rested, face down, beside a decrepit armchair and a smashed vase. Her shoes were off. Several toes stuck out of a hole in her stockings. He stood up.

The policeman said, 'Mrs Cronin inherited a substantial sum of money from her father, a year ago. Several million dollars. Properties, shares, the lot.'

'That's potentially worth killing for.'

'But there's more. Mrs Cronin's an incredibly wealthy woman herself. You know Healthy Hunny?'

'Yes. My kids love it.'

'Mrs Cronin owns that company. Making a fortune in sales while other bee farmers struggle. She's come up with a new way of keeping bees, that's cutting down bee deaths. She's also able to produce a range of different honeys here on her farm. Revolutionised honey production.'

'Here?' Cameron stared at him. 'This house is about to fall down.'

'Yes, she's a known miser. Wouldn't spend a cent on anything that didn't bring in money. Her honey production outfit is over the ridge, behind the house. Huge setup.'

'Where's her husband.'

'In their bedroom. Name's Darryl,' the policeman said.

'What do you know about him?'

'Widower. First wife was much older. Fell down the stairs and broke her neck. Tragic accident.' The policeman led the way to the bedroom.

A dark-haired man had almost been swallowed by an oversized armchair. He had a thick beard and moustache, but didn't look much over thirty-five.

He glared at them, 'I didn't kill her, Detectives.'

'Yet you have the perfect motive. Her money.'

'You have no idea!' He slammed his fist down on the chair.

'Help us understand why anyone would want to kill your wife.'

Darryl crossed his arms and looked away.

'You haven't been married long, have you?' Cameron broke the silence.

'Six months.'

'How did you meet?'

'She's my ex-wife's friend. I offered to do general maintenance around here, and we fell in love. That happens, Detective.'

'Can you tell us what happened this morning?'

'Margaret and I got up, and I helped her to the kitchen. She hurt her hip last week and was hardly able to walk. She made her usual, tea and toast and I helped her to the lounge. I went out to feed the animals. When I came back, she was dead. I didn't kill her, Detective. Eunice did.'

'Who is Eunice?' Julius spoke.

'Didn't anyone tell you Eunice was here? Too quick to lay blame on me to consider anyone else, hey? Eunice. Our neighbour. Bee farmer also. Almost bankrupt. She came to see Margaret this morning, I passed her on the step. I know Margaret was going to offer to buy her property. Good, flat land, perfect for bees. I heard Eunice yell that she'd rather see Margaret dead than sell her anything. I heard something smash, raced in and saw Eunice had hit Margaret with the vase. But Margaret told me to leave them alone, so I did. Go arrest Eunice.'

'Eunice did not kill her! How dare you say that. You killed my mother. I heard you arguing last night, about her money.'

Julius spun around. In the doorway stood a tall, blonde woman. Her eyes were red and swollen, her hair swept into a ponytail. She wore a short blue dress, high heels and more jewellery Julius thought possible on the human body, in one go. A little white fluffy dog cradled in her arms began to yap like only little dogs can.

Darryl leapt up out of the chair. 'I wanted to take her on a holiday. Mind your own damn business. You, with your stupid little dog and your stupid paintings. You wanted her money.'

'I'm a bestselling artist! I don't need her money!'

The policeman walked over. 'Miss Cronin, back to the study, please.'

The woman pivoted on her heels and clacked her way down the hallway, dog still yapping. Moments later a door slammed.

Darryl shook his head, 'Nasty piece of work. Came back here after our wedding and stayed.'

'Where was she previously?'

'She went to the city to become an artist, apparently.'

'Let's talk to her,' Julius looked at Darryl, 'How did Margaret hurt her hip?

'Tripped on a loose step. I hadn't got around to fixing it.'

The detectives walked to the study, assailed by the barking of the dog.

'Hermoiny, be quiet sweetheart, these nice detectives are taking that bad man away for killing your grandma.' Allegra kissed the dog's head. The dog, with her bejewelled collar and underbite, bared her teeth and snarled.

The study smelt of mothballs and dust. It was dark in the room, the curtain melded to the wall, there was no end to the greyness of either. Cameron flicked on the switch, and a thin circle of light chased back some of the shadows.

'Sorry it's so dark. Mother bought bulbs that used the least amount of electricity. She'd do anything to save money.' Allegra moved uncomfortably in her chair. A tear in the side of her dress flashed pale skin.

'Was your mother always like that?'.

'Yes. Soon as I was old enough to work the bees, she fired most of the workers and I'd have to do it.'

'What about Darryl? Did he help out?'

'No. Lazy as.'

'You know bees and honey making?'

'Yes. Couldn't wait to get away from here. Nothing but slave labour.' Hermoiny wriggled in her arms and Allegra kissed her head. 'It's okay precious baby, we won't be here much longer.'

Julius asked, 'Why return if you hate it here?'

'Because she sent me a text announcing her marriage. I flew home to stop her, but it was too late. And now he's killed her. Like he killed his first wife.'

'Would you say you and your mother had a good relationship?'

Allegra glanced down at her dog. 'She annoyed me, like she'd never throw anything away, never wasted anything. She'd cut mould off food and use teabags twice. But we were very close. I loved her.'

'What happened this morning?' Cameron's voice was soft.

'I got up and made Hermoiny her breakfast. I heard my mother call out, then a bang. I raced into the lounge, and she was on the floor. She was vomiting and shaking. She said, 'Honey bear,' then she died. I couldn't help her.' Allegra's voice wavered and she began to cry.

'Honey bear?'

'Yes, that's what she called him. Honey Bear. He called her Honey Bunny. Made me sick. I know she was telling me he killed her.' She moved Hermoiny and reached for a tissue. Her forearm was covered in a white bandage. Several blisters on her fingers and palm were inflamed, her nails ragged and dirty.

'You hurt yourself?'

'It's nothing.' She jerked her hand back. 'I dug up some weeds on our boundary fence that caused a reaction.'

'Still working on the farm then?'

'Mother insisted. I'm currently her only worker.'

'Any unhappy workers who may have a grudge against your mother? Other bee farmers?'

She laughed, 'All her staff hated her. They didn't understand her. As for the other bee farmers, they all despise her. She's taking all their business. She's too smart and they're jealous.'

'What about this Eunice? She's a bee farmer.'

'Eunice Burns. She's the sweetest lady. No. She wouldn't kill Mother.'

'But Darryl says she's bankrupt. And she hit her.'

'Don't believe what Darryl says! Eunice would never hurt Mother,' she paused and wiped her mouth, 'though if she was bankrupt and blaming mother... I saw her head down to the bees before Mother collapsed. She has some equipment in our shed. I bet she's still down there.'

'That's all our questions for the moment. Let's go find Eunice.'' Cameron said. Allegra slumped down on the desk, face buried in her arms.

Cameron led the way outside. The men walked around the side of the house, past a dilapidated shed. Its walls were pockmarked and the gutter had rusted through. An old truck with a flat tyre was still connected to a large trailer covered with a tarp.

Julius untied one corner and lifted it. The trailer was full of dying plants, maybe eight feet tall. Their leaves were long and thin, their dying pink flowers still pretty.

'Don't touch it,' Cameron called out. 'That plant's poisonous. It looks like oleander.'

'How do you know?'

'My mother grew some. Thought it would attract bees.'

'Did it?'

'If nothing else was flowering, they'd go into the flower, but if they made honey from it, it'd be poisonous.' Cameron shrugged. 'Dad fell into the plant, got a vicious blistery rash, and destroyed it. End of oleander.'

'Can see why Allegra pulled it up. Couldn't have that growing on a honey farm.'

Cameron tied down the tarp. 'Let's go.' They skirted around a little sports car; its front end destroyed. 'Someone hit something hard.'

They trudged up a large hill, sweating and cursing, then stopped at the top.

Sprawled out in front of them were several commercial greenhouses, alien igloos clinging to the ground. The white walls were blinding in the midday sun, and the rounded tops glowed.

Cameron shaded his eyes, 'Clearly spends her money on the bees.'

'Do you know bees often see a dermatologist?'

'What?'

'For their hives.'

Cameron groaned and began to walk down the hill. Julius followed.

They stopped at a massive shed which shone with a silvery newness. The padlock on the door denied them entry, and the tinted windows gave nothing away. The air smelt of honey.

'Eunice might be in with the bees.' Cameron headed towards the first greenhouse. The hum of bees sounded like a well-tuned motorbike.

'Sure are loud. Hey, what do you call a quiet bee? A mumble-bee.' He peered through the transparent door of the first greenhouse and whistled. It was like an oasis. The plants inside were vibrant green, with a carpet of purple flowers. Bees were flitting around the flowers or flying back to their hives, perched like miniature houses around the edges of the greenhouse.

Each greenhouse had different flowers. Julius peered around the end of the last greenhouse. 'What's this?'

There was another greenhouse. Tiny. Made of cheap plastic. Tent pegs held it to the ground.

'Is that for real?' Cameron laughed. 'I have one like this at home. Park both my cars under it.'

'Maybe this is for a small crop. For a special kind of honey.' Julius walked over to it and unzipped a flap. 'Empty. Well, no bees at least.' Thirty large pots were lined up in rows of five. Each of them contained soil but were devoid of plant life. From the dirt on the ground and the dirt leading to the main flap, it was clear the plants were removed, dragged from their pots and out of the greenhouse. 'Guess it was a failure.'

He bent to zip up the flap. Several pink flowers and a bee had been crushed into the dirt. Julius pushed them away with his boot and zipped up the flap. 'Well Eunice isn't here.'

'Someone's here.' Cameron pointed to a figure limping towards them, cane raised over her head.

'If you're real-estate agents, get out of here now! My land's not for sale.'

'Ms Burns?'

'Get out!'

'Ms Burns, I'm Detective Cowley and this is Detective Simmons. We'd like to talk to you.'

'You're not real estate agents trying to work out the value of my property?' She lowered her cane.

'No.'

'Margaret rang you, didn't she? About the vase.'

'When was the last time you saw her?'

'This morning. Yes, I threw the vase at her. How dare she offer to buy my property. It's her fault I'm struggling. She undercuts my prices. If she put her prices up, I wouldn't be broke. But no, she has her bees all safe here, and different flavours of honey. She can sell her honey cheaply. I can't compete. I'm almost bankrupt. And she offers to buy my land. The ultimate slap in the face.'

'Margaret is dead, Mrs Burns.'

Eunice lifted her cane. 'I didn't kill her. She was alive when I left.'

'Mrs Burns, we'll need to interview you. Please, just go home, and we'll send someone over to talk to you, soon.'

'Probably killed herself to frame me. Old cow. I'll be waiting at home. With my lawyer.' She hobbled off.

Back at the farmhouse, both men headed into the kitchen. An old wood stove crouched in one corner, beside a prehistoric fridge. Fliers for holidays were stuck to its door. The kitchen bench was strewn with clutter, a battered toaster next to an ancient kettle, a bee smoker, hive tools, bee brush, and an uncapping knife with a serrated blade. A bottle of prescription pain killers sat beside a chopping board covered in toast crumbs. Julius slipped gloves on, picked up the bottle and read the label. 'Margaret's painkillers.' He opened the bottle. 'Almost empty. Only purchased a week ago.'

'That's because Allegra takes them.' Darryl stood in the doorway. 'Hurt herself when she crashed her car. Didn't have the money to buy her own. Like her mother. Won't spend money on herself. That's why Margaret and I argued last night. I wanted a holiday and to hire workers to harvest the honey, she said no, I was to do it.'

'Do you know anything about honey or the small greenhouse?'

'No.'

'Did you dig up the plants in the trailer?'

'No.'

An awful yowling came from down the hallway. Hermoiny's high pitched yap sounded seconds later, both sounds travelling at speed towards the kitchen. A large cat burst into the kitchen, skidded on the lino, slipped around a corner, then disappeared. Close behind came Hermoiny. She scrabbled on the lino, slid straight into the bin, and knocked it over. Rubbish spilt over the floor.

'Hermoiny! Come to Mummy!' The dog bolted after the cat, and Allegra's voice rose. 'Bad dog!' She hurried through the kitchen.

Julius leaned over and grabbed a small container which had lost its lid and begun to spill its contents across the floor. 'What's this doing in the bin? A full jar of honey.'

Hermoiny trotted back into the kitchen and stopped at the spilt honey. Cameron pushed her away. The dog growled and lunged at the honey.

Allegra hurried inside, stopped and screamed, 'No! Hermoiny!' She picked up the little dog. 'Did she eat any of the honey?'

'Possibly.'

Her face paled, 'I, um, have to take her to a vet.'

Julius looked at her, 'Why?'

Allegra sobbed.

'Why?'

'She's eaten the honey.'

'So? Honey is fine for dogs.'

'Umm....'

'Unless that honey is different. Honey made from oleander plants kept in a small greenhouse down the back of the farm. Plants pulled and placed into a trailer to be taken away. Plants that burned and blistered the hands and arms of the woman who pulled them up. The same woman who left out a jar of poisoned honey and allowed her mother to spread it on her toast. The same woman who threw that honey into the bin. The only person here who knows bees, plants, and honey. That's you, Allegra.'

Tears streamed down Allegra's face. 'Please, take us to the vet, don't let Hermoiny die.'

'I'll take you if you tell me the truth.' Julius' voice was calm.

'I killed her. With the honey. I killed her. The hateful old woman.'

'Why?'

'Because she wouldn't give me any money. My paintings didn't sell, and she wouldn't help me out. I crashed my car and she wouldn't fix it. Now please, the vet.'

'The honey kills almost instantly, doesn't it?'

'Yes. Mother ate several mouthfuls, vomited and died.'

'Honey Bear?'

'She said, "honey bad" She knew.'

Julius turned to the policeman. 'She's all yours now.'

Allegra grabbed Julius' arm, 'But the vet?'

'If your dog had eaten the honey, it'd be dead now.' He leant over, took the snarling dog from her and lowered it to the ground. It bolted.

Her mouth opened then closed. 'Oh. No, I can't go to jail. Who will look after Hermoiny? Hermoiny!' She hurried after her dog.

The policeman followed her. 'Miss Cronin, I'm arresting you...'

Cameron clapped him on the back, 'How did you know?'

'The crashed car, the torn dress, the lack of pain killers. Allegra clearly had no money to spend on anything. Also, Margaret wouldn't waste mouldy food. There's no way she would throw a full jar of honey in the bin, no matter how awful it was.'

They walked to the door.

'You know that old saying,' Julius paused.

'What saying?'

'A fool and her honey are soon parted.'

'Stop it,' Cameron shook his head.

'Bet her favourite book was The Great Gatsbee.'

'Stop.'

'Who's a bees favourite singer?'

'No.'

'Bee-oncé.'

'It's going to be a very long drive to the station.'

NOTHING EVER HAPPENS IN ANAFI

ELIZABETH SPRATT

This was the day to unearth the family skeletons and solve the mystery. Let this be his last visit here. He'd said that for several visits now. Confidence raced through his veins. But Jamie could not afford for Aunt Lottie to find out his motivation or she would continue to clam up. He ran from Aunt Lottie's white stone house where water lapped just metres from her blue front door. The ocean views stretched to the horizon and in the distance the nine-hour ferry chugged along. Tomorrow it would take him back to Athens.

Of all the days to have slept in. He zig zagged over a trail of black stones on the golden sand. Reaching the dirt track his footsteps further weaved the path that hugged the shoreline. He glanced up at the clifftop church, its shadows looming over him. Strange the church bells had not woken him this morning. But

Beatrice, Lottie's long-time housekeeper insisted they'd rung. She hadn't displayed her normal disdain of him. There'd been a hint of a smile from her.

There seemed to be more rocks by the path than yesterday or was it the ouzo from last night.

Probably from last week's landslide that had cut them off from the hilltop village, he reasoned.

He halted and gazed at the water, it seemed like hundreds of diamonds glittered on the surface. Pity his mum hadn't told him more from her death bed. His foot kicked something that glinted in the sun. He reached down. A brooch. Minus the pin. He picked it up and raised his arm towards the ocean. Aunt Lottie's sullen mood would worsen if she discovered she'd lost any of her trove of gaudy jewellery. He shoved it into his pocket. He'd seen the pictorial listing for every tacky piece. Some even looked real.

Beads of sweat dotted his hairline. He wished he could have found his hat, the morning sun was relentless. Back home materialistic Izzy with her fiery long locks, was always asking about the family jewels. One word summed up their last conversation. Disaster.

The last night of his London West End production, well, it wasn't quite in the heart of the theatre district. And not exactly in a theatre. On the fringe was more apt. A decent size room above a pub. Just not a watering hole frequented by theatre patrons and tourists.

But hey, he'd got an audience each summer evening and on the opening night the room was full. All thirty seats occupied. He'd never achieved a full house before. Everything was great until Izzy dumped him, for a seventh time, forcing him to come to this remote whitewashed island alone. *Well, someone else could turn her from a make-up artist into a Hollywood star.*

He walked a few more minutes along the path until he reached concrete and the white stone taverna came into view. Steps led down to tables dotted across the sand. There she was under the solitary pink and yellow striped umbrella. Aunt Lottie was always the first customer of the day. You could set your watch by her.

His hand shot up and scratched the back of his neck. He knew one juicy storyline could be the next epic production. To date, all his returned scripts bore similar labels. "Rejected." "Already done." "Lacks a good romance." He dreamed of a script that would be explosive and shocking. According to his late mum, his family history was all that and more. There must be a reason why Aunt Lottie kept coming to this island.

He rubbed his unshaven chin. Hard to believe that this morose pasty skinned woman with garish jewellery decorating every one of her fat dimpled fingers was indeed his mum's sister. The best time to talk to her was after her morning shot of Greek coffee served to her at exactly 10.05am.

Approach and be firm. That's right, one foot in front of the other. 'Morning Aunt Lottie. Isn't it a beautiful day? I leave tomorrow, well assuming the ferry isn't cancelled again.' Escape from this sun and all the white houses. 'Now, the family secret. You did promise to talk about it.'

He skipped the step and plopped onto the sand. Yuck. Fine white grains slipped into his sockless boat shoes. He glanced at the table. Bare. No coffee. That's not good. Her bright orange lips set in a tight straight line. Stephanos, the taverna owner should brace for the expected rebuke.

Speaking of Stephanos, where was he? He rolled away from the typical silent treatment of Aunt Lottie and those black sunglasses that covered half her face. Footprints. Good Stephanos must have gone to get the coffee. Hang on the impressions led to the water's edge.

Focus Jamie. 'Mum told me that it was imperative to our family's reputation and business that the family secret must always be protected. Well, Aunt Lottie it's only you and I left now.' He twisted to watch her reaction. 'No other relatives.'

Come on. You can tell me? 'I want to help you to safeguard the secret. You can trust me.'

He rubbed his hands together and gazed out to the deserted sea.

'Okay Aunt Lottie. Do you want me to get your coffee?'

He pushed himself up. 'Aunt Lottie?'

'Wake up.' He stretched out his hand and stroked her arm. No. No. She felt cold. He prodded her. Oh no.

Her arm was stiff. He shouldn't have touched her. This wasn't good. *Get a grip Jamie. She's had a heart attack.* A sickening sensation grew in the pit of his stomach. The last person guarding a life-long secret dead at fifty-nine. Perfectly healthy. No reason for her to die. Could this be murder?

He took a step backwards then another. He spun round and halted with one foot mid-air.

A shirtless Stephanos in tight ripped jeans leant against the door frame of his beachfront taverna.

Uh-oh. 'Help. Stephanos. Help.' He staggered up the sand towards the concrete slabs that surrounded the taverna. 'It's, well it's... it's Aunt Lottie. Something has happened to her.'

Stephanos rolled his eyes, straightened up and reached back inside the bar. He came out carrying a white shirt and gave it a sniff before he shrugged his arms into it and padded barefoot towards Jamie. 'She's early, that's what has happened.'

Jamie shook his head. 'No, you're late.'

Stephanos paused, tucked a strand of wet hair behind his ear and pointed at the hilltop church. 'The bells have not rung. It isn't ten o'clock. I don't open until I hear those bells.'

'No, Beatrice told me I was running late if I wanted to speak to Aunt Lottie. She heard the bells. She told me that she did. I slept in.'

Stephanos muttered and went over to the chair that propped up Lottie. He leapt backwards.

'She's dead!'

Jamie wiped under his eyes and stumbled towards Stephanos. 'Yes, I know.'

'You said that something happened to her. Not dead.'

'Well, that is something. Look, here comes Beatrice.'

They both took a step further away from the body. Beatrice, in sensible black lace up shoes, a crisp white blouse tucked into her standard grey straight skirt and a wide brimmed hat, strode towards them.

She pushed past the men and spoke to Lottie. 'Your nephew has been messing with your will.'

Jamie's head jerked. He'd never been able to locate any will.

'You were right to...'

'Beatrice, Aunt Lottie's dead.'

'Dead.' Beatrice took a step closer and picked up Lottie's wrist. Seconds later she let it slip from her grip. 'No pulse. Stone cold. Dead for hours.'

'Hours. That can't be right.'

'The stress you caused your aunt. She warned you to stop with your wild fantasies of a family secret. You've killed her.'

He ran his fingers through his hair. He thought he'd been discreet, but nothing got past miss busy body. Well, he knew a secret about Beatrice, that the police would love to hear about.

'No.'

She turned and wagged her finger at him. 'I know you stole her new will.'

Stephanos raised an eyebrow at him.

Beatrice turned sideways. 'She'd added a new heir and you didn't like the fact you would have to share her estate.'

Bingo. Confirmation there had been another child. It had always worried Izzy that he might have to share his inheritance. 'Rubbish.'

'What's this then?' She waved a wide brimmed sun hat at him.

'My hat. Where did you find it?'

'In the rubbish bin. With her new will stuffed inside it.'

'I've never seen her will.' He grabbed the papers from her outstretched hands and skimmed through the pages. The family secret was in here.

Stephanos laughed. 'Didn't think you had it in you to finally do the old bag in. I'll never have to hear that sour voice dictating to me that 'coffee should be hot but not enough to burn my taste buds'.'

Both Beatrice and Jamie turned in shock to Stephanos. He'd mimicked Lottie's voice to perfection.

Jamie felt dizzy. The way Stephanos' lip curled up was a mirror image of Lottie. The final piece in the puzzle fell into place.

Beatrice snatched the will back. 'You murdered her.'

Jamie felt a trickle of sweat run down his back. 'It's a heart attack. It has to be.'

Stephanos took a step closer to Lottie and peered from top to bottom. 'There's no obvious sign of any injury. Hang on. There's something in her hand.'

'Don't touch anything. Leave it to the police.'

Stephanos snorted. 'They won't come for at least a week.' He pulled a piece of paper from the swollen purple hand and started to read.

'Interesting. Old Lottie snuck out to meet someone at midnight. And it wasn't me Beatrice, I have standards.'

Beatrice snatched the crinkled paper from Stephanos. A button on her shirt popped open. 'This is your handwriting, Jamie.'

'No it isn't.' He plucked the paper and from Beatrice and blushed when he caught sight of her lacy bra. He wouldn't have thought that she owned anything verging on sexy. 'Well, yes. How strange. It is.'

Stephanos advanced towards him.

Jamie backed away. 'Wait, this has been cut from my latest script.' That bra reminded him of Izzy. His eyes became fixated on

Beatrice's chest. The brooch. She usually wore it pinned between the second and third button of her blouse.

Beatrice cackled. 'Another flop you mean. Lottie was not going to finance any more of your productions.'

Jamie shoved his hands into his pocket. 'You hated her Beatrice. I saw those looks you gave behind her back.' He squeezed out a tear and sniffled, 'You're the only one talking murder.'

'Stop snivelling and blow your nose.'

Jamie yanked a hanky from his pocket and the brooch went flying.

'My brooch. That was in the drawer with the will, your aunt gave it to me for safe keeping.'

'Liar. Aunt Lottie wouldn't give you a legal document for safe keeping. And this brooch, I found it on the path this morning. You had it on last night when you brought in Aunt Lottie's bedtime tea.' He snatched the brooch up. 'Proof you killed her.'

Beatrice ignored him. 'Stephanos, keep an eye on Jamie. This worm would frame anyone. Like his mother. A sponge. Stay here. I'm going to the house to find her lawyer's number and call the police.'

'Wait.' Stephanos bent down next to the table. 'What's this?'

Jamie moved closer. 'A gold chain, broken.' He recognised it from the pictures. He kicked at the sand; the blue stone was missing. 'She's been robbed.'

Beatrice glanced at her watch. 'That could belong to anyone.'

He stepped behind Lottie. There was tiny red mark on the back of her neck. 'No, it's Aunt Lottie's. Mum said she kept something close to her chest. I thought she meant secrets, but it must be this necklace.'

'Rubbish. Your mother was forever filling your head with nonsense. Now I'm going to call the police.'

Stephanos rubbed the chain through his fingers. 'It's not tarnished. There hasn't been anyone else here for over a week.' He nodded up the hill. 'Not since that landslide.'

Jamie pointed at the footprints. 'Someone was here last night or this morning.'

Beatrice tucked the will under her arm. 'Another nocturnal visitor Stephanos.'

Stephanos winked. 'Jealous?'

Beatrice narrowed her eyes. 'Stephanos, keep Jamie locked up in your store- room until I return.'

Stephanos locked his arm through Jamie's and dragged him towards the taverna.

'Please. Stephanos, I'm innocent. Someone's setting me up.'

'Who? Sit in that chair and don't move.'

Jamie sank into a wooden chair. 'I don't know.'

The peel of bells caused both men to turn to the open door.

'I told you, it wasn't ten o'clock.'

Jamie leapt to his feet. 'Beatrice! She set me up.'

Stephanos picked up a checked tea-towel and started to wipe a table that held two wine glasses. 'What are you saying?'

'Beatrice. She was the one who told me it was after ten. She wanted me to find Aunt Lottie dead.' He clicked his fingers. 'She hid my hat. She created that fake will. Did you see the page where this new nameless heir was added?'

Stephanos shrugged and picked up the glasses.

Jamie scratched his head. 'No, well there was no signature on that page, yet every other page had a signature.'

He got up and paced the pristine floor. 'This morning when I knocked on Beatrice's door to ask where Aunt Lottie was, there was noise coming from inside her room. Someone else was in there. That's why she rushed out without her shirt done up properly and closed the door behind her. No brooch. That's why her blouse gaped open.'

Stephanos poured the dregs from the glasses into a bucket.

Jamie spotted a gold pin and bent down to pick it up. It wasn't an ordinary pin it was a bar pin that belonged on a brooch. His eyes bulged and he stood up to face Stephanos. 'You're in this together.'

Stephanos flung the tea towel on the bar. 'What are you on about?'

Jamie returned to pacing. 'You lured Aunt Lottie down here in the middle of the night. One or both of you killed her. Then you went back to the house. No wonder you gave me so much ouzo last night. You didn't want me to hear the two of you.'

Stephanos started to clap. 'Great story. What's my motive?'

Jamie licked his lips. 'Lottie's love child. The new heir. You're the reason she keeps coming here.'

Stephanos grabbed hold of a chair. 'Impossible. She's not old enough to be my mother.'

'She had a baby at fifteen.' That much he did know; he was just never sure if it was Lottie or his mother that had given birth. 'My grandparents were going to claim they had another baby. But with your olive skin, no one would have believed them.'

Stephanos pushed the chair over. 'No. Not true.'

'Yes. You both have the same nose and lips. I should have spotted it sooner.'

'I'll ring my mum now. She will tell you I'm not adopted.' Stephanos picked up the telephone. 'The line is dead.'

Jamie stopped pacing. 'Then Beatrice ...'

'We need to stop her.'

Jamie shook his head. 'Stephanos, you're not going anywhere.'

'You want to let your aunt's killer escape.'

Jamie backed towards the door. 'You are both her killer.'

'Not this again.'

'You beat me back here this morning to help frame me.'

'Impossible. You would have seen me on the path.'

Jamie stood in the doorway. 'Not if you swam back here this morning and then walked backwards, so it would look like someone had left the island rather than arriving.'

'Fine. I had a visitor last night. She left on a jet ski before sunrise.'

'Nice story. You always wear black pants to work, not ripped jeans. So, they are either wet or still in Beatrice's room.'

'We will both go to the house. I don't trust either of you. Beatrice called you James. Is that her pet name for you?'

He hated Izzy calling him that too. She wanted him to be more sophisticated.

'Perhaps the two of you are setting me up with this nonsense that I'm the new heir?'

They both glared at each other then ran to the rocky path.

Stephanos out sprinted Jamie and bounded up the flights of stairs yelling for Beatrice. Jamie arrived panting. All doors open except one.

245

'That's Beatrice's room.'

Stephanos rattled the handle. 'It's locked.'

Jamie bent over hands on his knees and sucked in some air. 'Break it down.'

Stephanos crashed against the door, splintering the wood in all directions.

Beatrice with her hair down round her face, in a yellow matronly night dress lay bound and gagged on the bed. She jerked her head towards the open window.

Jamie and Stephanos raced to the large window. A jet ski roared towards the open water. Long red curls swept up in the air.

'Izzy.'

'Last night's beauty.'

Stephanos turned back to the bed and started to untie Beatrice.

Jamie smiled. He'd underestimated both Izzy's make up and acting skills. Then again, she would have perfected that on her secret holidays with her Aunt Beatrice.

Whoever said that nothing ever happened on Anafi was so wrong.

Jamie leant out the window, caught in the wooden ledge was an empty syringe.

Izzy raised a fist and the sun glinted off a brilliant blue item. The stone. Ah, greedy Izzy had fallen for his story that Lottie possessed a rare blue diamond worth millions. He'd gone on and on about Stephanos the local love god and the line of women who snuck into his taverna after closing time. Perfect bait for her to sneak onto the island by jet ski from Santorini. Twenty-eight kilometres for her was nothing. She always slept round after she dumped him. Bonus it was with Lottie's love child. It would look like they conspired together to kill poor Aunt Lottie and rob Jamie of his rightful inheritance.

THE EYE OF PICASSO

JENNY WOOLSEY

This was the day Three-thirty. Two hours and this shift would be over. And at six I'd be on my third date with gorgeous Lily. My heart quickened whenever I thought of her and her warm smile. We'd met by accident at Tiffany's. It was Mum's fiftieth birthday, and I couldn't decide on the South Sea pearls or the emerald and diamond necklace. Lily, the patient assistant, told me they were both exquisite, but her favourite was the pearls. My heart had triple jumped at her dimples, lyrical voice, and her shiny honey-blonde hair pulled back in a ponytail. Without hesitation, as she settled the pearls in a navy blue gift box, I was completely and utterly entranced and took the chance to ask her out on a date.

On my security guard round of the art gallery, I passed the girl in Marie-Denise Villers' painting, *Young Woman Drawing*. Those blue eyes, petite nose and apricot lips were similar to Lily's. The next painting, Georges de La Tour's, *The Fortune Teller*, made me chuckle. A wealthy young man, engrossed in having his fortune told by an old hag, was unaware that the surrounding women were pick-pocketing him. Daylight robbery. Ha! I bet he didn't expect this reversal of fortune.

Beside the imposing sculpture of Michelangelo, I watched the public admire the rare European paintings hanging on the walls, and the sculptures and artefacts displayed on plinths. A set of three small Picasso plates sat on one of them. To me, the faces on them looked like something a kid or even I could do.

Being the middle of the week, this was a slow day and my mind wandered back to my first encounter with the gorgeous Lily. I smiled at the memory.

I shook myself back into the present. I was supposed to be guarding these priceless artworks. I focussed first on the girl seated on a padded black seat. Your typical Goth type. Black shoulder-length hair, dark makeup, a black overcoat, a dark top and miniskirt, torn fishnet stockings, tattoos on her legs and to finish the look, Doc Martins. A sketchpad rested on her lap.

Over in the left corner, a loved-up couple stood with arms wrapped around each other in front of a Monet, the guy caressing his lover's bum. Lover-girl, adorned by a knee-length flowing scarf, pointed at the lily pond and spoke in what sounded Scandinavian.

A blind lady, her mobile phone out and earbuds securely in place, paused in front of Caravaggio's, *The Musicians*. Her guide dog stood beside her. Bent forward, she listened to the audio descriptions, her face close to the painting.

On the other side of the room divider, a clean-cut suited-up gentleman was focussed on the painting of Rembrandt's, *The Night Watch*. He moved his gaze around the painting as if studying the brushstrokes. After his examination, he wrote something in a small notebook.

Having overheard him speak to the lover couple, I knew he owned a private art collection and loved European masterpieces. He had asked them where they were from – they had told him Denmark.

Four-thirty and just an hour and a half until I would meet Lily at the fountain at the end of the mall. I'd planned a special night of wining, dining and dancing. The venue overlooked the river lined by a corridor of trees and sparkling lights. I wanted to impress her.

I moved from my station and repeated a slow wander around the room, checking each piece.

'What the?' I spat, as I looked at the Picasso plates.

My skin froze like a windscreen in winter.

'Oh, crap!' I spun around and scrutinised the five visitors. They were the only people who had been in this room since I had done my last round.

One of them must have switched a plate. Two of the pieces were the same. One wasn't. It was close but not exact. What the hell was I going to do?

First, I needed to stay calm. My hands trembled, my gut squelched, and my head spun. The rule in the case of suspected theft was to report it to the office. If the perpetrator was believed to be on the premises, we were to detain them until the police arrived, noting anything said. But if I did report it, could I lose my job for incompetence and being distracted? I needed this job – Lily liked it.

I stared at the plate. This one had an identical face, but the colours were slightly off. Most people wouldn't know the difference, but I did. I had an eye for detail. It definitely wasn't the Picasso. How was I going to figure out the culprit?

Fingerprints? Probably a waste of time but I examined the plinth anyway. I couldn't see any.

The only thing I could do was to suss each person out and ask them questions. But I could hardly come out with, *'Did you steal the Picasso plate?'* They'd probably lie in defence. I had to think like a detective.

Who would I approach first? Who had the best opportunity? I didn't really know. And wouldn't the thief have left by now? One would think so, but no one had entered or left so it had to be one of these in the room. Maybe they were planning on stealing more pieces or they thought I wouldn't notice.

Who would I approach first?

The Goth girl's overcoat was now buttoned up and belted around her waist. She was suspect number one. I had to think up a ruse to search her coat.

'Excuse me,' I said.

She still sat, with her sketchpad resting on her lap. I could see she had been drawing. 'I like your sketches. You're pretty good.'

She flicked her black kohl-pencilled eyes at me. 'Thanks, I'm studying fine arts.'

'I noticed you have a patch of white chalk on your back. Can you take your coat off please so I can brush it off? It could damage the masterpieces.'

The girl replied, 'Do I? Geez, this is my new coat.' She stood up, undid her belt and unfastened the buttons. I held my breath. Nothing fell out.

'Here, let me do that for you,' I said, reaching out to hold the collar.

'Thanks,' she said, pulling her arms out.

I spun the coat away from her and pretended to brush the non-existent chalk off. It was light.

She wasn't the thief.

'Thanks,' I said, handing back the coat. 'Have a nice day.'

Who would have done it then?

I stared at the couple and the guy in the suit. Could it be?

'Excuse me, Sir.' I strolled up beside my next suspect.

The man jumped and turned towards me. 'Yes?' he asked.

My eyes darted to the bulge inside his suit jacket. My heart hammered. Was it the plate?

'The museum is always looking for volunteer guides, and I was wondering if you have a business card?'

'Really? I would enjoy that. I won't be too willing to talk about Picasso, though. I think his stuff is rubbish,' he replied.

I nodded then acted casual. That comment could be a diversion tactic. He opened his jacket and pulled out his wallet and notebook from his inner pocket. He opened his wallet, pulled out a shiny black card with his photo and gold writing on it which he handed to me.

'Thanks, Gerard,' I said, having read the name.

I scanned him once more. Damn. There was nowhere else on his body he could hide the plate... so it wasn't him. Well, that left the amorous couple as the blind lady wouldn't be able to see to do it. They had moved on to the Matisse. Lover-girl now held her scarf folded like a present in her hands. Lover-boy didn't have his arm around her anymore.

I watched them for a minute. What was I going to ask? They had to be the thieves.

Five o'clock. The museum closed in fifteen minutes. If I didn't solve this quickly, I was going to be late for Lily!

'Excuse me, do you like this Matisse?'

'Oh, yes,' said Lover-boy. 'I like his use of bold colours.'

'He's a bit like Picasso,' said Lover-girl. 'That lady's face reminds me of a Picasso.'

A zap traversed my spine. This must be them as Lover-girl liked Picasso. I had to keep going with my questions.

'I noticed that beautiful scarf you were wearing,' I said, directly to Lover-girl. 'It's very pretty. Who's the designer?'

Lover-girl's face suddenly changed. Her mouth turned downwards, crimson enveloped her face and her eyebrows furrowed.

I put my arms out in case she ran. I had her!

'I think you better—,' I started.

'He bought me this and said it was an original,' she squealed. 'He just admitted it's a fake from Asia and I don't want it anymore! He's a bloody liar.'

'I didn't tell you that!' Lover-boy spat.

I placed my hand on her arm. 'Come with me. I—'

Lover-girl threw down the scarf. It landed on the wooden floor in a heap.

Crackkkkk.

'Bloody hell, they're fake too!' Lover-girl screamed at her partner. 'Just like you!'

I stared at the large translucent beads that scattered in all directions across the floor. The scarf contained a necklace, not the plate.

No... I had cleared my last suspect.

Goosebumps covered my arms and my head began to spin. I would have to contact the front desk and tell them the Picasso piece was gone, and I didn't know how it happened. I bet I would lose my job. I would also lose Lily.

Lover-girl wasn't picking up her beads. Instead, the two lovers stood staring at each other. Her eyes were cold, like glaciers. His voice, soft and pleading with hands outstretched towards her crossed arms.

I bent down and started to gather up the beads. They were a safety hazard. With seven in my hand, I took them over to the seat where the Goth girl had sat. She was no longer there.

I looked around at the other beads, strewn like tiny golf balls on a driving range. I didn't want to pick them up, I wanted to find the culprit.

A few had rolled over near the blind lady and her guide dog. She was busy, absorbed in her audio guided tour, in front of a Turner landscape.

I went over and bent down to retrieve them.

'No way!' I murmured, straightening up. 'Excuse me,' I said to the lady, as I touched her arm.

'Yes?' she replied, removing her earbuds and turning towards me.

'I'm the security guard here and I need you to come with me.'

'The Metropolitan Museum of Art will be closing in five minutes.'

Please make your way to the exit, boomed over the intercom.

'Where to?' she asked. 'I can find the exit on my own.'

'I'm taking you to the entry,' I said.

'I really am right, but if you are going that way...'

'Yes,' I said, my shoes clicking on the floor.

As we walked, the lady told me, 'This has been such a lovely exhibition. I really enjoyed it and I'm going to tell all my friends about it. The little bit I could see was complemented well by the audio feed.'

'It's impressive,' I said, running my hand through my hair. She was the only one left to interrogate and she was acting very cool. I had to think of something to not arouse her suspicions that I was onto her. I needed a trap.

I led her past the front desk and into the back office where another security guard sat. I raised my eyebrows at Matt.

'Before you go, would you be able to answer a survey on the audio descriptions?' I asked her.

'Ah, yes,' she said, 'I believe I have time.'

'That's good. There's a seat behind you. The survey will only take five minutes,' I said.

Matt raised his eyebrows at me and I pointed downwards. I then reached down and slid my hand underneath the guide dog's harness coat and retrieved what I was looking for. 'Ma'am you're not really here for a survey. You are in the security guard office. Can you please explain why your dog has a Picasso plate hidden under its harness?'

'That's his drinking dish,' the lady's voice squeaked. 'It's not a real Picasso.'

'No, it's the real deal,' I stated.

'Someone else must have put it there,' she said.

'I don't believe you. No one else went near you,' I said, trying to get the truth out of her. 'It was you, wasn't it?'

The lady didn't answer. She wasn't going to come clean easily, it seemed.

'The police are on their way and you *will* be charged with stealing an artwork. If you don't confess to me, then you will need to confess to them,' I stated.

A strangled gasp escaped from her lips, her shoulders slumped, and tears welled in her eyes.

Matt shook his head.

The black Labrador sat up and put his head on her knees. She twisted her hands together.

'Make this easy on everyone and confess,' Matt said.

'I'm telling you…,' she replied, tears falling down her cheeks.

I checked my watch and listened to the ticking of the clock on the wall. This was annoying. I had to go. I didn't want to keep Lily waiting. If this woman would just fess up, I could leave her with Matt.

I stared at the suspect, her face bent and a trembling hand stroking the dog's head.

A knock sounded on the door.

'The police are here,' I said, crossing my arms in front of my chest.

The lady's hands went up to her face.

'Afternoon,' the first copper said as he entered the room.

'This is—,' I began.

'Ohh,' the lady wailed interrupting me, *'I am a fool. It was me.'*

257

I spun my head from the coppers to her.

'What?' I asked her.

'It was me. I'm so sorry,' her voice quivered. 'I had my replica Picasso plate in my bag and I swapped them when I heard you talking on the other side of the room. But I didn't come here intending to. I just did it when I saw how beautiful the real plate was.'

My mouth dropped open.

'I love Picasso and I've even been to Spain to see his home. I could never afford one and I didn't think you would notice the difference.' She ran her hands through her hair. 'It was a really stupid thing to do!'

'I thought you were blind,' I spluttered.

'Many people with guide dogs have some sight,' I said. 'Can I please return it? I will never do it again!'

'Over to you,' I said to the coppers. My job was done. A lesson learnt that some people with guide dogs can actually partially see. I glanced at my watch. It was five-fifty-seven and my hands shook with anticipation for my date with Lilly.

LAST KILL AND TESTAMENT

GARY DAVID

The only way to know if you're predator or prey is when the lights go out.

I listened for others in the room. Three wheezed as their throats tightened in fear, while one sounded calm. My breath rasped through clotting blood until I spat onto the floor.

'Who's there?' Mother's voice echoed off the walls.

'Paul,' I answered.

Her chair scraped on the floor. 'Oh my God, Paul, can you help me?'

Even now, with me banged up, she thought only of her needs.

'Why am I handcuffed to this bloody chair?' Uncle Tony called out. His chair screeched as he struggled.

Mother replied, 'I'm handcuffed, too. Who else is here?'

'Me,' Aunt Tanya slurred. 'Was I drugged?'

'We all were.'

'Wait, is that Detective Covey?' My mother was always good at identifying threats. 'Why have you got us here?'

'I'm handcuffed too, genius.'

'Bullshit, pig,' Uncle said.

Handcuffs rattled from the direction of the detective. 'Your messed-up family has a lot of enemies, but it makes no sense why I'm stuck here with you mobsters. Something else is going on here. What's everyone's last recollection?'

Aunt blew out a noisy breath. 'I was preparing for Father's birthday. Then I woke up here.'

'When I get the dog responsible, I'm going to slit their thr—' Uncle's threats turned to screams.

'What's going on?' Mother called.

Uncle gasped for air. 'Ch... chairs... electrified.'

'Hang on, these are the chairs from Father's safe room?' Aunt scraped hers about the floor.

'The old coot has finally lost it,' Uncle said.

'I'm not sure he has,' the detective announced.

'What would you know, pig?'

'For starters, metal handcuffs on metal chairs, everyone's chair screeching with the slightest movement. And yet, the counsellor seems able to lean forward and spit without a sound. He's not cuffed. But he's your son, your nephew, your family lawyer. He wouldn't turn on you... unless... something happened to his grandfather. Isn't that right, counsellor?'

I pushed a button on a remote. Light flooded the room.

Uncle's face turned between the other four people seated around the table. His eyes followed electrical cables attached to a car battery, cables running to all chairs except mine. 'What're you up to, boy?'

I stood, placing my remote on the table next to the empty naloxone syringes, a knife and two guns.

'I asked you a question, boy!'

'As the detective said, Grandfather's dead.'

Aunt's eyes widened. 'What, how?'

'I caught him in the kitchen trying to sneak some of his birthday cake for tonight's party. When he slid the knife in, it activated a pressure bomb. I made it, he didn't.'

'You think it was us?' Mother put on her best offended expression.

'You all had motive.'

'Motive?' she asked.

'Monday morning, he was selling the family business and writing you all out of his will, leaving everything to charity. Now he's dead, and conveniently, the old will stands. Unless I can prove any of you had something to do with his murder, you'll all get equal share of the empire.'

'Well, it wasn't me, boy. Let me out of these handcuffs before I—'

I tapped the remote. Uncle's body shook as I picked up a case from the floor and placed it on the table. He didn't seem nervous enough to be the killer, but I couldn't be sure. When I released the button he slouched back in the chair, wheezing through clenched teeth.

'What happened to you?' Mother motioned toward my bloody nose and neck. But it was clear she was questioning my unfamiliar behaviour.

'I'm not sure. When I came to from the blast, I could no longer, well, feel things.' I struggled to translate my lack of empathy for them. A lifetime of loyalty that excused their behaviour, now gone.

'What're you going to do?' Aunt asked.

'Find out who killed Grandfather, and kill them.'

Mother spoke up. 'He was our father. No one in this room would have killed him.'

'Not one. Two.'

'Two?' Mother queried.

'Two differently designed bombs. The pressure bomb in the birthday cake, and this little case bomb I found in here.'

'And me?' The detective raised his eyebrows.

I shrugged. 'You dedicated your life to destroying our family. You have informants. Between your illegal investigations and my client privilege, the two of us should be able to find the killer.'

'And if we don't?'

'Then it was probably you.' My finger ran over the cold metal lock of the case until it clicked open. A red LED timer continued counting down.

The detective laughed in disbelief. 'You're kidding me. Is that live?'

'I thought the countdown would provide motivation for its owner to cooperate and deactivate it.'

'Why would anyone deactivate that bomb if it means a death sentence?' Mother asked.

'I don't care about attempted murder. The person in charge of this bomb goes to jail and loses their inheritance. The person in charge of the cake bomb gets a bullet.'

Uncle spat his words, 'I'm going to slit your—'

I pushed the button on the remote. The current suffocated his threats. I released the button.

The detective chimed in, 'I, on the other hand, will absolutely help you, if you electrocute that prick one more time.'

Uncle braced himself. Instead, the detective shook, then gasped for air.

'Don't test me, Detective. Either play the game, or you'll become it.'

'I can't feel my balls.'

'Let's begin.' I directed the detective. 'What do you know that I don't?'

'You don't want to know what I know.'

I sent a short jolt of electrical current to persuade him otherwise. He dragged back a hissing breath, eyes jerked open as wide as ping-pong balls.

'Okay, okay, felt my balls that time.' He took a breath. 'Your mother here runs prostitution and drugs for the family. A real psychopath.'

'Don't, you fat piece of bacon!'

I silenced her with a button. She looked up, stunned I would shock her.

'A reaaaaaaal psychopath,' the detective goaded her, hoping she would take the bait again. 'Do you know you had a brother once, Paul?'

Mother's lack of eye contact confirmed I did. It was becoming difficult to control my anger and the room at the same time. If she could hide that, she could hide anything.

The detective continued, 'After your father found out who and what she was, he left and took his son – your brother. He was about to learn the hard way why you should never piss off a psychopath. She had the boy kidnapped and discarded him into the sex slave trade. She did this to her own first born, while carrying you. She made sure your father received graphic images to make him suffer for crossing her. He agreed to turn state's evidence in return for help locating his son. That's when she had your father killed.'

'That's a lie! I tried everything to find my son. I was the one who discovered the kidnappers, I tried to negotiate with them. But the police arrived, stuck their noses in, and the kidnappers died in the shootout. I had nothing to do with that.'

'Maybe, but if the boy did return, he would be a threat just like Sarah, your sister's daughter, and you would have a lot of questions to answer. Now, your sister Tanya on the other hand, a master of finance and money laundering, lived by your grandfather's law, to give criminals who crossed them one warning to do the right thing. If not, she had them arrested and charged on something unrelated. Once in prison, her goons cut their throats.'

'What do you mean, a threat like Sarah?'

'Unlike you, your cousin Sarah could stand up to the family. She'd been one of my informants, until your mother and uncle found out.'

'Another crime family was responsible for killing her,' I corrected.

'Pretty sure you're wrong there, counsellor. Shortly after her death, I started receiving a lot of anonymous evidence. Details of crimes committed by your uncle and mother.'

'You bitch,' Mother fired at my aunt, before my electrical current focused her.

'My thoughts exactly,' the detective smiled. 'This suggested your aunt knew they were behind her daughter's murder.'

Aunt's face tightened and confirmed his suspicions.

'Until you shagged it all up.' The detective smirked.

'Me?'

'Your grandfather knew I was about to deliver the family a whole load of life sentences. His offspring were out of control trying to kill each other, so he decided it was time to get out. The plan was yours, wasn't it?'

'What plan?' Uncle asked cautiously, eyeing the remote in my hand.

I turned towards each member of my family. 'We were selling everything to the government. They'd get our contacts, methods and billions back in record-breaking busts. The family would be set up financially and completely protected with immunity.'

'Exactly, and if your aunt's psycho siblings got immunity, she couldn't get them offed in prison. The best way to get rid of them was to remove the one protecting them.'

'That's preposterous,' Aunt protested.

The detective smiled, seeming satisfied with her reaction. 'Only the part about you killing your father. A far more interesting person is dear Uncle Tony, the most unforgiving arms dealer on this side of the planet. A man with the contacts to source a cake bomb and the ability to sneak it through his father's security.'

'Why would I kill my father in a way that would lead straight to me?'

'You kept a file of every bomb you procured. In case the family ever turned on you, you had all the evidence you'd need to convince them otherwise.'

'How do you know about that, pig?'

'Your sister does, so I do. If you would be so kind as to provide us with the password?'

'There's no way I'm giving you that password.'

'Counsellor, I think we can take this as a sign of guilt.'

I picked up the blade from the table. 'Password!'

'I'm not afraid, you pathetic little weasel. You're a filthy lawyer, not a killer. You don't have the stomach.'

I sliced the inside of his thigh, just enough to puncture an artery.

'I'm going to kill you when I get out of here.'

'In a few minutes you will bleed out. Tell me the password... or don't.'

Uncle Tony, assumed the old me would fold. The silence drew out. His eyes rolled as his blood puddled around my shoes.

'All right, all right.' He dictated the cloud address and stuttered through the password.

After a few minutes I relayed, 'No matches on the bombs.'

'I told you. Now get me to a hospital.' His threats reduced in intensity.

Aunt Tanya roared. 'That doesn't make him innocent.'

Uncle struggled to take a breath. 'It's not about innocence. We kill to protect our family.'

She spun to face Uncle. 'But you killed our family, you bastard.'

'I arranged the bomb. The family gave the order.'

'You mean you and her.' She nodded to my mother. 'Our family always gave one chance to do the right thing before killing.' Her distress calmed, before returning an unnerving predator's smile. 'But now... you're dead!'

Aunt Tanya's eyes swung in my direction.

'Look for the bomb that killed your father,' Aunt said.

What? My father? I wasn't prepared for this. I thought I knew all their crimes. I was wrong. I scrolled as far as I could, 'Records don't go back that far.'

'Detective, were there any bomb signatures that matched his father's bomb?' demanded my aunt.

'Yes, two.'

At that point Uncle exploded into a rage of threats as the detective gave me the details of the bombs. I scrolled through the document on my phone. Adrenaline raced through my body as I stared at the guns on the table. I contemplated my next move. My gaze silenced the room, except for my uncle, who began to plead. I picked up one of my guns and walked to his chair. I ripped the cables from it and sat in front of him.

'Wait, what are you doing?' He was already getting weak from the lack of blood.

'My cousin did the right thing and you killed her. My father did the right thing and you killed him. Consider this your one chance to do the right thing ... before I kill you. Who else was involved?'

He spat in my face and I shot him in the stomach. I took the wires and inserted them deep into his wound. The deeper I shoved, the harder he screamed. 'You're about to be fried from the inside out. Who else was involved?'

'Fuck you.'

I pressed the button. He spasmed violently until his head fell forward, lifeless. I released the button. I released my breath.

'You stupid bitch,' Mother fired at Aunt, breaking the silence. 'Now you've killed our only way out of this.'

'He deserved it.'

'No bitch, your daughter deserved it. She was destroying our family.'

'We always give people the opportunity to do the right thing before we kill them. Always.'

'She had chances. You endangered everyone by not keeping that feral under control.'

'Feral? You forget, I didn't do this. I know you killed our father, and I know how to prove it,' Aunt accused.

'Don't bitch.'

'Her executions are always unique. It's her cover-ups that leave sloppy patterns.'

'The trail ran cold when the cake delivery guys were killed,' I said.

'How were they killed?' Aunt asked.

I felt stupid at not seeing the connection earlier. 'Shoot-out with police.' My heart raced.

'That's circumstantial,' Mother dismissed.

I pointed my gun.

'Wait, baby. Two different bombs, two different siblings, you said it yourself. If I deactivate that bomb, that proves she's the killer.'

'Code!'

'It's bio-reader sensitive. I'm the only one that can key it in.'

I grabbed the back of her chair, dragged her to the bomb, and unlocked one of her cuffs. She punched in seven keys till the bomb status turned green.

I pressed the gun to Mother's head. Her confused look bounced between me and my aunt.

'A bomb in a bomb-proof safe room, set to go off when everyone was scheduled to be somewhere else, would have done absolutely nothing.'

The detective joined in. 'Unless she knew about the main bomb. This was the exact room your grandfather would go to if the first bomb failed to kill him.'

Mother leaned her head into the gun barrel, unafraid of the trap she had just walked into, smiling at me as if I was prey. The bomb beeped red. Only now she had grabbed several of the wires.

'We're not going to hurt each other, are we now?' She smiled.

I backed away, not taking my eyes off her.

'Don't move,' she ordered.

I continued backing towards the door.

Mother reached into the bomb and reduced the amount of plastic explosive connected to it.

I rushed to punch in the door code. My aunt charged, dragging the chair she was cuffed to, colliding with my mother just as she threw the device. The bomb narrowly missed me, hitting the door. The detonation dislodged my gun as I thumped against the wall. Mother shoved her sister off her and staggered up from the table. Without hesitation, she grabbed my other gun, and fired two bullets straight into my aunt's forehead. She turned the gun towards the detective, almost out of his cuffs.

I cocked mine.

She paused. 'Okay then, kill me.'

I hesitated.

'Can't do it, can you?'

'Why kill Grandfather? He was saving you,' I said.

'He wasn't saving anyone but his own soul. He bred me to kill for his profit. By the time I realised I didn't want this life, there was no way out. No immunity deal was ever going to stop our enemies' bullets.' She looked at the detective. 'You two idiots are a lot alike. You both believe victims need protection from the criminals. But there's one thing you never got. Criminals are someone else's victim.' She raised her gun to my chest.

I sucked in a breath to protest, when the detective slammed into my side, throwing me to the floor. The bullet meant for my heart burned into my shoulder instead. The detective rolled off me and fired a bullet into my mother's chest with the gun he'd snatched from my hand.

She fell and reached for her gun, but her bullet wound prevented it. The detective lowered his weapon, walked to her and knelt in her blood. 'Your anger killed my father, and now it has killed you.'

She cleared the blood out of her throat with a cough. Her face turned to disdain ready to spit a vile reply. He shot her in the head, leaving her as incomplete as she had left him.

He walked to me, offered his left hand, but his right hand still grasped the gun.

I refused the help and we assessed each other like two attack dogs in a stand-off, unsure who was the alpha.

'Well brother, I was going to say, you still need to work on standing up to your family, but it appears they're all dead.'

The realisation left me trembling. 'Why did you save me?'

'Someone has to take that money and help all those people your grandfather wanted.'

'And if I can't?'

He smiled at me. 'Then I guess I'll just have to give you the opportunity to do the right thing.'

A CASE OF HONOUR

SHARON THRUPP

It was 2006, a pleasant November morning, when a young man was found bludgeoned to death. Our small community was rocked by the news of the death, a murder of one of our own.

I was sitting in the concrete dungeon that I called an apartment when there was a knock. I stood and opened the door. My friend Ant was standing there.

'They found a body this morning in the churchyard. It's a foreigner,' she said standing arms by her side, tears streaming down her face. I reached out and put my arm around her, guided and sat her down on the nearest chair in the room.

A foreigner is anyone who is not Indian in McLeod Ganj, a hill station in the northern part of India.

'Who is it? Do you know?' I asked. My heart quickened, as I thought of all the foreigners that I knew. After living in the small town and teaching at an English school for Tibetan Refugees for three years, I thought I knew most of the young people.

'It's David.'

I stare at her in disbelief, confused 'David? David Huntley? 'Are you sure?'

'Yes, he was found in the churchyard earlier this morning. His face smashed in by a rock. The police identified him by a bank card in his pocket,' she said as she choked back the tears.

My stomach knotted, the bile rose in my throat. 'Who would want to do such a thing?' Despite the coolness, sweat gathered on my forehead even through a sharp chill seeped in through the windowless room.

We sat in silence opposite each other, lost in our thoughts. 'I thought you might want to know,' she said as she stood up to leave.

'Let's get out of here', I said as I led her by the arm from the apartment. We walked silently up the stairs to the top floor of the square concrete building. The Himalayas in the distance seemed almost within touching distance. Even with this calming view, my hands were shaking as I fumbled to find the phone in my pocket.

'I'll call Sarah, she'll know happened,' I told her, wanting to confirm what was too shocking to comprehend at that moment. We all worked together at the local English School and like us, she is an expat living in this small town. We lived under the umbrella of the Dalai Lama's spiritual presence from his monastery on top of the ridge with the majestic mountains as a backdrop.

Sarah and David knew each other well, coming from the same place back home had started a charity in India together. Still feeling sweaty and scared, my fingers hovered hesitantly over the flat screen of the phone. I dialed Sarah's number, leaving out the formalities and got straight to the point. 'Is it true? I have just heard that David was found dead this morning.'

'Yes, it's true,' she replied, her voice as cold as the room I had just come from.

'Oh god! What happened? Someone told me that he was found in the church yard,' I said feeling like I was on the edge of a precipice ready to topple into an abyss. The churchyard was one of McLeod Ganj's tourist attractions and part of St John in the Wilderness Church built in the British Raj times.

'I can't talk now, I'm in the morgue identifying the body,' she said, her voice grew distant.

'I'll come around to your place in the morning,' I said before hanging up, not mentioning that I was planning to bring Ant, our mutual friend, along for moral support.

'Okay,' she says, her voice clipped and hung up.

I relayed my conversation back to Ant. We agreed to meet up early the next morning for a quick breakfast at a café near Sarah's place and then walk to her apartment.

Ant and I stood in front of Sarah's door, our eyes darted from one to the other, looking for reassurance. I knocked. She answered in crumpled pajamas, her long brown hair a tangled mess. She looked as though she has just gotten out of bed even though it was mid-morning. She blocked our entry, her body covering the doorway. Her brown eyes—usually open and friendly—flashed aggressive and defiant.

I opened my mouth and stammered, 'I'm sorry.' The tears welled up in my eyes and I reached to give her a hug.

She stepped back, folded her arms and said, 'He didn't do it. He was with me.'

There were no hugs. She was agitated and on edge. 'He was with me the whole time. He never left my side. We were watching TV.' She was referring to Manoj, her Indian husband. After a whirlwind romance they married in the traditional way six months before.

Ant reached out to Sarah as I diverted my eyes to the shadows of the room for Manoj, but she was alone.

'We are so sorry, Sarah, you must be devastated. We are all in shock this could happen to David. How could anyone hurt him? He was so kind and gentle.' Ant's voice was soft, her words kind and compassionate, attempting to connect to Sarah who was clearly avoiding any kind of eye or physical contact.

'Let me know if I can help in anyway,' she said as Sarah shut the door in our faces. Ant had been Sarah's best friend and bridesmaid just months earlier but at that moment Sarah's coldness pierced and confused both of us. Something was very wrong. David was now a corpse in the morgue and Sarah, his friend was focused on protecting her husband. We walked away quickly and silent. My thoughts turned to Sarah's adamant defense of her husband.

Soon after the wedding, I met Sarah on the street.

'How's married life?' I asked. Her face looked drawn and her eyes puffy.

'It's tough, Manoj has become so controlling, always checking who I am talking to on the phone and asking me where I am going,' she said.

I remembered a time when she would call me often but I hadn't only heard from her briefly since her wedding and was beginning to understand how difficult life had become for her.

'If David or any other male volunteer comes to the office, Manoj hates it and makes a big deal out of it. The situation is unbearable. As a new bride, I'm supposed to be happy,' she said as she looked down at her set of bangles traditionally worn by a bride on her wedding day and for a period after; 'Manoj's jealousy is making me so miserable,' she said. 'He controls my every move and monitors who I talk to and looks at every male, especially David with suspicion. He watches me by day and spends most evenings, late into the night, drinking and smoking (drugs) with his relatives. I didn't get married to have a life like this and be alone,' she said she wiped the tears from her eyes.

The ancient culture that Sarah had married into is one of patriarchy, where the man is the head of the family. After the wedding, Manoj had 'ownership 'of Sarah, by the mere fact of being married to her and wanted control over any relationship, professional or otherwise, with his wife.

David was the main target for Manoj's jealousy and subsequent honour had been fuelled by his new wife's revelations as she told me as part of the earlier conversation.

'David and I had a short romantic fling a couple of years ago,' she said

'Oh really,' I said knowing there was a familiarity between them.

'It just kind of happened.'

'I thought you were family friends,' I said.

'Yes, we are, it was over in a short time and not a big deal,' she said as she shrugged her shoulders.

'Until now!' I said. She nodded in agreement and I was thinking of the large age gap between them. She was in her early thirties at the time and David in his late teens.

'But the problem is that I have told Manoj,' she said.

'What! Why did you do that?' I stared at her in disbelief. It is tradition, that as brides, Indian women are expected to be virgins. 'I thought there shouldn't be any secrets between us after we were married.' The problem is now he hates David and thinks we are still having an affair, even though I have told him it was over a few years ago. He doesn't believe me,' she said.

David and Sarah had spent a lot of their time together prior to the marriage to set up the charity. At that time they were still volunteering at the English centre by day and working on the charity in their spare time. They formed a working bond in this new environment.

The charity was doing well around the time of the murder, helping to provide foreign volunteers for health care and schooling for the nearby slum camps. Sarah's family was well connected back home and raising lots of money.

I struggled to make sense of what had happened, and started to delve into why such a tragic event could have occurred. I started with David and wondered how his worldview changed when he travelled to India to volunteer as a teacher. He could have been described as a 'clean cut' young man, tall, thin, blue eyes and short wavy brown hair.

It was alleged that David did not die where was found, in the churchyard. The theory was that he was hit over the head with a piece of concrete, taken somewhere, perhaps inside a building close by and left there to die. Had there been a plan to hide his body far from where the murder took place? The police thought he was bludgeoned many times over the head and was unconsciousness before succumbing to his injuries approximately a day later. Was his body was removed from the murder site early the next morning and taken to the cemetery? There were unconfirmed sightings to indicate this is what happened.

The significance of where David's body was found caused a lot of speculation in the town as it was the only Christian Church in the district. David was a religious man, but this was only known by people close to him.

The local police in charge of the investigation took Manoj and Sarah into custody within two days of David's body being found. It appeared to be an open and shut case.

The next series of events are my assumptions based on my own detective work. Manoj and Sarah, the prime suspects were released. As there were no other any arrests I retraced the events leading up to the murder.

It was confirmed David saw a movie in town with a friend late on Saturday night. The pair lived in close proximity to each other and they decided to walk home together. His friend's house was the first stop, a hundred metres from Manoj's tea shop. My guess is that Manoj and his gang were sitting around a small fire at the front of his tea shop, drinking and smoking hashish when they heard David talking to his friend outside her guest house. As David left to walk home along the small winding path, Manoj and his gang of trusty sidekicks confronted him and began arguing. At the time there was a lot of construction work next door with piles of broken concrete close by. The argument escalated and David was hit over the head with a piece of concrete many times.

Once David had been bludgeoned and unconscious, Manoj and his gang would have panicked. The small rudimentary stand-alone tea shop was in a vacant allotment, next to where Sarah and Manoj were living. There would have been a lot of confusion. Maybe they dragged David into the tea shop, leaving him there on the cold concrete slab. My theory is that the murderers—Manoj and his gang—didn't know what to do when they had bashed David unconscious on his way to a slow, painful death.

My guess is that Manoj would have been blamed Sarah for what had happened. 'This is your doing and your fault,' he might have said making sure that she was implicated by deciding where and how to dispose of the body.

When David's body was found in the churchyard under a pile of stones, his hands were tied behind his back. I suspected that it was an opportunistic attack rather than premeditated. While all the focus was on Manoj, it was a family effort and part of its obligation to protect his honour the motive for the killing. In the past it was a widespread practice in India to justify the act of murder, due to the perpetrator's belief the victim had brought shame or dishonour upon the family. There are still stories in national newspapers of such killings.

Leading up to his murder, David knew of the threat to his life. He had told his friends that he was scared something would happen to him. Police told a newspaper. 'We've found diary entries on the deceased's laptop where he writes he was being threatened.' The diary told of hearing noises, "like someone trying to get in" and of men's voices outside his flat late at night. In another entry, he tells that Manoj and his friends make verbal threats and wouldn't permit him to enter the charity office. He believed that Manoj and his gang were closing in and getting out of hand. One of his diary notes said he was pinning his hopes on Sarah's mother, an old family friend of his parents, to arrive so that he could convey his fears. He thought he could trust and count on her to sort out the whole sorry mess. Unfortunately, she would arrive too late.

Manoj was extensively questioned by local police, but no charges were ever laid. The murder was huge news in India and back in Sarah's home town. She claimed she could provide an alibi for Manoj. However, she did admit that Manoj had great difficulty in accepting her social interactions with her fellow male charity workers. 'My husband often fought with me over this issue', she told a major British newspaper.

Sarah's mother arrived from the UK a few days after the murder. Sarah was released from custody soon after and Manoj followed. It was rumoured amongst the local community that Sarah's mother had paid a substantial bride to the police for both their releases. Was it a case that Sarah couldn't live without Manoj and told her mother that her release was conditional on his?

As I watched the television coverage where Sarah repeatedly defended her husband's actions, it was clear they were intimately involved. Ant and I distanced ourselves for our own protection. To date there has never been any arrests for the murder of David Huntley in India. The file was closed but later reopened. Sarah and Manoj left India a short time later and returned to her home. There is an extradition order out for their arrest should they try to enter India again. Is it an unsolved case of honour?

I recently tried to find out more information by contacting a couple of well-connected people to fill in the many gaps that remain. As the case wasn't solved, all the police case notes were destroyed which happens often when there is pressure from their superiors.

In a world that is raw, full of contradictions and flaws, India, as one of the world's most populist countries has very limited resources to ever bring justice to David's family, something that haunts me every day.

LIBERUM MORTIS

LR JOHNSON

*T*he roar of the wind was so loud that from the front door Larry barely heard her scream.

A vicious sandstorm scoured the adobe desert homestead. Solar panels and satellite dishes rattled as sand whipped against metal. On the horizon, the tempest screamed through husks of abandoned aircraft. The wind and sand stripped the carcass of a wild dog to the bone in minutes.

Larry's broom clattered to the floor as he raced to Mrs Sanchez's cry.

Larry knew her family had left to secure livestock from the sandstorm and been forced to shelter with the animals. Mrs Sanchez, the property owner, had permitted four travellers to take refuge with her. First was Inadra Kinos, then separately, on her heels came the other three: Joe, jack-of-all-illegal-trades, desert huntress Khiradi, and finally Larry Ross.

In the foyer Larry crossed paths with Joe. Joe had one hand clamped over his nose and mouth, with red spots on his shirt, and where Larry headed to the dining room Joe hurried towards the guest rooms.

Larry passed Joe in the foyer, as Joe headed in the other direction, toward the guest rooms with one hand clamped over his mouth and nose.

Larry flung open the dining room door to find Mrs Sanchez standing over the source of her dismay.

Inadra Kinos, aircraft-salvage operator, infamous member of the largest criminal cabal on the continent -and Larry's current target- lay in a pool of spreading blood.

Crouched over her like a vulture, the dark-skinned Khiradi pressed bloody fingers to Inadra's wrist.

Larry yanked Khiradi away. 'What have you done?' He snapped.

'Nothing!' She held her hands up. 'I was trying to help.'

'Well, I'm the Detective so I'll be taking over now.' He flashed a badge and stepped over the victim. He nudged aside a fallen vase and crouched to press a finger to Inadra's throat. He pursed his lips. 'She's gone.' He rolled the body forward. Khiradi had packed a headscarf against it, which he removed. A neat incision two inches wide revealed they'd gone for her kidney.

He shook his head. 'Knife wound.'

Khiradi chewed her lip. 'Her desert-salvage team will kill us when the storm ends and they catch up.'

Mrs Sanchez scowled. 'She wronged a lot of people...' She turned on Khiradi. 'But how dare you do this in my house!'

'I came when you screamed!' Khiradi countered.

Larry let the body drop and stood. 'Hold still Miss Khir...?'

She rolled her eyes. 'I told you when you arrived, Khiradi. Kee, radi.'

He patted her down for a weapon and found none. Mrs Sanchez volunteered a show of her trouser pockets. Nothing of use.

Inadra's' team was notoriously violent. He had to work quickly.

Mrs Sanchez had left a dusty trail of footprints from the kitchen into the dining room, but it wasn't enough to go on. He needed something more.

The big brass wall clock chimed the hour.

Khiradi pointed at the coat rack by the door to the yard. 'One of these dining-room sand-cloaks is gone. Maybe the killer fled outside.'

'Maybe,' Mrs Sanchez agreed, 'But did you know Joe is Inadras ex-husband, and I saw them arguing earlier. Where did he go?'

Joe was in the bathroom. Built like a wrestler with brawler's scars, he was scrubbing blood from his hands and face. Detective Larry met Joe's eyes in the mirror, and Joe stopped mid-action. 'What?' he demanded. 'Ain't never seen a man with a bloody nose before?'

The Detective scoffed. 'Plenty, most coinciding with murder. She punch you when you attacked her?'

Joe frowned. 'Murder? Who?'

'Inadra.'

Joe sagged against the sink, face white. 'No. No!' He wiped his stubbled face, tore his bloody shirt off, and hurled it into the bin as though it were to blame. 'I told her working with the cabal would get her killed.' He took a deep breath, sniffed, and scrubbed his eyes. 'Where is she?'

Before the big man could stop him the Detective grabbed Joe's backpack and emptied it onto the bed. Illegal tech, but nothing even close to a stabbing weapon.

'You think I killed her?' Joe asked.

'Where were you, Joe?' Larry pressed.

Joe snatched the pack, crammed his belongings back in, and yanked on a fresh shirt. 'Working out. We crossed paths, remember? Follow the bloodstain.'

Larry did. The maroon stains led from the guest rooms they'd been assigned on arrival, to the foyer, and stopped abruptly at the stairs, far from the dining room door. The coppery scent was legitimate. Joe had an alibi.

Larry turned and crossed his arms. 'Mrs Sanchez says you were arguing earlier.'

'Mrs Sanchez can mind her own.'

She snorted, 'All these years you've let everybody remotely associated with you know 'If you can't have her, nobody can!'

Larry raised an eyebrow. 'Joe, you followed her into the desert to...?'

Joe shrugged. 'Heard she was out of chances. Might leave the cabal and give me another go. You know, reconcile.'

Larry pursed his lips. 'She turned you down, and you killed her in a moment of anger, right?'

Joe grabbed Larry's shirt in a meaty fist. 'I didn't kill her. Got it? Can't reconcile with a dead woman. I get bloody noses when the weather's irritating, you know, like a sandstorm? But that don't make me a killer.' He shoved Larry backward. 'So, Mr. Detective, do your bloody job, all right?'

Detective Larry wasn't as tall as Joe, but he'd put down larger, more violent men. Larry's boss was more terrifying. He'd had a string of bad luck lately, and this job had been given to him on a platter. If he didn't take care of it properly his boss would kill him. If Inadra's team caught up, he didn't have a perpetrator to show them, they would burn the homestead to the ground with Larry in it. But, Joe had a point- this wouldn't close the case.

Larry smoothed his shirt front without breaking eye contact.

Joe looked at Khiradi, and snapped 'Why you even asking me squat when she's got blood on her clothes?'

'I tried to help her!' she protested.

'Yeah right, help your finances more like. I recognise that tribal scarring on your temples! You're a bounty hunter after Inadra!'

'Idiot!' Khiradi advanced a step. 'I needed her alive!'

Joe snorted. 'No pulse no pay? I guess you screwed up.'

'Where were you, Khiradi?' the Detective asked.

'The library next to the dining room. Mrs Sanchez was there before me!'

Larry sniffed. 'Unless you left the room and returned when she screamed.'

'I didn't have bloody hands until I tried to apply pressure to the wound!' she cried.

Larry squinted at her scars. 'Your tribe doesn't allow bounty hunting unless there's been a significant injustice.'

She clenched her jaw. 'It's personal.'

'It always is. Tell me.'

'No.'

He waited, let the silent void stretch fat and uncomfortable, and finally, she groaned.

'She scavenged on our land without permission.' She spat. 'People died.'

Joe leaned against the doorframe. 'Mrs Sanchez knows a little something about that don't you old girl?'

'Shut up Joe.'

'Didn't get any work-related death compensation did you?' he pushed.

The older woman's face went pink with anger. 'She lured my son to work for her with big talk and big pay-cheques that he never got to spend!'

Larry turned to face her in one smooth motion. 'Is that why you killed her, Mrs Sanchez?'

'What!?'

Khiradi's face lit up. 'You came from outside! You left sandy footprints from the kitchen!'

'I didn't kill her!'

Larry crowed, 'You couldn't resist! Inadra here, with no allies, and two enemies? You attacked her in the dining room, then took a cloak from the rack, disposed of the murder weapon outside, and came back through the kitchen, but forgot about your sandy shoes, giving you away.'

'Lies!' she cried.

Joe slammed his fist into the doorframe. 'Let's go have a lookie eh?'

The missing dining room cloak did not hang on the kitchen coat rack. One, however, was covered in fresh dust, which Detective Larry squinted, and nodded at.

He turned back to the elderly woman. 'So you were outside.'

'Oh for goodness.... Fine! I was locking the cellar.'

'From outside?' Larry pressed.

She threw her arms up. 'Every time vagabonds like you beg shelter in the storms, you back up a vehicle to the outside cellar loading door and empty it as you leave. It was the first chance I had to use my nice big new lock. That's why I've got dusty shoes! Happy?'

Larry narrowed his eyes. 'Marginally.'

Joe pointed into the storm. 'Let's go look.'

Khiradi nodded. 'A sand-cloak will give us a few minutes protection.'

The Detective chewed the inside of his cheek. That wasn't what he'd been hoping for. If he didn't agree he might lose control of the situation. He needed a moment to think, away from scrutiny.

He summoned a fake smile. 'Well, I have to take a leak. Let's meet up in the dining room in a bit.'

They looked a little nonplussed, but Larry didn't care. He hurried to the bathroom, closed the door, and sagged against it with a sigh.

Surely he could crack this case. Three people had followed Inadra across the desert. She sought shelter in the house of a forgotten enemy.

Mrs Sanchez had come from the kitchen with sandstorm-sandy shoes.

A sand-cloak was missing from the dining room. There wasn't an extra in the kitchen, but one was used. The cloaks only protected the wearer from a sandstorm for a few minutes, so the perpetrator must have returned to the house. Anyone outside without a cloak would be dead.

Maybe Mrs Sanchez had been locking the cellar.

Joe had motive but didn't have the opportunity. His bloody nose alibied him. He and Inadra, two separate pools of blood, with no connection.

Khiradi had been hands-on with the body, but he'd found no weapon, not even improvised.

He closed his eyes and sighed. The storm was forecast to end today, but it was still too intense. The perpetrator couldn't escape yet but Larry was running out of time.

He glanced at his wrist and swore.

He hurried back into his guestroom. He tore back his sheets and blankets, got on hands and knees, and searched under the bed. He upended his belongings, dug through them, then crammed them back in the bags. He swore again and kicked the bed.

Sweat stung the skin of his wrist.

This could be a problem.

Mrs Sanchez shouted again, and Larry resisted the urge to add to the body count as he stormed out of his bedroom and slammed the door.

'The body's gone!' she cried, pointing at the bloodstain on the dining-room floor.

Enraged, Detective Larry turned on them. 'Are you screwing with me? I excused myself for five minutes! Where's the body?'

A new round of infighting ensued. Larry stuck his fingers in his mouth and whistled to silence them. 'We'll search the house. Split up-'

Khiradi scowled. 'No. All together. There's a murder among us, remember.'

Larry pursed his lips. 'Fine. Let's go.'

Bedrooms, bedsits, bathrooms, washrooms, and all other places were searched. Under the Detective's supervision, Joe rummaged around in the cellar while Khiradi ferreted through a pile of hessian bags by the pumpkins.

'Nothing,' she huffed.

Joe kicked a loose pumpkin. 'She ain't here either.'

'There's just one more thing to do then,' Khiradi posited. 'What we planned- go look outside.'

Joe and Mrs Sanchez nodded, and Larry forced a smile.

The storm threw curtains of sand through the dining room doorway as Khiradi and Joe, shrouded in sand-cloaks, ventured out to shuffle around in the sand drifts.

Larry scowled through the dining-room window. He couldn't go outside. The masks of the other dining-room cloaks had been ripped out, and Joe claimed the only one from the kitchen that would fit Larry. All Larry could do was supervise from inside with Mrs Sanchez.

Joe pointed at the cellar door. Khiradi nodded and came closer to shout that it was padlocked. They pawed through knee-high sand drifts, searching for buried answers. Joe got to the well and found its cap blown away. He looked inside. 'Not here!' he shouted, then he stopped, bent, and from the sand drift against the well-wall retrieved something.

Detective Larry's lips compressed into a tight line. He'd missed it.

Khiradi and Joe returned inside and inspected their prize: a bloody hunting knife inside a plastic bag. The bag was blood-smeared inside and wrapped tight around the handle up to the hilt.

Larry inspected the weapon, turned it over in his hands.

He turned to face Mrs Sanchez. 'Very clever. Stab her with a plastic bag over your hand to stay clean. Then pull it over the knife to keep all the blood inside the bag.'

Joe's mouth fell open, but Khiradi spoiled Larry's triumph.

'What's the time Detective Ross?'

He frowned. 'Excuse me?'

'You haven't gone outside since the murder, have you?' she pressed.

His skin went clammy. 'I am the one asking questions,' he reminded them.

Khiradi looked down. 'Take your shoes off.'

292

Larry stiffened. 'I am the law enforcement here.'

Joe frowned, clenched his fists. Every knuckle cracked. 'Take 'em off or I will.'

Reluctantly, Larry did, and sand showered from the inside of the boots onto the floorboards.

Mrs Sanchez muttered at Joe and Khiradi nodded slowly. 'Now show me your wrists.'

Larry's shaking hands fumbled for his handcuffs. 'You're all under arres—!'

Joe tore them from his grip, and Larry went cold.

Khiradi with hands on her hips. 'You didn't look at Inadra's hands, Mr. Ross—#'

'Detective,' he cut her off.

'There was blood under her nails.' she continued. 'I believe, Mr. Ross, she saw you coming, reflected in that.' She pointed at the brass wall clock. 'Inadra saw and grabbed at you. Scratched you, maybe tore off your watch.'

Cold sweat broke out, and Larry's heart kicked up a gear. The damn watch he hadn't been able to find. 'I'm not the one under investigation!'

Khiradi raised an eyebrow. 'So if we search near this fallen vase we won't find it?'

Joe dragged aside the little table where the small vase had stood, and there on the floor was the detective's watch.

Khiradi nudged it with her boot. 'Expensive for a government employee. Genuine, unlike that badge of yours I'd guess.'

She turned back to Larry. 'You used the bag trick, stabbed her, got scratched, and lost your watch. But before you could finish the job you heard me in the library. So, you fled through this door in the missing cloak. I think you threw the knife at the well and missed. Then you circled around to the front door, shed the cloak, and swept clean your boots to hurry here to the dining room.'

Larry saw Joe disappear from the corner of his eye and his whole body tensed. He scoffed, 'That's not my watch.'

'Show us your wrist.' Khiradi countered.

Larry held up both hands. 'Let's just everyone calm down.'

Joe returned. 'A filthy coat at the front door, and mess on the floor.'

Steel-sprung nerves launched Larry at the outer door.

A mountain collided with him. Arms like iron wrestled him into a grip so tight he couldn't move. He was handcuffed to a chair with his own cuffs.

Khiradi yanked up Larry's sleeve to reveal deep, fresh scratches.

'I'll bury you,' Larry growled. To be undone by some desert brat set his flesh on fire.

Khiradi gave him a tight, sweet smile. 'Others have tried, all will fail. And no one will be burying Inadra, not yet.'

His ire faltered. 'What?'

'She wasn't dead,'

Larry clenched his jaw. 'How?' he demanded.

Khiradi crouched to be eye-to-eye. 'She was in shock. During your absence, I fetched a doona from my room and rolled her onto it to prevent drag marks. I stole a med-kit, and Mrs Sanchez' vodka to take care of the wound.'

'Where did you hide her?' Larry demanded.

'In the cellar... under the hessian bags by the pumpkins.'

Mrs Sanchez gasped. 'That's why you searched so thoroughly there.'

Larry frowned, 'Why save her? For the bounty?'

'I'm appointed to bring her to justice, not execute her. A dead woman cannot learn, or change.'

Joe snorted a laugh. 'She'll never change.'

'I can if you keep my survival a secret, Joe.'

All eyes swung to the doorway between the dining room and kitchen.

Inadra gave them a weak smile. 'Detective. Nice disguise, Larry. It took me a while to recognise you were today's cabal hitman.' The pale woman leaned heavily against the door frame. 'I've been thinking.' She took a shaky step into the room and grabbed a chair to steady herself. 'Many want me dead. You were all only in the desert because you were after me. Khiradi's tribe is a merciful one. I wonder if Inadra shouldn't die, and a new me surrender.'

Khiradi warned her, 'You will pay for your crimes.'

'Good enough for me,' said Mrs Sanchez with a jerk of her head.

Inadra queried, 'By death?'

Khiradi pondered. 'Perhaps.'

Larry shook his head vigorously. 'If she lives our boss'll kill me instead!'

'Oh hush,' Inadra winced. 'I figured he had a hit on me. Why do you think I travelled separately from my team? They'd cash me in any day. Tell my team you killed me, fed me to the pigs.'

She took off her watch and pulled a ring on a chain from around her neck. Joe gasped. She tucked them into Larry's shirt pocket. 'Wedding ring and SmartWatch. Every bit of blackmail I own is on files in this. I'd die before parting with it, until now. There was no use ditching them without a good fake death. Use these as proof, split the bounty with the team.'

Larry deflated in relief.

Khiradi narrowed her eyes. 'I can't let you go, Inadra.'

Joe straightened. 'I won't let you take her.'

'Joe, shut up.' Inadra let herself slide gingerly into a chair, one hand to her bandaged side. 'Khiradi, I surrender. You saved my life once already. That indicates good odds. Joe, come with me.'

The big man melted to her side, and she let him take one of her hands in his.

Larry could hear the ferocity of the storm lessening as the gloomy light brightened. He looked at them all in turn. 'So, as long as I tell our boss I killed you, and we pretend you're dead, we all get what we want?'

Inadra smiled. 'In death, I am free.'

TWICE A KILLER

DIANE K EDWARDS

Suzanna knew Nigel was watching her. He was always watching her.

Still, she didn't look up, she didn't have to. He wore his navy-blue jacket around the house. He was a debonair chap, her husband.

Suzanna Jones' last days were spent sitting at the kitchen table. She always sat at the kitchen table these days. Her eyes downcast darted back and forth across the timber grain. She ran her fingers over the tiny, new scratch marks. It had been her mum's, and before that her grandma's table. Suzanna sighed heavily.

When Nigel left the house for work each day, he wore that same jacket at his office desk, on the bus to and from Paignton Town Centre, even relaxing at home.

He was known for his navy-blue jacket.

He always placed his left hand in his pocket. Never did he place his right hand in his pocket. He was left-handed you see, so there was never an occasion for him to change his ways.

Nigel was watching her again. She wished he wouldn't. It was bad enough she felt wretched under his scrutiny.

Murphy and Bow Accountants had furloughed Suzanna from her job as a senior bookkeeper . Mr Murphy himself had beckoned her into his office to deliver the distressing news.

'Suzanna my dear,' he drawled, 'Suzanna.' He stopped.

What? Has he second guessed his recollection of my name?

'Suzanna,' he began again.

She wished he'd get on with delivering, what she was sure would be devastating and life changing news.

'My dear, it is with regret that I inform you are not required at work, until further notice. What this means is, of course we will pay you what we owe, however the firm cannot keep you here while this dreadful pandemic is rife through our town.' Suzanna had mentally switched off. *What will Nigel think?* she thought.

Mr Murphy stood in front of her, his eyes solemn and imploring.

What now?

'Suzanna?'

Mr Murphy said nothing more so she stood up and walked out of his office. On her desk was a letter that explained everything. *Mr Murphy could have saved his breath.*

Suzanna caught the usual bus home. After putting her work satchel behind the door, she sat down on the same chair as always.

In fact, she hadn't really moved from this spot except to go to bed.

Suzanna knew her husband worried about her eating. With his left hand in his pocket and the other cupping his chin, he studied his wife. Normalcy around the house was something she craved. Unfortunately, normalcy was something that would elude them, she feared.

Nigel left for work, as he did every day. *He* wasn't sent home from work. Oh no, apparently, they couldn't do without him. How was his role as a HR advisor so critical he became a 'key worker'?

Nigel stopped in front of her. She knew he wanted her to eat, or drink her coffee, even just a little.

Suzanna shook her head as Nigel tried to place a spoonful of food into her mouth. He replaced the spoon in the bowl and lifted her coffee mug instead.

'C'mon Suzi, the doctor said you need to eat, at least have a little coffee.' Not wanting a scene, Suzanna took the cup from him and held it to her lips. 'There's my girl,' he said.

Suzanna couldn't understand it, but the coffee always tasted bitter, and she always, without fail, felt sick once she had drunk it. She dared not run to the toilet though, for fear of arousing suspicion and chagrin from her beloved husband. He had previously accused her of bulimia and a dash for the toilet would surely give him the impression it was that which made her want to vomit. A dutiful wife would surely behave, she proffered a weak smile of gratitude for his caring behaviour.

Nigel was appeased, for now. She knew he would go to work a happy man. Once sure he was safely seated on his bus, Suzanna rose from the table and reached to the back of the highest cupboard in the kitchen. There among the 'odds and sods' were her 'little helpers'. Some years ago, Suzanna had procured, by dubious means, the dangerous relaxants. She had remembered her 'little helpers' the day she came home in a flood of tears, wretched and abandoned, and quite literally, useless.

Each day, she waited until Nigel left the house before she reached into the brown glass jar to retrieve her 'sanity saviours' as she affectionately called the little yellow capsules. Each day, she carefully broke open the capsule and poured the contents into her mouth, washed it down with the remainder of the coffee Nigel insisted, she drink. He would be so proud of her. Once the granules reached her internal system, it didn't take long until her whole body fell into a state of total relaxation, and she could rest her weary mind for a few hours, head on hands at the kitchen table, until Nigel returned.

Nigel thought long and hard about what he was doing. He knew the chances of being caught were slim. After all, the drug he was placing in Suzanna's food and coffee would surely end his miserable wife's life sooner rather than later. She had changed into a wailing shell of a woman.

His own role, was of course, of the utmost importance, and his boss Amelia, saw to it he need not stay at home for a minute longer than necessary. The relationship between himself and Amelia had blossomed of late. She was a little older than him, and outranked him as his boss.

However, such an appetite for sex was something he had never encountered before. The steamy, passionate sessions became more frequent. Amelia liked to leave him little notes. Notes that suggested different positions, different 'toys' they could use to pleasure her, different experiences for them both. It made Nigel quite hot under the collar, and he couldn't wait to get to work to see what Amelia's demands for him were going to be. He had been spending a little too much time and money on his mistress, but he pushed those feelings of guilt to one side with ease. Once Suzanna was dead, he could spend her life insurance on indulging Amelia.

Nigel thought Suzanna's time must come to an end soon. After all, the liquid arsenic he was giving her was considered deadly, as long as it was meted out over a long period of time. The prolonged consumption resulting in large quantities being ingested, and death.

Suzanna was very sad. She loved Nigel, but she didn't trust him. Especially now. Night after night, Nigel came home late. 'Busy at work', was his usual response when she bothered to enquire. That part of his job wasn't a lie. She knew about Amelia. It wasn't rocket science to determine who Nigel was having sex with. An exploratory journey into the right hand pocket of Nigel's navy-blue jacket, the one he never used, revealed secret, dirty notes left by Amelia. Notes that suggested all sorts of things. She knew Nigel was having sex with his boss. She had known for some time. The day she found the first note literally took her breath away. *How could he do this to me!*

Suzanna decided to exact her revenge.

She would not confront him. She would not ever let him know that she knew.

Suzanna hatched a plan. She started writing notes of her own that rivalled Amelia's. Her notes were not of a sexual nature, they were much more sinister. Suzanna's notes became a diary of sorts of how Nigel was killing her with the contents of little yellow capsules; the shell of which were also placed in Nigel's right-hand pocket of his navy-blue jacket.

She wasn't sure of how long it would take for those yellow pills to kill her, but kill her they would.

The next day, Nigel could not rouse Suzanna, and as a suitably distraught husband, he called the police. The detective questioned Nigel. The time of death was established as being between 8am and 8:30am that very morning. Nigel had returned home at 8:45pm that night to find his wife in her usual position; head slumped on her arms at the kitchen table. The detective believed the cause of death to be an overdose. 'Were you aware your wife was taking drugs of any sort?' asked the detective.

Nigel shook his head. He knew the drug he had given her daily was undetectable in Suzanna's bloodstream. The detective seemed to accept Nigel wasn't aware, after all an autopsy would surely pinpoint the cause.

As Nigel slumped his own head onto the opposite end of the kitchen table, the detective took the opportunity to gently lift Suzanna's head. As he did, he noticed the scratches in the old table. They appeared relatively new. On closer inspection the detective realised the scratches spelled out a couple of words: *Right pocket.*

The detective looked over at Nigel and said, 'Would you mind standing for a moment?'

Nigel heaved himself to his feet, as if the grief was too heavy to bear the load of his frame. The detective noted Nigel's hand was in the left pocket of his navy-blue jacket.

'Please empty your jacket pockets sir?'

Nigel obliged by producing a folded hanky, a bus pass, and a couple of coins from his left pocket.

'And the right one sir!'

Nigel's right hand went awkwardly to the right pocket, the one he never used. He went pale as he withdrew handwritten notes that exposed his affair with Amelia.

The detective read the first couple and glanced at Nigel. 'Quite demanding this Amelia person.'

It was a flat statement that Nigel was not expected to address. 'Did you love your wife Nigel, or did you want her out of the way?'

Nigel hung his head. He thought to answer with, *His wife was his life, and how could the detective think otherwise.* But refrained as he felt something else in his pocket. His hand wrapped itself around a small collection of plastic. The detective grabbed the contents from Nigel's hands. The two men stared at the empty pill capsules.

As the detective gathered the incriminating evidence, time stood still. The detective looked directly into Nigel's eyes and said, 'Nigel Jones, I am placing you under arrest for the murder of your wife Suzanna Jones.'

He was confused. How could this be? The drug was untraceable, and the autopsy hadn't been performed yet. Nigel was not aware of the diary-like notes Suzanna had herself written.

The proof of Suzanna's untimely death was in the pocket of the Navy Blue Jacket.

CONTRIBUTORS

JACK HEATH wrote his first novel in high school and sold it to a publisher at age 18. He's now the award-winning author of thirty-seven books for children and adults, which have been translated into eight languages and optioned for  film and TV. He lives on Ngunnawal Land with his wife, their two children, and several intimidating chickens. His new crime novel is Kill Your Brother.

You can find Jack at

Jack Heath (jackheathwriter.com)
Jack Heath (@JackHeathWriter) / Twitter
Jack Heath | Scholastic Australia

CHARMAINE CLANCY is an Australian author and educator.

Her works include novels for kids and teens, including the best-selling, *My Zombie Dog*. Charmaine also writes short stories for grown-ups and is published in various anthologies. She's even won awards for some of her stories.

Charmaine is very passionate about helping students who have struggled with literacy and inspires them to create their own stories they can be proud of. As well as teaching at high school, Charmaine presents holiday writing workshops for children of all ages and hosts the annual *Rainforest Writing Retreat* for grown-up writers.

All her books are written with humour and dogs. Life is better with both.

You can find Charmaine at

charmaineclancy.com

Instagram

ROGER BRAY'S life has been an endless adventure. Serving in the Navy, fighting in wars, and serving as a Police Officer. Each one of these have experiences brought him to the catalyst to write again.

Most recently, he was medically retried after being seriously injured while protecting a woman in a domestic violence situation. Roger fell into a deep pit of depression and rejection. Giving truth to the oft said saying, when one door closes, another opens. He now has a bachelor and master degree that has relit his passion for writing in a way that he hadn't felt since high school. He has always loved writing, putting words onto a page and bringing characters to life.

Roger has three books published, The Picture, Psychosis and Blood Ribbon, all psychological thrillers, with another on the way.

You can find Roger at

rogerbraybooks.com
Goodreads

CHRIS RADGE, is an Australian novelist based in Brisbane, Queensland where she writes fulltime and is a part-time stay-at-home NanMa.

Her published works include Anthologies, 'Smithy', in 'Short Stories of Mystery and Murder, 'Tinsel Fructify' in 'Short Stories of Forests and Fantasy', 'Ghost Writer' in 'Short Stories of Ghosts and Graves', 'Frankenstein's Legacy' in 'Short stories of Science and Space', and 'Feathered Hooves' in 'From the Edge' WAG.

Currently engaged in writing an Octology of YA Urban Fantasy books called The Elder Scale Series, and two Children's picture books Sneezes and Where the Lost Things Go.

She is a member of Queensland Writers Centre, BWG, Booklinks, Australian Fairy Tale Society, and looks forward to the Rainforest Writing Retreat every year catering morning and afternoon tea. With a 300 page recipe book called 'Nothin to it' full of easy fifteen minute recipes.

Chris is the editor/organizer of this anthology, and has loved each journey from beginning to end. She loves being busy. Lucky hey.

You can find Chris at

chrisradge.com
Amazon

GINA PINTO is a writer, editor, researcher,  and the recipient of an Award by the Consulate General of Portugal in Sydney for her nonfiction book *Partly Portuguese Almost Australian*.

Her past includes an honours degree in Languages and Linguistics, a job as Graduations Officer and *Student Guide* Online Content Editor at UNSW, and an MA (Writing) from Swinburne University of Technology.

At present, she has stories in several Australian Anthologies.

The future offers the opportunity to publish her own collection of short stories, a PhD, and another nonfiction book.

You can find Gina at

ginapinto.com
partlyportugueseproductions.com

EMMA RENNISON is a British-Australian author with one bionic hip living in Melbourne. She originally satisfied her need to write through a career in PR and communications, specialising in forestry and conservation. During this time  she ran campaigns about rare birds, forest fires and - the most controversial of all subjects - dog mess.

Enticed by her husband's vow to get her a cat if she emigrated, she hung up her wellies to move from the UK to Melbourne in 2008. It took seven years to fulfil that promise but in the meantime, she swapped her real hip for a prosthetic one and became mum to two beautiful children.

Her first published story, *No Guts, No Glory*, won the Editor's Choice Award 2020 in the RWR anthology, Short Stories of Science and Space. She was also runner up in The Burbidge Prize 2021 and shortlisted for the Newcastle Short Story Award 2021.

You can find Emma at

emmarennison.com
@emmajrennison

DR MEGAN STEELE, is a medical researcher who is more used to publishing research articles than short stories. Lately she has been rediscovering her childhood love of writing poetry and fiction. *Unsolved* is her first poem to be published.

You can find Megan at

meganleighsteele@outlook.com

When **HOLLY SYDELLE** isn't living in the jungle releasing rehabilitated sloths back into the wild, or helping save an endangered lizard out in the middle of nowhere in Western Australia, she spends her spare time writing fiction.

Soon to become a doctor of biology, Holly has a love for communication, from presenting at international science conferences, to publishing in scientific journals. Her joy for communication expands into a love of storytelling, a skill she has honed through Reading Creatively/Writing Creatively studies at the University of Western Australia, and workshop learning such as at the Rainforest Writing Retreat in Queensland, Australia.

Holly's scientific background gives her a unique and authentic perspective, particularly within the science-fiction genre, which is a perfect mix of her two favourite things: science and creative writing.

You can find Holly at

hollysydelle.com

JC LESLEY shares her house in the Brisbane 'burbs with, Boris her spoilt princess parrot, Elektra the rainbow lorikeet and her Dutch husband. In between sitting on health committees as consumer rep, she finds herself procrastinating over the second draft of her first novel with a blind investigator and her police guide dog Spike.

Before she went blind, Janelle had an international operatic career with the Australian and Frankfurt Operas. She is a media tart and is a regular conference presenter, with more than one hundred of her, arts, disability and health articles published.

She's the current National Champion in blind archery, and has won awards and short stories published in anthologies.

JC Lesley runs her own entertainment and production agency. She has recorded three solo CDs, boasts an extensive cocktail bar, and before covid, loved to travel overseas at least once a year to perform.

You can find Janelle at

JC Lesley Author | Facebook
Salubrious Productions

ALEXIA LEIGH has read so many books it has turned her brain. Growing up in the small country town of Bundanoon Alexia spent many hours in front of a roaring fire devouring whatever she could find to read. She now lives in North  Queensland. Alexia writes short stories, poetry, prose and hopes soon to turn her attention to her first Novel. She has contributed to multiple anthologies, these and her personal collections can be found on her website.

You can find Alexia at

alexialeighwrites.com

Instagram

ZZ ANDERS is an introvert and 'chocolatarian' (it's not only a word, it's a religion) who loves to read and currently dabbles at writing whenever time can be stolen. As with most writers (or wannabe writers) ZZ is hoping that one day,  writing will be a fulltime occupation. Until then ZZ must survive working a real job where often mistaken for an extrovert as ZZ tries to fake it through human interaction.

You can find ZZ at

zzanders.com

ROBIN MARTIN THOMAS is an author and teacher, who writes both adult and young adult romance. Originally from Canada, she now lives in Brisbane, Australia.

Her publications in YA sci-fi romance series are The Alien Chronicles includes *My Alien, The Alien Within, and Once an Alien.*

Her publications in adult books are the Short Sweetz series include High Stakes and Bonjour Cherie.

She is a member of Write-Links, for children's and YA writers, she has also attended many RWR workshops over the years. Robin also connects with writers and readers on her author's Facebook page or website.

You can find Robin at

Robin Martin Thomas Author | Facebook
robinmartinthomas.com

CHRISTINE BETTS is an Australian writer who left her heart in Paris years ago. Christine trained in education and the visual arts and spent many years creating giftware and art for interior designers.

A keen traveller, her first two novels are set in France and two works-in-progress are set in California and England. She is passionate about writing strong female characters, yoga, animal rights, and her family.

You can find Christine at

writerpainter.com

KATE KELSEN has received recognition from literary awards around Australia, including the Cancer Council Literary Awards and the Alan Marshall Short Story Award. At twenty-one, Kate published her debut novel, The Wilted Rose, a novel inspired by the true story of a Brisbane family's experience with mental illness in the 1960s.

In 2016, Kate published *The New Neighbors*, and *Paid to Dance: Stripping Past and Present*. In her writing, Kate explored various human experiences and perspectives, using her writing to help to share people's stories in the wider community.

You can find Kate at

katekelsen.com

FRANK PREM has been a storytelling poet for forty years. When not writing or reading his poetry to an audience, he fills his time by working as a psychiatric nurse.

He has been published in magazines, e-zines and anthologies, in Australia and in a number of other countries, and has both performed and recorded his work as 'spoken word'.

Frank has published several collections of free verse poetry – Small Town Kid (2018), Devil In The Wind (2019), and The New Asylum (2019). and A Love Poetry Trilogy (Walk Away Silver Heart; A Kiss for the Worthy; and Rescue and Redemption) in 2020, as well as a two part picture book – A Beechworth Bakery Bears e-Book and A Beechworth Bakery Bears e-Book (too) and Pebbles to Poems (2020) an e-book sample collection which includes extracts from each of his previous published works to act as a showcase for readers.

He and his wife live in the beautiful township of Beechworth in northeast Victoria (Australia). Get in touch below. He loves to chat with readers.

You can find Frank at

FrankPrem.com
Amazon

VICTORIA VANSTONE is a British-born mum, writer, and alcohol-free living advocate. She lives on The Sunshine Coast with three noisy children, a very patient husband, and a rather confused dog. Vic used writing as a form of therapy after deciding  to go tea-total in 2018 and her blog, drunkmummysobermummy. com, is a comedic and brutally honest insight onto her transition from party-girl to mum.

Vic loves writing about her zig zaggy journey to sobriety to help others understand they are worthy of seeking professional support. Victoria has written a book on sober parenting which she hopes to get published in 2022. When she isn't at her computer, or at the studio recording her podcast 'Sober Awkward' you can find her hiding from her children in the Aldi carpark or plunging her fork into a gigantic slice of chocolate brownie at her local café. After being inspired at The Rainforest Writing Retreat, Victoria decided to give crime writing a stab in the dark. This is her first fictional piece.

You can find Victoria at

drunkmummysobermummy.com

DEBBIE KAHL has dreamt of writing fiction since she was a teenager obsessed with the Sweet Dreams books that cluttered her bookshelf. Despite an ongoing battle with author imposter syndrome, Debbie has continued to write contemporary  fiction for tweens, teens and adults winning the inaugural Book Links QLD Mentorship and the CYA Conference Unpublished Chapter Book for middle grade readers, along the way.

When she's not writing, you can find Debbie teaching English and Japanese at a high school in Brisbane, where she finds lots of inspirations for her stories. Debbie is also an integral part of the CYA Conference team, which aims to provide professional development opportunities for young adult and children's writers in Australia.

You can find Debbie at

debbiekahl.wordpress.com
Linkedin

GEORGINA BALLANTINE, is a Sydney-based editor and author of speculative fiction for adults and children. The opening of her novel-in-progress, *Fire* — an alternate history, myth-laden tale of a girl whose skin burns to the touch —  won the 2017 CYA Conference Award for Young Adult fiction. Georgina also writes commissioned web content and articles on a range of commercial topics.

Georgina has over twenty years' experience in the publishing industry as a freelance editor and writer. She co-manages the Australian Science Fiction and Fantasy Writers' Association, convenes a speculative fiction writers group and has held positions on the Children's Book Council of Australia and Australian Fairy Tale Society committees.

You can find Georgina at

www.georginaballantine.com

LEA SCOTT has published three psychological thrillers, The Ned Kelly Game (2009), Eclipsed (2010) and One for All (2013). She acts as Chair of the Queensland Writers Centre and mentors new writers under their 'Writer's Surgery' program.

She has facilitated writing workshops and seminars and has appeared at writing festivals throughout Australia and overseas. She has acted as associate editor for a Special Issue of *TEXT Journal of Writing*. Lea is currently undertaking a PhD in Creative Writing and has also published academic research on writing about trauma and the transformative potential of creative writing.

You can find Lea at

www.leascott.com

DANIELLE HUGHES is a busy mother of four young kids, living in the south east suburbs of Melbourne and loves writing whenever she can. Her published books include The Lost Unicorn, Mystica: Book 1 and several short stories in  various anthologies. She is currently working on Book 3 of the Mystica trilogy, a fantasy adventure series for older kids aged ten and up.

Danielle can be found at

fourmoonspublishing.com

Blog Post Interview

PAUL SMITH is recently retired and started writing his first novel Walk with the Tiger, not long after. This is the first adventure/thriller book in the Jack Harrigan series set in the seventies. The second and third book in the series are in editing.  There will be four more Jack Harrigan stories after these.

Paul has also written two short stories, *Monty & Tomatso*. He is also featured in Oz Tales, Murder on the Mountain in Short Stories of Mystery and Murder, and Yowie on the Mountain in Short Stories of Forest and Fantasy. Paul's one and only Bush poem is Jack the Dancer, set in a country pub back in the 1930's.

Paul is part of the Rainforest Writing Retreat's crew assisting where he is needed from driving buses to making sure everybody has settled in to their accommodation.

You can find Paul at

PaulSmithAuthor.com

MARIA PARENTI is always up for an adventure with its dose of adrenaline. She has jumped out of a perfectly good plane and white-water rafted down a raging Tully River. When the chance came to get blood on her hands, for this anthology, she chose a knife – a fantasy knife to be exact. This is her fourth adult poetry story published with RWR. When each year's theme arises, she has hesitated/baulked/back peddled, yet through the supportive, nurturing environment of the three-day writing retreat she has explored these genres beyond expectations.

The freedom to write poetry stories has disengaged her brain from the constriction of formal structures. It has allowed her mind to fly with wings across her scenes as her characters unfold. She is proud to have been part of – forest/fantasy, ghost/graves, science/space and now detective/crime.

You can find Maria at

mariaparenti.com
Maria Parenti Author | Facebook
Maria Parenti Author | Instagram

RAELENE PURTILL'S short stories have appeared in many local and nation-wide anthologies. Her passion is Young Adult speculative stories. She loves to connect and network with other writers  at conferences, retreats and workshops.

Currently, she is a creative writing student at the University of the Sunshine Coast and lives in the northern suburbs of Brisbane with her long-suffering husband and their three millennials.

You can find Raelene at

rapurtill.com
Raelene Purtill Author I Facebook

MICHAELA SANDERSON has been writing YA fiction for most of her life. She works closely with young adults and is blessed to be able take inspiration from their antics. She mentors a student writing group, who have just released their first anthology.

Michaela writes short stories and has experienced success in several writing competitions. She is an avid fantasy writer but will venture into other genres with confidence.

She loves a challenge and has 'won' Nanowrimo for eight consecutive years, producing a new story each year. She is a member of several writing groups, and enjoys the different perspectives other people bring to her writing. Michaela has completed several online writing courses, and regularly attends the Rainforest Writing Retreat, where she is motivated and encouraged to keep on writing.

You can find Michaela at

Michaela Sanderson | Facebook
theyellowbird@hotmail.com

ELIZABETH SPRATT was born in Sydney and has lived there her entire life. From Monday to Friday she is a professional accountant, longing to find extra hours in the day to devote to her passion for creative writing. From a young age, Elizabeth  was always penning different stories. Over the past few years she decided to take the plunge and write her first novel. She is currently re-editing a second draft of a spy thriller.

Elizabeth loves mystery and crime thrillers. She loves to travel to all parts of the world. With limited travel options over the past year she decided to combine travel and writing together and attended the 2021 Rainforest Writers Retreat. She is thrilled to be part of the RWR anthology.

JENNY WOOLSEY, M.Ed. (Hons), is an author, ceramic artist, speaker and teacher, on the theme *Be Weirdly Wonderful! Embrace your disability and differences.* She was born with a rare craniofacial  syndrome, lives with low vision and uses a long cane. Jenny lives north of Brisbane, with her three children, three crazy cats and adorable dog.

Disability, difference and mental wellbeing are the focus of Jenny's Middle Grade and Young Adult novels and all-age short stories. Jenny's school visits and speaking engagements bring particular awareness to disabilities, facial differences, bullying and good mental health practices, and she encourages kindness towards others.

You can find Jenny at

jennywoolsey.com
Amazon

GARY DAVID has always loved the art of storytelling, and how we learn and grow through it. It may have started when he was reading stories to his foster children, or teaching kids to read in prison, or even living in remote areas working in community development programs.

With degrees in criminology and psychology, his interests have always lain in adventures that have taken him through third world regions across six different continents.

He believes we are drawn to crime stories as a biological need to sharpen our minds in the event we need to outsmart criminals to protect the ones and things we love. Can we solve the puzzle before the hero reaches the finale or will we be another victim to the plots of the criminal masterminds?

Gary David's true passion is found after the story in debate with other readers, over moral and philosophical themes. Especially when the debate gets more intense than a good crime thriller.

You can find Gary at

garydavid.com.au

SHARON THRUPP is a long-time traveller  and observer of life, writing travel stories for magazines and publishing blogs commenting on social issues whilst living in India for 14 years. Whilst in India she helped to establish a writing community in Dharamsala. Sharon also runs Mindful Writing Groups at her local Buddhist Centre on the Sunshine Coast and leads writing and literary tours in India. This is her second published work of creative non-fiction. Sharon is currently researching and writing her memoirs.

You can find Sharon at

Sharon Thrupp | Facebook
Unplugged In India

LR JOHNSON grew up in a rural Queensland town surrounded by heritage and dust. Always with a mind for storytelling, she discovered novels and writing in early adolescence.

Fantastical worlds and far off places penned by the likes of Tolkien, C.S. Lewis and Lovecraft have sculpted her imagination. She enjoys exploring the human condition of the individual, with themes of psychological growth.

She has a Diploma of Visual Arts majoring in Digital Illustration, and Jewellery Making. She also did a year of Graphic Design, but business logos are not her style of storytelling. She is also a painter, and pottery sculptor.

You can find Lucy at

deviantart.com/lrjproductions

DIANE EDWARDS often laughs openly about her writing journey as it is made up of so many different genres it's making her head spin!

With a manuscript almost ready to be published and several 'short story' compilations being copy-edited, Diane is looking forward to 2020 when it's all going to go public!

Previously published in an RWR anthology with the story *The Passenger* – an anthology of Crime stories by Australian authors, Diane has now been accepted into this publication in print.

A British born and Australian bred Lancashire lass, Diane has recently moved to the beautiful Cotswolds area of England in Oxfordshire, to continue writing a novel.

Her dream is to share her days equally between the home she knows and loves in Brisbane, and closer to her heritage in England.

You can find Diane at

Vixenpublishing | Facebook
dke@dianekathrynedwards.com

ACKNOWLEDGEMENTS

RWR would like to thank Chris Radge (Christine Titheradge), Charmaine Clancy, Anthony Puttee and Noel Morado and Victor Marcos for their hard work in assembling this anthology and also the warm staff of O'Reilly's who always treat us more like family rather than customers. Likewise, thanks are also due to the RWR retreaters/authors, without their work there wouldn't be a book. A big thanks to all the crew at the Self-Publishing Lab for everything you do. You can contact them at selfpublishinglab.com for all your setup and publishing needs.

And the biggest thanks to Charmaine who thought that a writing retreat would be a great idea and has run with it ever since.

The writers at the Rainforest Writing Retreat are an extraordinary breed—perhaps even an entirely different species. When I visited in 2021 I was astonished to find myself surrounded by such bold, enthusiastic storytellers, already confident in their own genres and eager to experiment with others. I expected their enthusiasm to wane after a day or two, but it did not. I've never had so many entertaining literary conversations in my life.

~Jack Heath

WANT TO WRITE A NOVEL?
DON'T KNOW WHERE TO START?

Join us at Australia's favourite writing retreat.

LEARN

Immersive workshops, mentoring & publishing tips from International best-selling authors and industry experts.

CONNECT

Find the support you need and new life-long friends who share your passion. Network, laugh and connect.

PUBLISH

Every year, RWR puts out a high-quality anthology only open to Retreaters for submissions.

SECURE YOUR SPOT!

Each year, 50 writers gather at the spectacular O'Reilly's Rainforest Resort in Lamington National Park. Many of our writers have gone ahead to publish their first works because of the ongoing support and guidance they receive. RWR can book out over six months ahead, so get in early and secure your place. Once you have become a Retreater, you'll also be invited to our private mastermind group, meet-ups, extra workshops and qualify to submit to our publications.

www.RainforestWritingRetreat.com